ALLIGATOR HUNT

*An empty stretch of swampy river, and a
silent and merciless death*

BOOK FIVE

AGNES MAKÓCZY

ALLIGATOR HUNT © 2020 by Agnes Makóczy.

For information contact :
www.agnes-makoczy.com

Photo of Girl in Red by Greyerbaby
https://pixabay.com/photos/girl-sitting-tree-water-river-826867/

Background artwork by Syaibatulhamdi
https://pixabay.com/photos/moon-trees-palm-branches-trunk-5161142/

Book formatting by Derek Murphy from www.CreativIndie.com

ISBN: 0-9774395-5-0
        978-0-9774395-5-3
Bobweiser Books

First Edition: July 2020

Contents

Introduction

The Storm

THERE WAS MUD EVERYWHERE ON THE FEEDER ROAD. It must have rained heavily while he'd been gone. A series of lightning strikes illuminated the distant horizon and then subsided. Chris Mouton—feeling the drop in barometric pressure in his bones—drove as fast as he could, like a maniac, avoiding the potholes, scattering wet pebbles under the tires of his truck, hoping to make it to safety before the heavens opened up and drenched the world. But already the winds were picking up and trying to blow him off the road. He could feel the strength of the gusts beating down on his truck, making it shudder, and he held on to the steering wheel as well as his meager frame allowed him to.

He looked up at the blackening sky and frowned. It would be tight, but he might still make it. Judging by the distance of the lightning, and a lifetime of experience in the wild and inhospitable swamps of Louisiana, he calculated that he had enough time. But just barely. He dreaded the idea of being stuck in the middle of a storm out in the open. Once the deluge arrived, the roads would flood within minutes and become impassable. He could easily be swept away, big heavy truck or not. And it wasn't so much that he was afraid of dying by drowning—God knew that everyone must die somehow, sometime—but he couldn't bear the thought of not being in control of his own destiny. This was his life, his story, and he still had so much left to do. He would have to leave the dying for some other time. Right now, he needed to get home.

Suddenly, appearing out of nowhere, a scraggly brown dog ran across the road, right in front of the truck. He slammed on the brakes, startled, and the truck skidded to a stop. He gasped. He'd barely missed running the dog over, poor beast. He felt a pang of sorrow for it, out in this weather.

He hoped dearly that it had a home, or at least a safe shelter, to run back to.

He took a few deep breaths and waited for his heart to stop pounding. Damned weather. It made you do stupid stuff. He should have been paying attention to the road, and he should have been wearing his seat belt.

He found the seat belt wedged behind the cushion, and he put it on. Minutes wasted—he grumbled—and the storm approaching fast. He looked around for the dog, but it had vanished. Nor was there another car on this stretch of the road as far as he could see. He hadn't passed one in forever. This was such a lonely stretch. Usually, he enjoyed the soothing solace of an empty road. But not on a day like this. Should he get in trouble this far from civilization, he would be on his own. He needed to be more cautious.

At the next intersection, he stopped, and with his left arm, wiped the fog off the windows and the moist sweat off his brow. He worried about missing the turn-off toward Mudville.

The wind had picked up big time now, flinging leaves and smaller branches at his window like projectiles, swirling around the truck, blinding him, disorienting him.

Knowing in his guts that his turn-off should be but a few hundred feet ahead, he drove on watchfully, upper body leaning into the steering wheel—the sweat pouring down his face, into his eyes—trying to see through the clumps of dirt and other flying debris, face as close to the front windshield as possible. His anxiety level increased as he counted the distance from the last intersection in his head and almost forgot to breathe until he saw the dead tree leaning against the abandoned remnants of the rotting fence that was his landmark.

Whew, he sighed with relief. He was almost there. He hated being away too long. He hated being around people and having to play nice. He was socially awkward and never knew what to say or how to behave. He was better off on his own, where nobody expected anything from him. Every day he thanked his dearly departed mother for having left him this little swamp house that was his safe haven.

Within minutes he was at the next turn-off, and he couldn't help smiling when he saw his shack, its rusted aluminum roofing peeking out from behind the clusters of trees and overgrown bamboo. Yup, it was still there—home—shaking under the onslaught of the approaching storm.

He had heard on the radio earlier that the tropical storm would become a hurricane by the time it landed, and he didn't doubt it. Already the gusts of wind arrived with brief, violent showers that pounced on the ground with peppered force, and disappeared within seconds, as fast as they had come, followed by that howling wind that put the fear of God into your bones.

As pleased as he was to be finally home, he cursed under his breath that he had wasted precious time. He hesitated. Didn't seem like he would have a chance to board up the windows. Didn't seem like he would even have the chance to unload the plywood for them from the bed of the truck. Shoot, he told himself, I'm too late.

He jumped out of his truck and ran to the door. He brushed away the swirling leaves that hit his face and got into his hair. He had to hurry. At least he should close the windows properly and fasten those worthless outdoor wooden shutters that were probably going to blow away at the first gust of wind unless they were boarded up.

He looked up at the sky, at a straggling flock of squawking birds flying away in a rush, and at the dark, angry clouds accumulating with a vengeance over his head. The weather looked threatening, but it was still holding. He decided that he would put up as many boards as possible before the full strength of the hurricane winds came his way, and he picked up some heavy-duty leather gloves and began unloading the truck.

Chris worked hard. He worked fast. Years of experience made the process automatic. He had the tools, he had the knowledge, and the anxiety gave him a speed he rarely experienced. He was usually more of a laid-back beer drinker who took his time to accomplish stuff. But he loved his shack, and today, anxiety lent him wings.

His shack—his home—was in a small clearing surrounded by forest lands, and swamps, and gigantic centenarian trees that had already been saplings when the French had stepped foot in Louisiana for the first time in the year 1717 or so. Its lonely location was its safety, but it was what made it so vulnerable as well. A fire, a bad storm, and out there, nobody would ever find out that someone might have lived in that secluded shack and died.

Before he finished nailing up the last board, he turned around toward the thick of the shrubbery, thinking that he had heard something, but there wasn't anything there. Just a quick light brown shadow that seemed to whizz by, and then nothing. Some wild animal, running from the storm. He had no neighbors, and he lived alone. Nobody ever came all the way out there into this Southern nothingness but him. Or his brother, when he needed something. Of course, there wasn't anyone there.

Pleasantly surprised that the weather had held long enough, he finished nailing on his last plywood board and walked to the house, fighting the wind. He thought he heard a small girl crying out a name repeatedly like she was calling for her cat or her dog, and he turned to look toward the swamp, startled, but nothing. Of course, nothing. He was imagining things again. That was what always happened when he stopped taking his pills. Or was it because of the pills? Chris shook his head and went into the house, locking all the locks on the door behind him. Then he walked from window to window, testing each one of them, making sure that they were all secure.

But he couldn't stop thinking of the little girl. Was she real, or was she a ghost? Was she out there? Was she lost? Did she need help? He couldn't let it go. By habit, he walked to the window to look out, but it was boarded. He shrugged. There was no way to look out. He would just have to let it go. He took a beer out of the refrigerator and pulled the tab off. The cold froth sprinkled his face, and he laughed. It was always that same excitement, opening a can of beer.

He pretended to forget the little girl and drank his beer, but he drank it down fast, in big gulps. He couldn't get her out of his mind. He decided he was going to go outside and see, real quick, make sure that she wasn't lost, or in some kind of trouble. He couldn't just sit down and enjoy his hurricane in peace when there could be someone out there needing help, now could he?

When he stepped through the door, it slammed against the wall behind him, and almost blew off its hinges. The wind had picked up tremendously. It was going to be a big one, they said. Everyone, get out while you can, they had said. But Chris was going nowhere. He had survived every major hurricane that had struck South Louisiana in this same shack ever since he had been a kid, and he wasn't about to run now. No, sir. He had enough beer for two weeks at least, plenty of dried meats, and a larder full of canned goods big enough to feed him for two straight years. Then, there was all that bottled water, and of course his beloved generator. That blessed thing had been his paw-paw's, and it was still running as good as it had back when. Yup. He wasn't going nowhere.

He stepped onto the front porch and admired the all-powerful strength of the storm, feeling it in his bones, in his soul, sheltered in a corner from the worst of it. He inhaled with his eyes closed. The air smelled of rain. It smelled of impending storm.

The bushes and the weeds shuddered under the onslaught of the wind, and soon, huge fat drops of water began plopping on their big shiny leaves, making drip-drip sounds before they slipped onto the wet ground. He opened his eyes, amazed and humbled by the power of nature. Smaller trees were bending over, from side to side, as if following a rhythm of their own, left and right, left and right. Soon the dancing would be over, and they would be torn out of the ground and thrown aside like so much refuse. Bigger trees would lean over for a while, and after they could lean no more, they would get picked up by the hurricane winds and pulled out of the ground. They would twirl around and around in their own tornado, their roots dangling about them, flinging the dirt and the worms, and the ants and everything else that lived on that tree, onto the ground, and the wind wouldn't stop until everything was dead. Dead. He had seen that before, so many times.

Then he heard the cry again, and it startled him out of his complacency. He squinted toward the thick of the forest, trying to see through the gathering darkness. This time he knew he hadn't imagined it. It had been loud enough to be heard over the howling wind, and he knew exactly where it had come from, too. He patted his side where he carried the gun in its holster and picked up the machete from the floor by the front door, and with his courage right where it belonged, he started walking that way.

Things scratched his face as they were blown by the wind. Some of them even hurt. Pecans, small twigs, pinecones, God knew what else. But he didn't falter. He brushed his face. He was going to find out what was going on. And if someone out there was in trouble, he was going to do something about it. His conscience wouldn't allow him anything less.

He followed the path, cutting shrubs down with his machete where he had to. He knew his way around every bush, every swampy puddle, every cypress tree. And on he went, obsessed, bowing his head against the wind. Within minutes, complete darkness fell, and he unhooked his flashlight from his belt. Not that it was going to be needed much, because lightning kept striking methodically, sort of keeping the way in front of him illumined. With that and the flashlight, he would be okay. Besides, it wasn't like he could ever get lost, right?

The wind was intense. The rain was pouring so hard now that he could barely see two feet in front of him. The full force of the hurricane had arrived. The sludge under his feet quickly became deep and slippery, and it sucked him down, turning every step into a struggle with the muddy ground that was trying to swallow him.

Then, suddenly, a small tree, a sapling, got uprooted, lifted into the air and tossed right in front of him, barely missing him. And then another one. And then, whole clumps of vegetation flew in front of his eyes, and he knew that if he didn't move, he would be next.

This was not good. Maybe he had been too hasty. He hadn't heard the cry in a while. For all he knew, he had imagined hearing the voice. Wouldn't have been the first time either. He stopped. This was ridiculous. He was going to go back home. But where was he? How far had he walked? He turned about, suddenly disoriented. He looked around to see which way he had come from. The trees were all so tall, so dense, and the wet night so disorienting, that he felt suddenly lost. And that howling wind!

He groaned with despair, turning around and around, trying so hard not to panic, thinking about what to do next, when he saw it. He didn't believe it, but he did see it. An enormous alligator, white as a demon ghost, shining as if it was made of light, slowly making its way through the trees, barely a few feet from him. He stopped and stood still, scared to breathe. He had never seen any gator this big in his whole long life. Gaping, he watched as the beast made its progress slowly heading away from him, never looking his way. But that was not what took his breath away, no. It was what the alligator had in its mouth. The unholy creature was dragging the body of a man, his blood obscenely red against the maw of the shiny white beast.

Chris finally reacted and took his gun out and got ready to shoot, but his guts failed him. Before he knew what he was doing, he realized he was running away, running as fast as the wind, as fast as he had ever run before. The man had been alive, God absolve me, he would never forget, and he would never be able to forgive himself. The man had been alive, and—like a coward—he had run away.

Chapter 1

The Party

ODETTE ALVES STEPPED DISCREETLY INTO THE CROWDED BALLROOM, sticking close to the wall, staying behind the enormous flower arrangements that were strewn about the magnificent room on marble columns and display tables. A small orchestra—in a recess at the end of the hall—played softly for the beautiful people of Half Moon Bay who mingled and gossiped and laughed happily, tended to by an army of waiters and waitresses carrying drinks and hors d'oeuvres on shiny silver trays.

She looked toward the balcony and saw right away that Vinnie was there already, waiting. She had business with him tonight, but she didn't want to be seen. She found it frustrating that she had to sneak around like this. Vinnie had a way of always complicating things. She also found it imprudent. If they ever got caught, they would both go down like dead weight in the murky swamps.

A waiter walked by, carrying in one hand a large silver platter full of champagne flutes, and Odette deftly picked one off, without being seen or felt by the young man. For a second, she admired his youthful good looks and the tight, well-formed body in the festive uniform, but then her focus shifted back to the job at hand. Objective: deliver the artifact. End result: a decent wad of cash. Or, if everything failed, well, she refused to entertain that thought.

Odette drank up the golden bubbly liquid in the champagne flute and placed it on the corner of a table, and she pulled down the black lace on her small evening hat so that her face was partially concealed. She hoped that it would be enough to make her hard to recognize. Then, swallowing hard, she walked straight to the balcony.

Meantime, two well-dressed men began arguing politics in the middle of the room, and everyone turned to look in their direction. Perfect distraction. She looked at her watch and smiled. Trust her friends to deliver. It was such an age-old deception, two men to distract a crowd, and yet it still worked. But she must hurry up. You didn't keep a man like Vinnie Chauvin waiting.

She pulled the balcony doors sideways, and they slid open in perfect silence. Vinnie—her beautiful, handsome, debonair Vinnie—was leaning on the balcony rail, the town, and the whole bay at his feet.

Rain was on the way. A low rumbling shook the sky, and a tight group of menacingly dark, angry clouds floated by, obscuring the twinkling of the stars, plunging the sparkling waters of the bay into darkness.

It smelled of rain, too, and of the pleasant musky cologne that Vinnie Chauvin was so fond of. She inhaled the heady scents with her eyes closed. What a shame that men didn't much wear cologne anymore. These days— at best—you would get their body odor, with the stale breath of booze, or not enough mouth wash. But Vinnie was all man. Didn't she know it?

"Hello, *ma belle*," he said, turning around, and giving her that dazzling snake-charmer smile that he was so famous for. "Long time no see."

Odette pulled up the lace from her face and leaned in for a peck on the cheeks. Vinnie looked good. Healthy, prosperous, full of vitality. It was always such a pleasure to see him.

"It's a shame that we have to sneak around like this, Vinnie. We never have quality time together anymore."

"I know, *sha*. But I'll be free after the party if you want to come back and spend the night. We haven't done that in a long time."

"I'd love to do that, Vinnie. I'll come back." Odette's heart pounded with desire, remembering the pleasure of feeling his warm skin against her naked body, and she sighed. Vinnie always had that effect on her. "I'll come in by the back door as usual."

"Wonderful. That's great. Now, did you bring me something?"

"I sure did." Odette looked back toward the room and noticed that by now, the argument had escalated, and her friends were about to hit each other. The guests had gotten even closer to them, surrounding them, full of curiosity. Then, assured that nobody was paying any attention to her, she pulled a package out of her purse, rolled in yellow silk, and handed it to Vinnie. "Be careful when you open it," she said. "It's in two pieces."

"Thank you, sha. Come back after midnight, and we'll settle."

"Why always the cloak and dagger stuff, Vinnie?"

"I promised to deliver it tonight. But I'll see you later. I want to talk to you, anyway."

"About what, Vinnie?"

"About us, ma belle. I miss you too much to see you so seldom. Maybe it's time that we made plans for the future. Together. But you better hurry now. The guests are losing interest in your friends."

And it was true. It was time to go. Odette pulled the lace back over her face and slipped out as the first drops of rain began to fall. She looked back at Vinnie one last time as she slid close the balcony doors behind her. There he was, smiling like a contented cat, that irrepressible snake-charmer smile, looking out into the horizon. She couldn't help herself. Despite everything, she was still madly and desperately in love with him. Then, with a sigh, she stepped behind a column and disappeared.

Chapter 2

Party II

THE WINDSHIELD WIPERS SWISHED LAZILY LEFT AND RIGHT, left and right, slapping away big, fat, random drops of rain as the skies shook with lightning and with rumbles of thunder, announcing the oncoming storm. It was not the best night to have an opening party for a new art collection at the Gallery, but the distraction-starved beautiful people of Half Moon Bay didn't care and flocked to the event anyway.

Brooks—dressed in a freshly-pressed Chauffeur's uniform—jumped out of the new Mercedes and hurried to open Margo Fontaine's door. Next to Margo, her cousin Robert's wife Madeleine waited for her turn, sitting pretty in the back seat, her hands on her lap. He kept them dry from the scattered raindrops with an enormous umbrella, and they held on to his arms so they wouldn't slip on the wet marble steps.

Margo was wearing a vintage black, semi-sheer tulle gown with spaghetti straps and dark red rose appliqués that had once belonged to her mother, the famous opera singer Nicola Fontaine. Next to her sat Madeleine in a more somber burgundy velvet dress with a discreet side slit. It had been quite an accomplishment getting Madeleine out of her house. Ever since Robert had vanished, she had become a recluse, shunning all social events in favor of sitting at home with her three horrible children, reading, or doing needlepoint embroidery in front of the television set.

As they walked up the wet, slippery marble steps to the new Lafitte Art Gallery, Margo rejoiced in the rare chance to wear an elegant long gown for the sophisticated evening. Moments like these came too seldom to the small South Louisiana coastal town of Half Moon Bay where everyone usually wore shorts and flip-flops.

For a fleeting moment, Margo remembered her mom Nicola, and the frequent concert tours and after-parties they had attended together while she had been alive. She would have given anything to go to one last event with her mom, who had died oh, almost at the same age she was now. She had been just a chubby teenager with braces back then. Now, this slender, sophisticated dress fit her like a glove.

She still remembered the recital vividly. It had been in Prague. Nicola had sung excerpts from Bizet's opera Carmen. It had been very appropriate, the long black dress with the dark red appliqués, for the story of an ill-fated love affair between Carmen and a torero—a bullfighter—with the red roses reminiscent of the gore and the spilled blood of the bullfights. She patted down the front of the dress wistfully, happy to have a chance to wear it, to feel close to her mom again.

Margo had never recovered from the shock of her death, but it wasn't until that famous *séance* a couple of years earlier that had brought back long-buried memories of her being the one to find her own mother, lying in a puddle of blood, a grotesque carving knife sticking out of her chest. No wonder she had blocked that recollection completely. And then, in the end, her killer was never found. But she kept alive the hope that one day she would find the murderer and bring him to justice.

But much water had flowed under the bridge ever since, and the pain wasn't as poignant as it had once been. She had learned to enjoy those moments that life allowed her regardless of her tragedy. She reminded herself not to mope, for the sake of her cousin Robert's wife, who in a way was also in mourning. She allowed the sad memories to flit by and came back to the present.

Already from the street, you could hear the Chamber Orchestra over the pitter-patter of the rain. Margo looked around and admired the line of fancy cars idling in line, raindrops glistening on their shiny, elegant bodies, waiting for their turn to drop the guests off at the front door.

Thankfully, the weather had held so far, for the most part, anyway. And all the lights had been turned on, on the street and this newly renovated building on West Albatross, barely a half block from the Opera House, making the venue shine as bright as a stadium on game night. Until recently, it had been a movie theater, one of those colonial throwbacks that even though having fallen into disrepair, had maintained the charm of the Art Deco building style of the turn of the 20th century.

Margo chuckled with glee. She had a fascination for old buildings—a passion she shared with Father Armand, the middle-aged heartthrob that was the much-loved priest at St. Quintian's, the local Catholic Church. He'd been invited, for sure, and she wondered if he would show.

The magnificent original glass and chrome front doors were wide open. Two porters in Plantation-style livery—one on each side—greeted the guests and discreetly looked at their invitations.

The floor in the entrance hall—long stretches of rose and white-colored marble—had been lovingly preserved, restored, and polished. And an old-fashioned wooden circular staircase with carved banisters, set to the right side of the striking reception hall, was painted an antique white that brought out the gold veins in the pink marble.

Suddenly, she felt Madeleine pull on her arm, and she realized that she had been gawking. Her cousin's wife, finally free from her self-imposed exile, was too excited to stand still and admire her surroundings. She was ready to party. She pulled Margo toward the staircase at the foot of which, ushers also in Plantation-style livery were mingling with trays full of champagne, directing the guests upstairs.

There must have been a hundred people in the large room upstairs, at the very least. They stood in small groups, chatting, laughing politely, the women well-dressed and coiffed, heavily weighted down with fashionable gowns and priceless jewelry, and the men exuding power and success. Their educated voices mingled with the gentle background music, and Margo purred contentedly. This was her idea of a perfect evening.

Then, she looked around, delighted. She had visited the downstairs Gallery on numerous occasions before, but she had never been invited to the ballroom upstairs. It was completely encased in walls of glass. Even the columns, covered in aluminum sheeting, gave the impression of being part of the dark outdoors. The light from the chandeliers reflected in all that glass and the scattered mirrors and gave the impression of being stars. It was like floating alfresco out there, in the open night sky.

Margo left Madeleine talking to some friends and walked around. A balcony stretched along the whole side of the building. It overlooked the darkness of the bay in which you could barely discern the yachts moored by the Marina. She had a great desire to go outside and admire the view, but two men deep into some intense conversation that included a lot of hand waving had taken up outside the balcony door, and she felt that she couldn't go out and intrude. So, she kept circulating, looking back curiously toward them from time to time.

From another set of windows, she beheld the Pirate Bay Hotel, as brightly lit as a Christmas tree against the stormy sky. Mimi, the owner of the Pirate Bay was talking to someone, sweeping her arm toward her jewel of a hotel, probably showing it off to the guest. When Mimi turned around and saw Margo, she quickly waved and sent her a kiss.

That was always mildly disturbing, and today was no exception. Whenever Mimi saw her, she was always so kind and friendly, and Margo had gotten many unsolicited—although not altogether unpleasant—hugs from her. And yet they were strangers, nothing more. A lovely middle-aged woman of dark skin and extravagant black curly hair, Mimi had kept the voluptuous body of her youth, and was usually much admired by much younger men. But Dr. Gabe, the local pediatrician, kept a vigilant eye on her, standing firmly by her side as if making sure that nobody absconded with his girlfriend. Mimi was much older than Dr. Gabe, but somehow, they made a lovely couple.

Margo put down her empty champagne flute and picked up another one. This was the lifestyle she loved, a bigger town with more of a social life. At times, Half Moon Bay was stiflingly small. Small town, big hell, as her mom used to say. Maybe it was time that she talked her beloved Pierre into moving to some exciting place where they could both enjoy living a more socially active, more challenging lifestyle.

She looked at her watch. Talking about Pierre, he should have arrived already. She worried about him driving such enormous distances every time he came to visit her. South Louisiana roads were famous for the speed with which they flooded and became deadly. She frowned with worry and looked around, wondering if she had missed him, although he would have been hard to miss. He towered over the local men, and he was outrageously handsome, so much more than anyone else.

As she sipped on her champagne, she walked around, keeping an apprehensive eye out for Pierre. She mingled, said hello to the people she knew, and she was just about to go look for her cousin's wife Madeleine to check on her, when a shrill scream followed by a hollow silence pierced the enjoyable atmosphere in the room. The orchestra stopped playing, and the people stopped talking.

She turned in the direction of the scream. It had come from the balcony. She took a step in that direction, but a powerful sequence of lightning strikes tore through the sky blinding her, and almost immediately, a violent rumble shook the building, making the glass walls quiver. The storm had arrived. And as another bolt of lightning illuminated the sky, Margo saw—as clear as day—the body of a man, out on the balcony, lying in a pool of blood.

Chapter 3

DAY ONE: The Dead Man

MARGO'S HORRIFIED EYES SWEPT THE ROOM, hoping to see her friend Sam Stark among the guests. She knew for a fact that—as the local Sheriff—he would have been invited. But, as far as she could tell, he was nowhere to be seen. Surprising, as he was known to enjoy social gatherings.

She quickly dialed Sam's phone number and let it ring for a long time, but there was no response. Where on earth could he be? He always picked up his phone. How exasperating. The one time she needed him, too. What should she do? Having worked with Sam on so many suspicious death cases, she was aware of the importance of securing the scene. You didn't have to be a full-fledged detective to know that evidence needed to be preserved. That man lying in a puddle of blood on the balcony could have died as a result of an accident, but he could have just as easily been murdered.

She also knew from Sam—because he was always harping on about it—that curiosity from spectators was one of the worst nightmares for investigators. They trampled on everything, leaving footsteps, contaminating the scene with hair and other organic debris. Action was needed.

She positioned herself in front of the glass doors leading out to the balcony, and she nervously watched the crowd. At first, they pretended nonchalance and barely glanced toward the dead man as if they were not that interested, but as the seconds ticked by, she noticed their attitude change. They were edging closer, slowly, step by step, even gently pushing each other to get a better look at the dead man.

Margo's palms began to sweat. She had read about crowd behavior or collective mentality, and about the intensification of emotion that's driven by mutual interaction. Without an authority figure that commanded enough respect, they would become impossible to control. They would do whatever they wanted, and they were unpredictable. She was already seeing the first signs of it. Her forehead and her neck were moist. Her heart was beginning to beat much harder. She was going to have an anxiety attack if they kept getting closer. She could almost smell their excitement, their morbid curiosity, their need to see the gory spectacle.

She considered calling for order, but the idea terrified her. The more she thought about it, the faster her heart beat. She was a nobody. The guests around her were older, more seasoned, powerful people. People who commanded attention and were used to bossing underlings around and didn't like being told what to do. And then there were their scary wives. She was almost more afraid of them. Because, honestly, none of these very important pillars of Half Moon Bay society would listen to her—a mere female, and young at that—if she tried to keep them away from the balcony. They would push her aside and trample her down. So, she sweated and trembled with indecision as she watched the mesmerized guests slowly approaching her, whispering to each other, crowding her out of their way, moving her to the side, so that they could take a better look at the dead man.

Finally, Margo knew that she had to do something, otherwise, there would go the evidence, should there be any. And it would all be her fault for being a coward.

"Everybody, stand back, please," she yelled out—too loud—waving her arms nervously, reclaiming herself some space by the balcony door and facing the startled crowd. "Everyone needs to stand back. Please, let's not contaminate the scene. Can someone call the police station?"

Some people hesitated and stepped back an inch or two. She saw a couple of men whip out their cell phones and dial. Others, especially the women, simply ignored her, pushing her out of their way, shoving each other, getting as close to the glass wall as they could, taking photographs of the dead man, for their social media for sure, leaving handprints and traces of their warm breath on the glass. Someone asked loudly, "Was he murdered, do you think?" Suddenly, the question was taken up by the guests, and the murmurs became agitated and aggressive. It was fast becoming a mob scene.

Margo was on the verge of panic. She looked from side to side, realizing that she was unable to handle the situation when she saw Dr. Gabe approach, and she let out the breath she had been holding back. He had a standing in the community. Everyone knew him. He was also a tall and imposing man with a very deep voice that elicited respect from all of those who met him

Dr. Gabe spoke and everyone turned toward him. Loudly and with determination he asked everyone to please move back, and the guests immediately stood aside to let him pass and give him space. Margo tried not to dwell on the fact that as a young woman, she had carried absolutely no authority whatsoever, and had to wait for a man to come and rescue her. What was important was that things were in good hands. Dr. Gabe was not only St. Hildegard Hospital's Pediatrician, but he was also the new Medical Examiner.

"What happened, Margo?" he asked, approaching her with a worried look on his handsome face and putting his hands gently on her arms.

"I don't know. I heard the scream and hurried this way. When I got here, the balcony door was closed as you see it, and he was alone, lying there without moving. I'm quite sure that he's dead. His eyes are open, look, but he hasn't blinked since I've been standing here."

"This is not good," Dr. Gabe said, getting closer to the glass door and glancing up at the sky. "It's a deluge all right. Sheets of rain are falling on the balcony. He's already soaking wet. Expect fibers, hairs, footprints, fingerprints, etc., to have been washed away."

"I know. It's a disaster. Maybe we could cover him. There might be some evidence left that we could salvage."

"We can try, I suppose, but at this point, it's more than likely that the effort will be meaningless. The way the gale is blowing, any tarp, any cover, will be blown away. This is quite a violent storm, Margo. We'll be lucky if the poor man's body isn't gusted off the balcony."

"I feel horrible for him, poor guy. Let me try and find something to put over him anyway, Dr. Gabe. At least let me feel that I'm helping. I'll be right back." Margo looked despondently at the now raging storm for a second and then hurried in search of someone who could help her locate a tarp.

By the time Margo made it back with a shower curtain, the sporadic raging storm had turned into a ceaseless wall of water that came down from the skies as abundantly and violently as a waterfall. It poured down obliquely on the balcony, rattling the wrought-iron chairs and table ever closer to the edge of the balcony, making the dead body shiver and tremble as if it was still alive. Like the furniture, the dead man inched ever closer to the banister, furniture and dead body in danger of being swept away by the powerful wind.

Even though the glass walls in the ballroom shook with a teeth-grinding rattle every time lightning struck, their integrity held, and the balcony door remained closed. Outside, the dead man still stared with his eyes wide open—as far as Margo could tell through the pouring rain—and on the inside, an unpleasant chill had descended upon the gathering. Meantime, the crowd had thinned out. It was obvious that some people had left, and only the more curious ones lagged behind. Without a policeman to bully the guests into submission, everyone had done as they had wished.

"I'm sorry, Dr. Gabe, but this was all I could find," Margo told him, holding out a colorful, brand new stretch of plastic. "With all the fishes and shells on it, it's a bit too cheerful to cover a dead man, but there were no tarps, and the housekeeper gave me a shower curtain."

"I guess we can try to cover him up, but at this point, we might as well leave him be. As soon as the rain lets up a bit, I'll get the ambulance crew to come and pick him up." Then, Dr. Gabe looked into Margo's eyes. "I know that this troubles you, my dear, but nature has decided over the will of man, and there's nothing we can do about it. But let's make sure we find out what happened to him, and if he was murdered, we'll find the culprit and we'll have him or her punished. I promise."

Margo looked back at Dr. Gabe and saw the kindness in his eyes. He was a good man, Dr. Gabe. He was also a compassionate man. Mimi was a lucky woman. She nodded.

"Has anyone seen Sam or Maurice?" Margo asked.

"Not that I know of. Someone said that Sam was supposed to be here, but he didn't show, and Maurice, well, nobody calls Maurice when there's an emergency, right?"

"I guess not."

"Maybe we should call the State Police."

"No, please don't do that yet, Dr. Gabe. Sam would be very upset. I'm sure he'll be here any minute to take care of things. And while we wait for the ambulance, I can ask around to see if anyone saw or heard anything."

Chapter 4

Pierre At Last

MARGO RUMMAGED IN HER EVENING PURSE, hoping for a pen and a piece of paper. Despite Dr. Gabe's offhanded comment on Maurice, she had speed-dialed his number, hoping that he would pick up, to no avail. Maurice—while coming across as being a tad slow—was just shy and inexperienced. He had just recently graduated from the Baton Rouge Police Training Academy. People were expecting too much of him. After having lost Deputy Andy to criminal activities and life in prison, Maurice was going to have to learn to be Sam's right hand, even if he wasn't ready unless Sam finally made up his mind to look for someone else with more experience. But Sam hated change, and he had been so very fond of Andy, that they would all have to wait for him to be done mourning the loss of his deputy. None of which was good news for Maurice.

Unfortunately, Maurice liked being the man behind the desk at the tiny Half Moon Bay police department. He was friendly and gregarious. He liked chatting with the people who occasionally walked in with a complaint, helping sort out their minor problems, or answering their lesser questions. Andy had always been the go-getter, the one who saw the bigger picture, who had the tracking skills and the knowhow to pursue a perp to the ends of the earth to get justice and retribution. On the other hand, Maurice—who hated outdoor activities—sat contentedly at his desk, holding his telephone in his hand at all times. Margo had long suspected that he was quietly playing video games. He was probably too young for the job, after all, and people tended to forget that, and that was why they had gotten in the habit of thinking that it would be pointless to call Maurice if the emergency was too dire.

She watched Dr. Gabe stride over to the waiters who were standing restlessly in a corner. After a brief conversation, a couple of bigger waiters who looked more like bouncers nodded to Dr. Gabe and walked over to guard the door, presumably so that not everyone would vanish into the rainy night. Margo grunted with frustration. Unless Sam or Maurice showed up, she and the good doctor would have to do at least some basic form of interrogating all by themselves before the guests mutinied and left.

She watched the balcony absentmindedly while she organized in her mind the questions she should ask. As she got lost in her thoughts, she didn't realize that someone had seized her from behind and given her a warm kiss on the neck. Startled out of her reverie, she jumped and turned around, hand out to slap the cheeky fellow, when she noticed that it was Pierre who had finally arrived.

She fell thankfully into his arms. She felt so loved and so safe when he hugged her. Any time Margo saw Pierre after a long absence, her heart skipped a beat or two. And it wasn't only because he was so tall, dark, and handsome, but because he made her smile, and laugh, and they had so much fun together. Pierre filled her life with happiness and left a sad, gaping hole in her heart when he was gone.

Tonight, she was especially happy to see him. With a dead man on the balcony and no Sam, she had felt lost, torn between the desire of going home and letting someone else handle the situation, and the responsibility of probably being the only person in the room with any remote idea of police procedure. Would Sam be disappointed in her if she left? She looked at Pierre and wondered if she should ask him what to do. But she hated herself immediately for thinking like that. She should be able to make her own decisions. Maybe always feeling so vulnerable in Pierre's arms was not such a good thing.

"Hello, pretty girl," he said with his perfect smile, giving her a twirl. "You look ravissante tonight, ma chère." Margo smiled back happily.

"What's going on," he asked. "Why is everyone looking so distressed? Why is the music not sounding? I heard sirens coming from afar when I stepped inside the building."

"That must be the ambulance on the way. There's the dead body of a man on the balcony. It's probably murder, but it's too early to say. After all, he might have tripped and fallen against the wrought-iron table, hitting his head fatally. We'll find out soon enough."

"But who is he?"

"He hasn't been formally identified yet, but I knew him well enough to be sure that it's the owner of the Gallery."

"Vinnie Chauvin? Where? Here?"

"Yes. Outside, on the balcony."

"Oh, that's terrible. I feel sorry for the man. And what a bummer for you, ma petite détective. That rain's going to wash away all your evidence, I'm afraid."

"Yes, I know. And Sam's AWOL and Maurice still hasn't answered his phone, and the guests are beginning to get restless. I'm afraid they will leave before we have a chance to ask them some questions. Someone should have a talk with them. But they probably won't listen to me."

"Is that why you're looking at me like that? With so much expectation?"

Margo laughed. "Yes, Pierre. You have that presence. If you ask them to sit and behave, they will."

"I can do that and more for a decent kiss. Is there a place where they can go and sit, and be comfortable, while the Sheriff shows up?"

"Manuel's working here tonight. I can ask him. I'll be right back."

As Margo walked away from Pierre, she had the feeling that time was distending and that the event had been going on for hours. Yet, she checked her watch and noted with surprise that it had been merely a half-hour since the scream by one of the guests had alerted her of Vinnie Chauvin's death. She sighed, and then, she hurried on.

Chapter 5

Pierre And The Dead Man

MARGO WENT IN SEARCH OF MANUEL, and Pierre's eyes followed her as she walked away, swaying elegantly in her evening gown as she went. He saw how at the end of the Gallery, Margo grabbed Manuel's arm, and with an easy intimacy that bothered him, he watched them leave. There was this whole hidden side to Margo's life that he knew almost nothing about. He was aware that she and Manuel knew each other from way back, from when she spent summers at her aunts' rambling mansion waiting for that bon rien Jack who had been her first great love. He had heard the stories. And then Manuel had swiftly risen from being a lowly waiter at the Pirate Bay Hotel to Mimi's right hand and confidant, and it bothered him so much. For some reason, he didn't like Manuel.

Embarrassed about his feelings, he turned back to the murder. Margo was right. The guests were getting restless. They had formed tight groups and were whispering amongst themselves at sotto voce, leaning toward each other, yet darting curious glances around from time to time. A group of well-dressed older women huddled by the glass wall for selfies, moving one way or the other to conveniently allow the dead man a corner of their photographs.

Pierre wondered for a second if the murderer was still among them, and he looked keenly around, hoping to observe someone's odd behavior. Something out of place that would give the murderer away. If he, himself, had the guts to kill someone, would he remain at the scene of his crime, out of sheer bravado, or a ghoulish interest? Or would he have gotten out at the first opportunity?

Curiosity—he pondered—was a strange thing. Just a few days earlier he had observed an older man being pulled out of the Vermillion River, back home in Lafayette. Ambulance first responders and a handful of policemen huddled around his inert body. They had laid him on a stretcher, on the muddy bank, but there was a disturbing lack of action around him. He expected there to be efforts to revive him or to check on him. So, he stopped. Inquisitive, unable to look away, he watched for a while, although nothing was going on. He couldn't tell if the man was dead or alive. He was too far away. He told himself that he would wait to see what happened. Then, suddenly feeling disgusted with himself, ashamed of his desire to ogle, he looked away and began to walk. It was then that he noticed how many people were standing at the riverbank as well, mesmerized like he had been, staring.

Pierre tried to ignore his inner dread of death and walked closer to the balcony. People parted to let him through, and he noticed that the women—particularly the women—beamed at him with big dazzling smiles. As they closed ranks again behind him, he heard them gossip in their soft, educated tones. Margo shouldn't be so worried. These people were going nowhere. This was probably the most excitement they had felt in a long time.

Pierre was an avid detective-mysteries reader, and he followed Margo's investigations closely, proud of the way she could solve her cases. But he, himself, he preferred his dead bodies in the pages of a book.

Poor Vinnie Chauvin. Who could have hated him enough to murder him? And in such a brazen way in front of all these people? Because, regardless of what Margo had told him, his gut feeling told him that this was no accident.

Besides, and first and foremost, even he had heard about the art dealer's reputation, and he didn't even live in Half Moon Bay. He imagined some rival mobster had done him in. You couldn't deal with the kind of people Vinnie did business with and not expect to be offed by them sooner or later.

The whole thing looked hopeless. Good luck to Sam and Margo if they were hoping for clues. Nothing would survive the onslaught of this storm. Already the blood—if there had been any—would have been washed away. They would be fortunate to find something legible in his pockets. For sure, everything else would be gone.

Pierre stood quietly as he analyzed the scene. The glass wall that surrounded the room was so crystal clear that it made you feel as if you were outdoors, floating over the city and the bay, in the middle of the darkest night. Far away, the city lights twinkled in the falling rain. The big, fancy, modern edifice to his left—Mimi's Pirate Bay Inn and Hotel—was brightly lit by multicolor neon signs. At its feet in the bay, blurred by the distance and the curtain of water, yachts, and boats rocked on the angry water, their tiny lights shivering in the storm. He saw Mimi at the far corner of the room, talking to her daughter and her politician fiancé, all three standing apart from the others, all three, looking worried. He knew from the local gossip that Mimi held a treasure trove's worth of other people's secrets in her heart, and he briefly wondered whether she had anything to do with this here murder.

The black or dark green wrought-iron furniture that was now pushed against the edge of the railing by the tempest had once been scattered around the large balcony—he presumed—and the low table with the glass top must have originally been next to the body, to its left. Logically speaking, the man could have slipped and hit his head as he fell, knocking him out and outright killing him. It happened. The man wasn't young anymore. Could he have been drunk and fallen backward?

Maybe. That was going to be his first question to the guests. Had anyone seen him stumble? Fall? He went through his pockets and found a pen and a wrinkled envelope he had previously thought about discarding. He wrote his question down. Then, he took his phone out and began photographing the entire scene, including the balcony door, the handle, the floor around it. Sam and Margo could examine the pictures later, and maybe find in them additional clues once the crime scene itself had been examined.

There was quite a lot of shattered glass on the balcony floor, blending in with the pools of water that formed rivulets around the body, and he zoomed in on the glass tabletop. From what he could see through the rain, it looked intact, though, so the broken glass was something else. Perhaps glasses, or a large ashtray. That would be his question number two.

And that was that. He frowned. In the stories, the detective always finds clues. Here, there was nothing. No blood patterns, no important objects on the balcony, no breached safe or cabinet, no shoe marks, nothing that would traditionally help in a murder investigation. But, hold on. Pierre looked down and noticed a very faint footprint, or rather a half print right by the door, on the inside, still wet, very slightly muddy. It startled him. He quickly looked around, but Margo wasn't back yet. The full responsibility of having found a real clue hit him. He took a quick picture, but that wouldn't help. He searched for information in his mind, and finally, he dug a quarter out of his pocket and placed it by the print. Otherwise, how would anyone know what size it was?

Then, fully aware that thoroughness is key, he went on a photo-taking frenzy and began a systematic sweep of all the guests, both of the groups they were huddling in, and of larger, individual ones. Everyone who hadn't snuck away in the initial confusion was photographed.

Meantime, the orchestra members were fidgeting, beginning to pack up their sheet music and their instruments, and it felt like a lull had fallen over the room, and the guests began to move toward the doors. But Pierre knew that Margo would be distraught if the people left, so he hurried toward the makeshift stage and asked the musicians to wait for a while. Then he stood on the podium and addressed the guests.

"Ladies and gentlemen, I'm sorry that all this has ruined your party, and y'all look like you're ready to leave, but please wait around a little longer. We must ask you a few questions as maybe someone can provide information about what happened here tonight. I'll ask the musicians to continue playing, and the waiters to keep food and drinks coming, so please be patient."

Pierre signaled to a couple of waiters to bring something to drink, and then he stepped down from the podium to go in search of Margo.

Chapter 6

Oops

SAFFRON SIGUR REALIZED—from the moment she stepped into the ballroom—what a terrible mistake she had made, and all for a furtive kiss in a dark alley that had really meant nothing. There had been a murder, just a few feet away from her, and, where was she? The Star Reporter? Well, not covering the murder, that was for sure. And now that she had sent her photographer home—after the aforementioned furtive kiss—she didn't even have a cameraman to cover the scene.

The ballroom was cold. She wiped the raindrops from her arms and shook her glorious mane of red hair, and a small shower of tiny drops formed a cloud around her, and the drops lingered in the air for a second before they plopped onto the marble floor.

Saffron looked around and saw no Sam. She didn't really know why she always looked for Sam when she entered a room, but it had become a habit. Next, she looked for Margo and laughed at herself. That too had become a habit, because whenever there was a murder, Margo was never more than a few feet away from it.

And as her eyes swept the room and took in the two dozen or so affluent and powerful couples she usually reported on in the Social Pages, she noticed a quiet shadow behind a marble column, and her reporter's antennas twitched. Without taking her eyes off the furtive figure, she pulled the phone from her purse and, as surreptitiously as she could—so as not to make the shadow bolt—she took a few photographs as she walked closer to it.

From the corner of her eye, she saw Manuel approach Pierre and talk to him, and saw Margo walking right behind him, and she got distracted for a few seconds. By the time she looked back at the column, the figure was gone. She hurried to the spot and looked around it, and then at the floor, but there was nothing, except for a small square of tissue paper with a smudge of lipstick on it. Did that mean that the figure had been a woman? Or had it been dropped on the floor by an earlier guest? She picked the tissue up with a piece of scrap paper she found in her purse so as not to touch it and soon forgot all about it.

Somewhere, a gong went off, and Saffron looked at her watch. Midnight, like in the Cinderella story. But the story she had just stepped into had a long and dark prelude, one that she was not prepared for, and it was one in which the redheaded princess would never see her prince again.

Someone had told her that there was a dead man on the balcony. She ran up the marble staircase and stood in the middle of the ballroom, and she knew they were staring at her. Statuesque and stunningly beautiful, daughter of Ava Sigur—the famous opera singer—and a pretty darn good singer herself, Saffron knew that she was not every wife's cup of tea. Because every man in the room was gawking at her like they always did. Her green, skintight sequins dress suited her complexion, and especially her magnificent red hair, and those large green bewitching eyes that every man coveted to possess.

And then she saw him. She hurried to the balcony, not believing her own eyes. She had to control her feelings because the room had fallen silent and everyone was staring, but she felt her universe collapse under her feet, and she had to hold on to the balcony door so that she wouldn't faint.

The fire of regret burned deep inside her, and a million thoughts raced through her mind. What-ifs followed what-ifs, but there was no changing the past, nor the present, for that matter. She would get over it, eventually. She had, once or twice before. After all, he'd never really been hers, and now for sure, he never would be.

It had been a long day, and she wished she could go home. She doubted that she had the courage to confront what was to come. As soon as she saw him from the middle of the room, she had known it was him. Even under that wall of rain, she knew. Even from that far away, she knew.

Agnes Makóczy

She watched Margo, Manuel and Pierre herd the guests toward another room, and soon the hall became empty. In the deep, dark quiet, Saffron stood by the balcony. Now that she was alone, she couldn't stop her tears anymore. The rain had stopped but drops hung onto the glass walls like tiny shiny crystals—as the teardrops running down her face—and down in the bay, the sea had calmed down, and the boats were no longer being tossed about like irrelevant toys, and Saffron put her right hand on her heart, hoping that it wouldn't break. Where are you, Sam, when I need you? She asked herself, and a vision of knowing Sam to be in danger ran through her like a premonition.

Outside on the balcony, the dead man slept. On the floor, diluted by the rainwater, reddish puddles luminesced in the moonlight. Oh, you poor Vinnie, what have you gotten yourself into this time? Saffron shook her head sadly. She wished she could step outside and quietly sit on the floor next to him, so she could put his handsome head in her lap. Maybe pray for him that all his sins should be forgiven, and he could go on to Heaven. She banged her fists angrily at the glass walls. How could this have been allowed to happen? How? But, deep down, she knew. This was the last scrape Vinnie would ever get himself into. That was for sure. But where was Sam?

Chapter 7

After-Party

ODETTE ALVES WAITED UNTIL THE LAST CAR VANISHED into the thickening fog and approached the Gallery from East Anchor Street, at the back. Boy, the party had lasted a long time. But finally, the alley was quiet, the Gallery dark. Only one tiny light flickered upstairs, somewhere.

She crossed the narrow street in haste, doing her best to avoid the puddles. The brunt of the rain had passed, but there was still an annoying drizzle in the air.

By the yellowish light of the flickering streetlamp, Odette poked about in her purse until she found the keys, and she gave her surroundings careful, paranoid looks before she inserted the key in the lock and entered.

She had done this so many times before. Even back when the structure wasn't yet The Gallery but just any old building. She moved around in the dark hallway with confidence and headed to where Vinnie's office was.

But it struck Odette right away that something was wrong. She tried to comprehend, sensing something intangible, something unusual, even as her common sense warned her not to imagine things. Because surely everything was just fine, as usual.

One of the windows was open, way at the back of the room. From where she stood, she could see the diaphanous curtains billow in the gentle breeze, under the tenuous light coming in from the street. Some cats under the window were making love—loud enough to raise the dead—and then a male voice coming from the alley yelled at them something rude and disturbing, concerning their need to shut up. And Vinnie didn't make a comment.

If Vinnie had been in the room, he would have cursed at the sudden disruption of his private silence. But not a sound broke the absolute quiet of the house, and the hairs on Odette's arms and back stood up.

She sniffed the air, realizing that she couldn't smell Vinnie's cologne. The scent of musk traveled with Vinnie wherever he went. You could usually tell he was in a room by the all-pervading scent. But as Odette sniffed the air, half feeling ridiculous, half worried, she just knew that he wasn't anywhere near.

She stumbled back toward the wall to look for the lights, feeling the empty space with her open hands, suddenly disoriented in the dark. Never had she been in this room in the dark. She didn't even know where the light switch was.

As the seconds on the grandfather clock ticked by in the echoing silence, Odette's anxiety grew. It took all her willpower not to bolt. By the time she finally found the switch, she was about to scream.

And when the lights came on, she did scream for real. And she screamed and screamed. The room was in complete disarray, as if a tornado had gone through it. All of Vinnie's beloved books—that had sat on shelves strategically mingled with statuettes, and vases, and other examples of ancient Houma native art—were all on the floor, strewn in disorganized piles. Many pieces of art had fallen or had been thrown purposefully on the floor and lay smashed into pieces. Others were missing. She knew all the pieces, most of which she had helped Vinnie acquire. She knew exactly which ones were missing.

She ran from one spot to another in a panic, trying to understand. Then she ran from room to room, turning lights on as she went, screaming for him, but finding the place empty.

She took the stairs two at a time, that horrible feeling crushing her chest. She ran into the ballroom and saw that the remnants of the party hadn't been picked up but had been abandoned, left behind. The building was deserted. Vinnie was gone.

Then, a flash of color caught her eye, and she went out on the balcony. The yellow strip of silk had been caught on a jutting piece of wrought iron and was fluttering in the wind, shining in the moonlight. It was the silk that the artifact had been wrapped in. But of the artifact, there was no trace.

Odette hung on to the balcony guard rail with shaking hands and looked out into the bay and watched the clouds drift by, and the little boats bob on the restless sea. It was over. Vinnie was gone, the artifact was gone, and the place had been abandoned in a hurry.

It was pointless to wonder what had happened. A cold dread spread across her whole body. She had to get out of town immediately. Vinnie was probably dead, and she could be next.

Chapter 8

Two Crows

THE ROAD TO TWO CROWS WAS LONG AND ARDUOUS. Deep in the heart of Louisiana, most of it was little more than dirt, with a few lonely stretches of paving.

Odette had taken this trip so many times in the last ten years that she had memorized every pothole, every abandoned gas station, and every burned down farm.

It was a solitary trip that took the driver from the modern seaside town of Half Moon Bay back in time, mile by mile, until—after five or six hours of grueling driving—you arrived at your destination: the Two Crows Reservation where she had been born and had lived until her mom—tired of being slapped around by an abusive partner—had run away with her little girl in the middle of the night.

But the abusive partner had eventually died of liver failure, years and years later, prompting her and her mom to return to Two Crows.

Then, on a quiet afternoon, as a couple of youngsters ran and hopped by the riverbank collecting shells, the life of the little town changed. It started with a thigh bone sticking out of the dirt, causing numerous adults to run to the site to investigate. Before long, they had uncovered pottery, a treasure trove of.

By then, Odette knew Vinnie well enough. She had gone to middle school and high school with his daughter. And she had always had a crush on her friend's handsome, outgoing, and charming dad.

Odette—missing the more exciting life of the big town that she had left behind—had grabbed the chance to go back and talk to him, to show him what they had found. She was well aware that he bought and sold art. And so, the idea was born.

And now, Vinnie had vanished. She had long suspected that what she and the rest of the village were doing was sort of illegal. They should have gone to the Tribal Council and asked what to do with the artifact trove. They should have shared the money that seemed to never stop coming with the others, but they were just so very poor, so very isolated from the rest of the reservation. So, they tacitly agreed to say nothing. After all, they hated giving up an income that was big enough for their tiny enclave, but not quite big enough to share with the whole tribe.

After reaching US-91, she drove North for a solid two hours, turned off at a feeder road, and then turned onto a narrow substandard road, and after a few miles, stopped at her usual Rest Stop to stretch her legs and use the bathroom. This was the last place with a bathroom until she reached home.

She walked around the parking lot for a while. There was a time when a woman had felt safe walking around by herself in the early morning. But now that the world had changed, she couldn't help but dart suspicious glances about any time that an unusual sound pierced the silence.

Soon, the sun began to awaken, tingeing the horizon with pale yellows and oranges. A few strips of angry clouds floated by, reminding her of last night's storm and Vinnie's disappearance.

She stifled a sob and walked to the WC building. After using the restroom and washing her face with cold water, she braced herself for the day.

With a couple of dollars, she bought enough coffee from the vending machine to refill her thermos, and then she went back to her car.

She looked around the parking lot, the semi-abandoned, decrepit rest stop, and made sure that nothing had changed. No surveillance cameras had been installed—not yet, anyway. So, she unscrewed her license plate and changed it for the one Vinnie had given her for an emergency. Then she pulled off the flower decals that she had wanted so badly at one time. Bought online on Amazon, they came off as easily as they had advertised. Old license plate and torn decals went into the trash bag on the back seat. No way would she leave them in the trash cans at the rest stop for the cops or the others to find. Vinnie had taught her well.

Odette quickly changed into men's clothes and tucked her hair into a baseball cap. Her body was angular enough and tall enough to allow her to pass for a man when viewed by a surveillance camera.

And with this, she'd done everything she could, to disappear. Now, she was going to go back to Two Crows and lay low and wait to hear from Vinnie. And never go back to Half Moon Bay until he let her know that it was safe. Unless he was already dead.

Fifteen minutes later, Odette pulled up at the last gas station. While the pump filled her gas tank, she looked around. One lonely person inside the building stood by the cash register and ignored her as she slapped a $10 and a $20 on the table. Whatever. She didn't feel like talking either.

The sun was completely up now, and the sky was clear blue. Trees and bushes sparkled like diamonds as the last drops of rain on their leaves caught the sunlight. The foliage behind the gas station was alive with birds chirping and with leaves rustling in the pleasant early morning breeze. For a second, she wondered about the strip of yellow silk fluttering on the balcony banister. Then, she hopped in her car and headed home.

Chapter 9

DAY TWO: Sam In The Swamps

SHERIFF SAM STARK DROVE PAST THE MARITIME MUSEUM IN THE DARK, slowly crossing small settlements, and lonely, crumbling farms with rotting lean-to barns, keeping to the lower speed limit. All seemed quiet. Town after town, farm after farm, the world still slept. No dogs rushed to the fences to stare at him or to bark suspiciously.

His window was open a wedge, and the cool air rushed in at him, bringing in the mildewy scents of the after-storm. Everywhere, puddles of water filled the potholes, and the trees still dripped after last night's downpour. Respectfully—to awaken no one—he drove on silently through the quiet towns, envious of their chance to sleep.

Once he hit the highway, the trees, the barns, and the empty roadside fruitstands around him became brighter and more discernable, as the awakening nature began lifting from the early morning fog. Spanish moss hung from the old oak trees that grew alongside the road and shivered in the early morning breeze. A couple of deer ran across the road in front of him and soon disappeared into the horizon. Some black and white cows walked out of the mist and looked at the truck curiously with grass hanging from their mouths. And Sam inhaled the sweet morning air.

The gas tank showed almost empty, and Sam turned off at the edge of Allons, the last town with a gas pump, into Lou's Gas Station, and grunted with disappointment when he saw that it was Lou himself at the pumps. Now he was going to have to play nice. He was in no mood to be amicable, but Lou was such a friendly guy. He didn't have the heart to be rude.

He got out of the car to stretch his long legs and get a whiff of fresh air, and he patiently listened to Lou talk about everything Lou liked to talk about while he tanked. Here and there he grunted a *yes* or a *no,* accordingly. Finally, with a big sigh of relief, carrying the Styrofoam cup of steaming-hot coffee that Lou had insisted on putting into his hands, that was over, and he hopped into his vehicle and drove on.

His head was still hurting from last night. There must have been something seriously wrong with that moonshine his cousins had cooked up. And being on duty on the road was not the way he preferred to spend the day after throwing up all night. But at least he hadn't ended up at the emergency room at St. Hildegard's like his uncle Joe, or like that other guy, friend of theirs, that died in the ambulance. Anyway, time was of the essence when a kid went missing. In this weather, and with the swamps full of snakes and gators, it would be lucky if she was ever found.

He thought about the previous night, and a furious blush of embarrassment spread across his face. He remembered getting ready for the Gallery opening, dressing especially smartly, knowing that Saffron would be there, looking forward to being with her, to holding her in his arms while they danced, and he gritted his teeth in anger. He banged a fist on the dashboard. What a fool he had been. Shouldn't have waited this long. By the time he had gathered his courage to ask her out, it was too late. Walking toward the Gallery building, after having parked his truck, he noticed that unmistakable mop of blazing red hair next to a corner under the street lamp, and the man who kept stepping up closer and closer to her and finally sweeping her into his arms to give her a passionate kiss. The shock had rooted him to the ground. That should have been him, not that stranger. After that, there was no point in going. He didn't particularly like parties anyway. He had only accepted the invitation because of her. He turned back to his truck, shaking with anger and frustration, and drove out to the dirt road in the middle of nowhere, where his uncle and cousins were having a fais do-do to taste the new batch of moonshine.

Following the truck's GPS directions, he stopped at the side of the dirt road at a clearing by the river, and he got out of the truck. It was good to stretch his legs, but he looked down at the mud with disgust. He was glad that he had worn his old, beat-up boots instead of his new KaiFeng Military Tactical ones. They might be waterproof and engineered for difficult terrain, and they might be shock-absorbent and more comfortable, but as his feet sunk into the gravelly wetness, sucked under by the mud, he was glad that he had saved his brand new KaiFengs for a friendlier occasion.

The early morning was chilly, windy, and he shivered in his jacket. It still drizzled in waves, the splatter barely drying up with the weak sunshine before another quick shower came down. The spot where the child had disappeared from was at the other side of the river, deep into swampland. Impossible to reach by car. He pulled an old, wrinkled Louisiana map from the glove compartment and he spread it out on the hood of the truck. He wasn't so good at map reading. Especially where every river's bend looked exactly alike. Still, he did recognize vaguely where he was, and he had a fairly good grasp on how he could get to where he had to go.

He walked down to the edge of the river and looked around. From where he was parked, he had seen a flat-bottomed boat at the edge of the water, pulled up onto the shrubbery. A lot of people did that out here, just left their boat right by the water. But that presented three, possibly four problems. First, he couldn't just steal the boat, Sheriff, or no Sheriff. It went against his nature even if by law he was allowed to do so. Second, he wasn't even sure how to maneuver a boat on a quiet river, much less how to cross a torrential, furious waterway like this one. Third, the place was infested with alligators. And lastly, but most importantly, he realized, the water—after all those rains—was too high for comfort. As if to prove his point, the bloated body of a dead dog floated by on the swollen water, and Sam almost changed his mind about the whole thing. He was not a tracker like Andy had been, and he was certainly no swamp man. He was a city man, and a sick one at that, and he really wanted to go back home and nurse his hangover. But again, worries about the lost child nagged at his conscience.

Sam squirmed, trying to make a decision. He had an enormous respect for the river and felt intimidated by it. But on the other hand, he was the only policeman left in Half Moon Bay—since Andy took up a life of crime—and someone just had to do something. And wasn't this the reason he had joined the police department anyway?

He remembered Andy, and he grunted with frustration. He had been fond of his deputy. They had worked well together. And now he was all alone in this. And he had at best a very vague idea of what to do.

But he was wasting time. The sun was just up, and he had a long day ahead of him. Might as well make up his mind and get going.

He shoved the cell phone into his breast pocket and buttoned it up, just in case. Then, he grabbed car keys, sunglasses, hat, and the map, and placed them in his regulation backpack. He was kind of glad that he had brought it along. It had crackers, protein bars, and about a gallon of water. He had no idea what he was getting into and came prepared as best as he could.

He walked over to the boat and stared at it. It had about two inches of water sitting in the bottom. He was going to get his boots wet. He hated that. First the mud, and now the water. Well, it was a boat at least, and there was a paddle in it. An oar? It had an engine as well, small, pulled out of the water. He wasn't even going to mess with that. He had no idea how it worked.

He pushed the boat toward the water and managed to jump in at the last possible moment before it floated away, carried by the current. Then, he grabbed the oar and rowed. As precarious as the going was, he soon got used to the rhythm of the gushing river and began to enjoy himself.

The morning was amazing. As the sun slowly came up, it colored the world around him, bringing it back to life, and the frothy, noisy, oily dark liquid of the muddy river shimmered. Every time he moved the oar, a soft whoosh tugged at his hand and moved the displaced water in ever greater circles. Pelicans, perched on the dead branches of swamp trees, watched him as he carefully paddled by.

Not a reader of poetry nor a soft-hearted man, he still couldn't help but enjoy the moment, the scenery, the birds, the power of the river. After rowing for a few minutes, he noticed another couple of boats, strategically bobbing in coves, almost hidden by the vegetation, where fishermen with floppy hats drank stuff out of steaming mugs while they held their fishing rods patiently. Old men. Old-timers, waiting for something to bite. Hardy ones, willing to be outdoors in this weather.

After about fifteen minutes of being pretty much carried by the currents, he hit solid ground close to the red, rusty water tank on stilts that was his landmark, and he jumped out, pulling the boat to dry ground. He turned around and scrutinized the horizon but couldn't see his pickup anymore. It kind of worried him, thinking that he might never be able to find it again, but he did have his cell phone, and it was fully charged and turned off to preserve the battery charge. He patted his breast pocket and grinned to himself. Amazing how having a cell phone filled you with confidence.

Well, and there he was. All he could see around him were trees and more trees. He looked at the sun coming up on the horizon behind the water tank, and he consulted his map and his compass and decided he knew which way to go, so he set off in that direction.

The kid had been last seen skipping and hopping into the woods right before the storm. The grandparents had told her in no uncertain terms to stay put, but the kid had just giggled and said she'd be right back. Anybody's guess where she was going. Probably to pick some figs or wild berries. And then the storm had barreled through, and the grandpa had gone out to look for her apparently without much enthusiasm and hadn't found her. That was the last time they saw her. And now, her daddy would be home from the oil rig first thing next Monday, and she could be God only knew where. And could y'all please find her.

The problem was that the previous storm had come and gone three days earlier, and they hadn't bothered to call the station until now when last night's new storm had rolled in. What kind of grandparents were these, anyway? And how long had the kid really been missing?

Sam looked at the map again. To his right, the decaying Hébert farm, his next landmark. Once very successful at growing sugar cane and fishing, the Héberts eventually got old and left their farm to their only son, who skipped town the day after his last parent died, never to be seen again. The neighbors finally had to come and rescue the dogs, pigs, and cows that the kid had callously left behind after hearing them cry for days on end. Now, even the neighbors were gone, having moved to higher ground when the river kept flooding their homes, ruining their crops, and killing their animals.

Not much farther, now. He walked carefully, at times slipping on the accumulation of wet, rotting leaves under the tree canopy. It wasn't a hot day, but the humidity was brutal, making him sweat profusely, the moisture dripping from his face, running down his neck and his back, drenching his clothes, sticking to his body. At least the rain had finally stopped.

Jungle sounds, he thought, listening to the myriad bugs chirping, and the birds twittering among the branches. Behind him, the swollen river roiled by in a foaming chocolate-colored mess, carrying debris and dead things, rushing to the juncture where it would join Shark Bayou, and from then on, the open sea.

From what he knew, the girl's mother was dead, and it was the dad who had been raising her. But she stayed with the grandparents when he was on his rotation on the oil rig. Not much love lost for the young child, then, he thought to himself.

And finally, the clearing. He stopped to get a sip of water and to look at the map and the compass to make sure he was still going in the right direction, and then he started walking again. After a while—mildly surprised that he had actually found it—there it was. It was a typical swamp house, at the edge of the water. Built on stilts out of what seemed to be recycled lumber and remnants of other materials thrown together in a mishmash to simulate a house. But he quickly checked his critical opinion. It was run down, granted, the wood bleached by the rough outdoors, but it seemed well built. Solid stilts. A boat tied to a pole on land, an ugly mutt—tied down to a post by the side of the house—barking wildly, announcing his arrival.

Again, Sam hesitated. If it hadn't been for the mutt jumping ferociously and straining on its chain, he would have just walked up to the house and knocked on the door. But he wavered. He knew these swamp people had their own rules, etiquette, whatever, and he didn't want to start on the wrong foot. Still, he didn't have all day. He approached the dog to calculate how he was going to get around it, but at that moment the door opened, catching both him and the dog off guard.

Chapter 10
Margo Looks For Sam

MEANTIME, MARGO RAN UP THE STEPS OF THE TINY POLICE STATION OF HALF MOON BAY and opened the door to the frigid headquarters of Sheriff Sam, and Maurice, the only policemen left in town. After all these years, the extreme cold temperature at which these two kept the building still gave her a shock.

Maurice—as usual—sat at the front desk, pretending to look busy, but probably just playing with his phone.

"Good morning, Maurice," she said with a big smile. "Is Sam in?"

"No, Miss Fontaine, sorry."

"Where did he go?"

"He didn't say."

"He didn't say anything?"

"Just that he had to go see about something."

"Come on, Maurice. Sam doesn't talk like that."

"He does, sometimes. He said that, and he left."

"Maurice, please remember. Before that, did he say anything? Did he give a hint?"

"Well, it's like this. I arrived on time as usual, and he was already here. Door unlocked and all that. So, I went into his office, and I found him with his boots on the desk, and his hands behind his head. He looked like he was thinking hard."

"Yes, and then what?"

"He asked me if I knew how to track someone in the swamps. Like I was an Indian tracker, you know, like a Coushatta."

"And?"

"Well, I told him no. Where was I going to learn that? I was just the little fat black kid that everyone made fun of in school."

"My God, Maurice, but you're not fat."

"Maybe not anymore, but I used to be. And I still feel touchy about that."

"Gosh, Maurice, that's nuts. You're tall and handsome, and you shouldn't feel insecure. Now tell me what else Sam said."

"What he says every day about missing Andy. So, I went to my desk. He came out a few minutes later and he said what he said. And he left."

And that was that.

Chapter 11

Sam And The Swamp Man

THE GUY STANDING IN FRONT OF SAM WAS OLD, unkempt, and grumpy looking. He wore stained threadbare jeans and a shirt that might have been a rust-red plaid at one time. And he had murder in his eyes. In case you doubted that, all you had to do was stare into the face of that powerful looking rifle pointed at your chest. And he looked the kind of man who was willing to pull the trigger at the slightest provocation.

"Shut up, you fleabag," the man snarled and kicked the unfortunate mutt for good measure. "And you, what can I help you with?"

"Is that a Timber Classic Marlin?" Sam asked good-naturedly, hoping to defuse the man's antagonism.

"Yes. Who wants to know?" The man aggressively took one step forward and touched Sam's chest with the barrel.

"You can point that rifle somewhere else, sir," Sam told him gently, raising his arms slowly and very calmly. "My name is Sam Stark. I'm the Sheriff of Half Moon Bay, and you must be John Armentor. Here about the granddaughter you reported missing."

"Oh yeah, Luna. Sorry about that, Sheriff," Armentor said, lowering the rifle and patting Sam on the back. "We've had too many strangers lurking about lately. Come in, come in."

The man turned toward the house and entered, and Sam followed. The mutt yapped a couple of times but retreated prudently to a corner. The man was shorter than Sam, but he was stocky, powerfully built. His hair was so oily that Sam had to wonder whether it had ever gotten washed.

Suddenly blind in the darkness of the small house, he blinked hard until his eyes adjusted, and he could see again. The one room in front of him was both living and dining, and to one side, a makeshift kitchen blended into the penumbra of the house. The sink was full of dirty dishes.

"Sit, sit," the man said. "Let me get you a cup of coffee, Sheriff. Just brewed it. Wife's out back, washing. She'll be right in if you want to talk to her."

"Yes, thank you." Sam sat cautiously on the soiled green sofa. He shuddered with disgust. It was moist and sticky from the constant humidity of the swamps, and it smelled offensively of mildew. It was a good thing he had a spare uniform in his office. After the mildew stains that would probably stick to his pants, he would have to change right away. "So, your granddaughter," he said.

"Luna."

"Yes, Luna. She's still not back, is she?"

"No. Haven't seen her. Ever since she said she'd be right back before that storm hit."

"But you waited three days and another storm to report her missing. Why's that?"

"Because she's always running away and then coming back by herself."

"I see. Can you show me the place where you saw her last?"

"Sure. Let me tell the wife that we're leaving. Finish your coffee. I'll be right back."

While Armentor was gone, Sam walked around the small house. The wooden floorboards creaked under his boots. The furniture was old, and other than a couple of nice antiques, looked haphazard and mismatched. A side table was covered with dusty odds and ends and a few photographs in frames. He picked one up, in faded color. A pretty girl sat on a young man's lap. She had her arms lovingly around his neck and was smiling into the camera. They were as alike as two peas in a pod, those two, and Sam figured they had to be Luna and her dad. Another older, much older picture in black and white of a young man standing by a dead alligator hanging on a scaffolding. It had been enormous, that alligator, and Sam winced. He wondered how the man had managed to fight and ultimately kill such a massive beast.

"That was a big one," the man said as he stepped back into the room. "I caught it back in 1960 something. Sold it to the tanner for a good bit."

"Is this Luna?" Sam asked holding up the picture.

"Yes, that's her and her dad. Brad's his name. You ready?"

Sam followed Armentor out and adjusted his backpack.

"Good thing you're wearing those high leather boots, Sheriff."

"Why's that?"

"Because of the snakes. They'll go for your ankles. But they won't bite through that leather."

"How about alligators?"

Armentor laughed. "They're not scared of leather boots."

They stepped outside into the grim humidity, and the muddy soil squished under Sam's feet. The day had become lighter, and the rays of the sun filtered obliquely through the tree canopy, and he realized that his surroundings were not as monochromatic as he had first thought. Wild stuff grew all over the place, and some of it pretty colorful. He inhaled deeply the fresh, clean air.

Armentor untied the dog which got all excited and jumped up and down despite the insults by his owner. It made him think of Andy, that faithless bastard, who had gone on a murderous rampage and left him in this mess alone. Andy had been good with dogs. And right now, he would know exactly how to track down a little girl in the swamps.

Chapter 12

The Swamps

THEY SET OFF QUIETLY, WALKING IN COMPANIONABLE SILENCE. The weakly shimmering sun crawled up the sky behind a translucent haze. A chilly breeze swept through the brush, whistling softly, making the smaller leaves of the bushes around Sam tremble. Oblivious to the cold, the mutt ran on ahead, following the trail, its tail wagging with enthusiasm, its warm breath forming a cloud around its head. From time to time, it turned around and came back to hop in front of the old man, but then it ran ahead again, visibly happy to be free. Sam figured it didn't get allowed off the chain too often and felt sorry for the poor devil. The existence of a dog out there, not so good, while the pampered dogs of Half Moon Bay lived out their lives in luxury.

Within a few minutes, he turned around to orient himself. The house had receded into the haze, its grayed wooden planks blending in with the foggy horizon. Already you could barely see it, it had become so small and indistinct. Sam felt a frisson of foreboding thinking that on his own he would probably never find this place again.

Armentor wasn't much of a talker, so he had a chance to look around. The woods were thick and overgrown, the trail narrow, the trees so tall that they seemed to reach the sky. Wet, dead leaves carpeted the ground and squished under his boots. They were slippery and made him walk cautiously. Around him, the wetlands sat treacherously deep, hiding in the gloom.

"Make sure you follow me and don't stray to the sides," said Armentor. "It might look like solid ground, but it ain't always so." So, he obeyed and followed carefully. In this strange and alien world, everything looked surreal to him. Dead trees with gnarled naked branches rose from the swamps here and there, and that ugly moss hung on everything. Large, scraggly birds perched on the naked branches and eyed them evilly as they passed. Other things hung too, from the lower-lying branches, and he found himself slapping them off his face and his neck. Swarms of mosquitos followed them, buzzing hungrily. As much as he tried to shoo them away, there was no getting rid of them.

"So, tell me, Armentor. Why are we coming this way? Was it this far out that you saw her the last time?"

"Nah, not this far out. But she must have come his way. It's the only walkable path that won't swallow you up. I can tell you that nobody ever comes this way. And I mean nobody, so how come I'm looking at those footprints and all that trampled weed? She had to have come this way or no way at all."

Sam shivered with dread. "Could she have fallen in and drowned?" he asked, hating himself for having to bring it up.

"Could be. Storm came up pretty fast." Armentor stopped and turned toward Sam. The mutt stopped a way ahead and looked at Sam as well. He thought that Armentor was about to ask something or say something, but the old man's bushy eyebrows just wrinkled, and he looked sadly at Sam.

Soon enough, the fog finally lifted and Sam, even without tracking skills, began to discern the footprints and drag marks on the ground. Footprints were good, they could follow those, but he was concerned about the drag marks. He didn't want to worry the old man, but it was obvious what the marks implied. Dead or unconscious. Being pulled as dead weight. But he wasn't about to say that.

"How about those footprints? Could they be Luna's?" he asked.

"Too big for a girl. They are boots. Look at the indent. And see, they become deeper here. Heavy square heels, sunk in the mud, big guy probably." Armentor shook his head sadly.

"Or one not so big, but carrying something heavy?"

"Could be," said Armentor. He stopped and turned around to talk to Sam but didn't make eye contact. He had that worried look again. "My son's going to be back in a couple of days, and his little girl's gone. There will be hell to pay."

"Then why did you let her go?"

"I didn't want to tell you this, Sheriff, but it wasn't me. I wasn't home. It was the wife. She doesn't care much for Luna. Was probably happy to be rid of her for a bit."

"But she's her granddaughter," said Sam, horrified.

"Nah, she isn't. She's a new wife. She doesn't like kids much, either."

After a while of walking in silence, Armentor stopped abruptly. He put a finger on his lip to signal silence and closed his eyes. Sam waited. Even the mutt waited, but then unexpectedly, as if someone had whistled to call it, the dog took off, with Armentor right behind it.

"Stop," the old man yelled as he ran. "Stop, you fleabag. Where are you going?" But the fleabag kept on running. And Armentor not far behind, in pursuit. Then, there was some commotion in the shrubbery some distance away. And finally, nothing. Suddenly, Sam was alone in the clearing, and where man and dog had disappeared, only an eerie silence and some broken branches testified to them ever having been there. What had just happened?

Sam's heart started beating wildly. What now? He was very confused. Should he wait? Should he follow? He looked around, disoriented. He had no idea what had happened. He had no idea where he was. He had been so busy following Armentor that he had paid no attention to the direction in which they were going. He should have been designating landmarks, as common sense and training would have dictated so that he could orient himself.

He turned around and around trying to figure out what to do. He yelled out to the old man, even whistled to the dog. But no sound answered. Even the birds and critters in the shrubbery had gone quiet. The absolute stillness made his skin crawl. But he couldn't stand there all day. There was nothing else to do but follow their route. Maybe he could catch up with them. Find them.

He started off, cautiously, following the trail left behind by the man and his dog. Pushing aside shrubs and hanging moss, he watched his feet, careful to not step on a snake or something worse, like an alligator's tail.

He tried to remember what he had heard about them. Eight feet long, the smaller females. The males, much, much bigger. Carnivorous. Jaws so strong that they can crack a turtle's shell. Swallow their smaller prey whole, but the bigger prey, they shake it apart into smaller, manageable pieces. Not so active in cold weather. Sam watched his breath mist as he exhaled and was suddenly grateful for the chill in the air. With some luck, the alligators would be holed up somewhere, keeping warm.

At the next clearing, he stopped. One single paw print in the mud and some trampled vegetation told him that Armentor and his dog had come this way. But where were they?

He took his backpack off and took out map, compass, and pencil. He wiped his wet brow and took a swig of water. It might not be hot, but it sure was humid. Then he placed the compass flat in his hand. He turned the degree dial until the arrow lines and the magnetic arrow both pointed North, and he paused to scratch his head. He consulted his map, made some notes. If he was really heading North—as he figured—and he kept on going in the same direction, for sure he was going to reach Shark Bayou. After that, there would be nothing else but open water.

He took the cellphone out of his pocket and turned it on. He'd heard that out here in the swamps, the reception was spotty. Unless there were small communities with repeating towers, there would be no signal. He walked around the clearing, moving the phone in one direction and then the other, but nothing.

He decided to keep going for 30 more minutes, and if he didn't find Armentor and his dog, he would backtrack his steps and look for a place where he could get satellite reception and call for some help.

Sam put all his stuff away. The phone got turned off and went back into his shirt pocket. The sun was up in the horizon now, and the weather had suddenly become very hot and humid. He took his jacket off, rolled it up, and put it in his backpack as well. Then, compass in one hand, water bottle in the other, he headed out.

He had no intention of crossing the body of water at Shark Bayou. Not even if he found an abandoned boat big enough and safe enough to make it to the other side. According to the map, Cypremort Point was on the South-West tip of the bayou, and there was nothing but marshes on the other side. What would Armentor and his dog be doing there anyway?

Besides, a mass of sharks had been filmed swimming around an oil rig off the coast of Grand Isle not long ago. He had never given a thought to sharks swimming in Louisiana waters, but now, faced with the idea of having to navigate the bayou, it became a reality, and an ugly one at that. The news, he remembered, had mentioned that sharks don't travel in schools, that they're solitary creatures. But there was nothing solitary about the gathering of sharks he had seen on TV. He wondered if they grouped around the oil rigs hoping someone would fall into the water, a disquieting thought, and the possibility of intelligent animals, working together.

Ten more minutes, he told himself, consulting his watch, and he was going to turn and head back. He stopped at the next clearing to have another sip of water and looked down about his feet. The vegetation was seriously trampled around him, and there was rusty red liquid shining on some wild grass. He took his backpack off and bent down on one knee. He brushed the coagulating liquid with one finger and sniffed. It was blood, all right. And he thought he heard dog whelps, but very faint, but he couldn't be sure.

Then he heard some rustling in the bushes. Startled out of his musings, he almost cried out a *qui va?* but a deep-seated instinct for survival urged him to stay silent. Maybe it would be better if he didn't announce himself. He quickly got up and hid behind the bushes. There was someone or something out there, coming his way, moving in a blur among the vegetation, but he couldn't tell if it was animal or human. He moved closer to the darkness of the tight-knit canopy and watched.

He tried to listen, but the bugs and the birds twittered wildly. Something must have frightened them. Still as a shadow, he took quiet, shallow breaths of air, hoping that the interloper couldn't hear his ragged breathing or his wildly beating heart. He shouldn't be in danger because he had hidden himself well. His hand went to his side, and he carefully retrieved his pistol from the holster, and he waited. And then he waited some more, counting the seconds. If it was an animal, it could be anything.

With no experience of wildlife, he had no way of telling if this was a raccoon—harmless—an alligator—not so harmless—or a two-legged foe. But what if it was Armentor himself, hurt, looking to crawl out of the bushes?

He waited, trying to be patient, listening intently, but the silence coming from the shrubbery was absolute. It was maddening this not knowing what was lurking out there, and he almost gave up. With sweaty palms, he held on to the pistol, working hard to control the urge to shoot at the bushes. Breathe, Sam, breathe, he told himself over and over again. The seconds ticked by, and still nothing. As if whatever had been moving in his direction had vanished.

Two more minutes, Sam, just two more minutes. He remained motionless, but it was killing him to be absolutely still. All his instincts were screaming to do something. He kept telling himself that he couldn't step out into the clearing shooting like a madman until he had an idea of what was out there. The hangover headache he had been nursing all morning now grew worse from the stress and beat a cruel tattoo against his skull as he struggled to think. He rubbed his temple with his left hand. What if he stepped out into the clearing, pistol in hand, shooting, and it was Armentor or the little girl? He couldn't allow that to happen.

After the two minutes were up, he figured that the danger was over and he was safe, and he stepped out from behind the tree and back into the clearing. But he must have been discovered, because, at precisely that moment, he heard the rustling again, and much, much closer this time.

He thought about taking off running. The silence around him, the sudden reappearance of whatever was following him, the darkness of the trees around him, the unfamiliar environment, had spooked him. He cursed himself for having abandoned his backpack with the map, the jacket, and all his supplies. At least he had shoved the compass into his pocket.

But he was no coward, so he hesitated. He turned toward the sound and aimed the pistol at the rustling bushes, ready to defend himself. Still unable to see the enemy, he held his position, his sweaty, shaking hands holding the pistol, ready to shoot. He could feel the terror of the unknown crawling into his soul as his skin shivered, and the hairs on his arm stood up. He couldn't take it any longer. It was time to run.

Chapter 13

DAY THREE: Trapped

AS SAM CAME TO AND OPENED HIS EYES, he became aware of a dull, throbbing pain banging mercilessly against his temples. The pounding ache was so unbearable that he could barely blink. He closed his eyes again quickly, hoping for relief. Why was he in so much pain? He tried to move his head but like a jagged knife wound, the pain lashed out at him again, and again, and he stopped. Better not move, for now, he decided, until the head stopped hurting.

He had a vague idea of having been in some sort of danger and recalled feeling an urge to run. Had that really happened? As he struggled to remember, little bits and pieces of memory that almost felt more like snippets of dreams fleeted by. He saw an old man walking in front of him under a thick tree canopy, and he saw a dog, prancing happily ahead of them. Then, the dog barked furiously at the shrubbery, making him uncomfortable. There must have been someone hiding in the bushes. But soon, the images changed, and he nebulously remembered himself being dragged by the feet for a good while. He thought about his back and his neck, and the burning ache that screamed every time he moved. Now he knew where it must have come from.

Then, one image popped into his mind so crystal clear that it startled him wide awake: watching the old man lying on the dirt as he—Sam—was being pulled by the feet, the old man abandoned to the side of the trail with a big gash on his forehead, blood on the spears of grass, and his eyes open, staring up blindly at the sky.

The memory was so vivid that it frightened him. That had been neither hallucination nor dream. And it all came back to him now: the howling of the dog—hurt—and then its sudden silence, its still body lying inertly barely a few feet away from its master, and Armentor, the old man—completely motionless—most probably dead. Had someone killed Armentor first, and then killed the dog?

But then why was he not dead as well? Why hadn't they killed him? It made no sense that the murderer should have killed the old man and his dog, but allowed him to live, did it?

He finally dared open his eyes, his painfully swollen eyelids, and he squinted furiously against the light coming in obliquely from a side window, a relentless sunlight that felt as if it was burning into his corneas.

As he made a move to touch his eyes, he realized he couldn't move his arms. He pulled at them, and he twisted his body this way and that, but he couldn't move. As his mind woke further out of the mists of confusion, he came to the awareness that he was tied up.

"Hello," he tried to yell, but only a garbled, gasping sound came out of his throat. He was desperately thirsty. His mouth was parched dry. "Is anyone there?"

Nothing stirred in the silence of the enclosure. He was alone, and he was trapped. He was hog-tied. Incapacitated. A terrible urge to survive rose from within his soul. He refused to die like a dog in such degrading circumstances. He must get away. He must get away from the madman who had tied him up like this. He threw himself against the ropes that bound him with all his strength. He might not remember so clearly what had happened to him, but he knew that he had to figure out how to escape. God Almighty only knew what they intended to do with him, but the same God Almighty knew that he wasn't planning on staying around long enough to find out.

First and foremost, he had to reconnoiter. He was in a not-so-large place. That was obvious. He noticed the roof. Aluminum. So probably not inside a house, although many rural houses did have aluminum roofs. But still, perhaps a garage, or a shed. In good condition, but old. You can tell these things. So, someone kept the place up. There were no cobwebs that he could see, no bird nests on the corners, no bat nests on the rafters. Place must still be occupied. Therefore, unless the kidnapper was a sadistic murderer with nefarious intents, he hadn't been abandoned to his fate in this place. The setup seemed to have a purpose. The owner might be back soon.

He must have been kidnapped by a man. Why? Well, that was obvious. It would have taken someone of enormous strength to get a big, tall guy like him here. People weren't really aware of how hard it was to drag the inert body of someone any kind of distance. But if his kidnapper was a man, it would also be harder to negotiate a release. Women tended to be more soft-hearted.

The minutes ticked by slowly, and the headache began to subside. Finally, carefully, he turned his head and looked around. The room was darker now, as if the sun were setting, or as if a cloud cover had moved in front of the sun. But he had no clue as to what time of the day it was. This time of the year the days were longer, but that information was of no use to him.

To his left, furs hung on pegs side by side, exuding an unpleasant scent of death and wet, sticky humidity. In the corner, bales of furs, tied together with ropes were arranged into piles two feet thick. It took Sam a few seconds to comprehend that he was in someone's fur house, and then a few more to realize that he had been trussed up on some kind of table and had been tied to it. He grunted with frustration. How could he have allowed for something like this to happen to him of all people, him being the Sheriff of Half Moon Bay?

After a while, he stopped struggling. He needed a plan. Besides, all the aimless twisting and twitching were just exhausting him and exacerbating the pain. His feet were tied at the ankles, and so was his chest. He closed his eyes and tried to think. Somewhere in his brain, there was information on how to escape a situation like this. We never really forget anything, he told himself. He knew of techniques to break free from a kidnapper's restraints. The data was in there somewhere. He scoured his memories trying to remember, fighting the headache, but the recollection was fleeting, and he began to despair. In his frustration, he tossed and turned, grunting. He couldn't help himself. There had to be a way. He dreaded not knowing what they wanted with him. He had to get away.

"It won't work," he heard a girl's soft voice say behind him after a while. Startled to find out that he was not alone, Sam tried to turn his head in the direction of the sound, but the owner of the voice was too far back.

"What won't work? I know what I'm doing," he snapped back.

"No, you don't. I bet you've never been tied up before."

Sam wanted to say something nasty. This was all he needed: to be trapped in a fur house—tied down to a table no less—with a know-it-all kid. But the anger boiled away quickly. She was right. What was the point of denying it?

"You're right, kid. I never have. But I always read the articles on how to free yourself from a bad spot, and I think I'll have a chance if I remember one of them. Besides, you could just come and help me out."

"I would, but I can't. I'm a prisoner too. Maybe you can reason with him, and he'll let us go."

"What are you doing here? Are you tied up as well? I can't see you."

"No. I'm in a cage. I've been here for a couple of days. Maybe three. I forgot to count them."

"Dear Lord, in a cage? Seriously?" The hair on his back stood up, and a shiver of fear crossed his whole body. He was dealing with a madman after all, just as he had assumed. "How did you get here?"

"I went for a walk to get away from Mona, and I got lost. Then, it started raining really hard, and I had to run. But I got more lost, and I saw some guys talking, and I was going to ask them how to get home, but one of them chased me and grabbed me and brought me here."

"But why?"

"I don't know. He never said."

"And you didn't ask?"

"No. I didn't want to upset him. Mona gets angry with me when I ask questions and hits me on the head with something. And the man looked angry, so I thought it was better to be quiet."

"Who's Mona, child?"

"He's my grandfather's new wife. She's as mean as a snake. She hates me."

"Is your grandfather's name by chance John Armentor?"

"It sure is. He's nice to me when she's not around. But I think that he's scared of her, so he ignores me when she's around."

"He's scared of Mona?"

"Oh, yes. Mais oui."

"Tell me something. The kidnapper, has he been mean to you?"

"No, not really. But I make sure that he has no reason to be mean. I behave very politely when he comes in to bring me food and thank him and everything. And I sit in a spot, very proper like, and I stay very still."

"I guess you're right, kid. That's probably safer."

"But I'm scared. I don't like being here. I want to go home."

"Don't worry. I'll get us out of here. So, you're Luna, right?"

"Yes, that's me."

Sam chuckled bitterly. "Nice to meet you, Luna. My name is Sam. I've been looking for you. Your grandfather sent me to find you. I haven't done a very good job so far, but I'll get us out of here somehow. I promise."

Chapter 14

Interrogation

WHILE SAM STRUGGLED WITH HIS ROPES, his terrified mind conjured up disaster scenarios. If only that pounding headache would ease up, so he could think. What was he going to do? What would happen if he couldn't escape? Would they kill him? And would they kill Luna too? Would they be tortured first? The anguish of his helplessness made him thrash against the ropes even harder.

He should have been able to loosen his ties by now. But it seemed like the more he twisted, the tighter they became. He kept on going, determined to tear the ropes with sheer brute force if he had to. But he was out of shape, and he didn't have the strength of his youth. He had to face it. He had gotten old.

Finally, the mental and physical toll of struggling against the ropes got to him. He had no energy left. He stopped. He told himself that a better plan was needed. One requiring brains, not brawn. Problem was that he was weak from hunger. He hadn't eaten or drunk anything since he had set out from home before dawn, and that had been hours ago. He was nauseous from the hunger, the hangover, and the headache. And part of him just wanted to lay there quietly, and close his eyes and nurse his misery, but he knew that he was never going to give up the fight. He couldn't. That was not who he was. Stay sharp, he told himself. Try it one more time.

Determined to get it done this time, he grunted and groaned as he renewed his efforts and strained against his restraints, trying different moves, hoping to loosen the ropes that bound him, wincing as they burned into his flesh but never giving up until he heard the little girl caution him.

"You might as well stop, Sam. He's coming. I can see him coming this way. He'll be angry if he sees that you're trying to escape."

"You're right, Luna. I better stop. Where did you learn to be so wise?"

"I learned from Mona. I'm very scared of Mona."

Sam allowed his muscles to relax. He took a deep breath. The last thing he wanted to do was antagonize his captor. All he would accomplish would be to be tied even tighter.

He saw in his mind little Luna sitting in her corner, hands in her lap, quietly being good. It was gut-wrenching. He never had the chance to meet the woman who had put so much fear into the child and the old man, but he imagined her a monster, and if they got out of there alive, he was going to make sure that Luna would never have anything else to do with her. He couldn't even fathom the unhappiness in which this child must have lived, to be so afraid of displeasing someone.

Then, he heard approaching footsteps crunching on gravel, and the silence was broken. The fur house door banged open, and a slender man stepped through the doorway, his features indistinguishable in the sunlight pouring through the door behind him.

Sam blinked hard, suddenly blinded by the sun's rays. A terrible pain tore into his retinas like stab wounds, and he turned his head away from the light.

The man approached Sam and looked down on him.

"I see you're finally awake. Are you all right?"

It was a strangely disconcerting question, coming from your captor, but Sam nodded. Now that his eyes were adjusting to the bright light, he noticed that the man was young, late twenties, early thirties. Short-cropped sandy blonde hair, wearing round-rimmed glasses. He also looked concerned, and oddly kind.

"I was worried that your head wound might be too deep, and you might die," the young man continued.

"Well, if you let me go, I can find my way back to Half Moon Bay and go to a doctor."

"I'm sorry, but I can't let you do that."

"Sure, you can. I won't tell anyone what happened here."

"That's not it."

"Then what?"

"My brother already knows you're here."

"And?"

"And he told me to keep you here until he arrived."

"But why? What does your brother have to do with all this? And what is he planning to do with us?"

"He won't harm the girl, I'm sure. He likes girls very much. But you, he'll probably kill you."

"But why? I don't even know who he is."

"He knows who you are. He said he couldn't let you live."

Sam turned his head to look at the man better. His neck was hurting so badly from turning that it nauseated him. He grunted with the pain. "Hold on," he said, trying to reason with his captor. "There's no need for this. Your brother isn't here yet, so you should let me go. Before things go any further." The man just shook his head from side to side. He took his glasses off and rubbed the bridge of his nose. There was a look of fear and worry on the pinched face.

"I'm sorry. I can't let you go. I want to, but I can't."

"I'm a police officer. You could get into a lot of trouble for holding me captive."

"I know you're the Sheriff of Half Moon Bay. Makes no difference. I do what my brother tells me."

"At least let me take these clothes off. I'm wet, and I'm cold."

"Sorry, can't."

"And I'm hungry, and I need the bathroom."

The man just stared at Sam sadly and shook his head. The answer was obviously a no to all the above. Sam was out of ideas. The man didn't seem violent, not even unfriendly. But whatever hold the brother had on him, it was unwavering, and it would be impossible to break. He decided to adopt Luna's approach and back off. Wait and see.

Meantime, the man had taken his backpack off, and he walked to the bench and opened it. He took out a bottle of water and told Sam, "Careful, Sheriff. I'll pour some water in your mouth. Drink slowly." And gently he lifted Sam's head with one hand and with the other, held the water bottle close to Sam's mouth so that he could drink. He gulped the water down gratefully.

"Thank you so much, man. I was dying of thirst."

The man nodded. "I'll put a sandwich in your hands. I know they're tied, but if you lean your head forward some, you'll be able to eat."

Sam was ravenous. His upper body was tied with ropes to the narrow table, and his hands were tied in front of him, but by inclining his head forward, he could push his hands far enough to reach his mouth. He thought about Stockholm Syndrome and how easily a prisoner could become grateful to his or her captor. Then he stopped thinking and ate his sandwich.

"Turkey, cheese, a slice of tomato, and mayonnaise," the young man said. "Hellmann's."

Sam nodded with satisfaction. "Awesome sandwich, thanks," he said.

His captor stayed next to him, muttering to himself, looking down at him and watched him eat. But Sam ignored him. It was dreadfully humiliating to be in such a position, eating like a dog, tied down. It was easier not to think about it.

And then—as he was chewing—he remembered. Funny how the brain works. A while back, he had read the true story of a person who had actually escaped a similar situation of captivity after watching a program on TV. It was a woman who had been kidnapped for a ransom that never came, and they had left her to die. Not only that. He clearly remembered what she had done to escape.

Sam grinned. He had a strategy. But for now, he was going to do as Luna did, and play nice. Whether the guy was crazy or not, there was nothing to be gained by making him angry. Be friendly, Sam. Don't antagonize. All he had to do was wait for his captor to leave so that he could put his plan into action. So, when the guy apologized for having hit him on the head and capturing him, he just said it was okay.

"But I hurt you. You're bruised and scraped. I didn't mean to hurt you. I'm so sorry."

"It's okay, man. It happened," Sam answered, watching the young man as he fiddled nervously with his glasses. You would think that they were two acquaintances, shooting the breeze.

"I shouldn't have done that."

"No, you shouldn't. And if you regret it so much, maybe you should let me go, right?"

"I can't. My brother would get very angry at me, and I'm more scared of him than of the law."

"It's okay, then. Nothing we can do about it." Sam turned his head away from his captor. It was impossible to negotiate with him. It was pointless to even argue. He could hear the fear in the man's voice. The kind of fear that would never waver. Whatever his brother said, he would do. And it was final.

Sam took pensive, quiet breaths. He watched the man curiously, trying to understand what made him tick. Because there was something off about him. He observed how his captor moved around the room anxiously, awkwardly, how he sweated, and how he darted scared glances at the door. Was he waiting for the brother to arrive, the dreaded brother he was so afraid of? Or was there something else? Something wrong? One thing that he was sure of, was that this man seemed unstable. And unstable men were impossible to read. The faster he left the fur house with Luna, the better.

Chapter 15
Self-doubt

CHRIS MOUTON TOOK ONE LAST LOOK AT THE SHERIFF WITH A HEAVY HEART and turned to leave. From here on, Sam's destiny would be out of his hands. And he had to let it go. He couldn't fight his brother any more than he could fight the floods or the hurricanes. But he hated being his brother's slave. A long, long time ago, he had dreamed of getting away as far as he could from his family ties, but he soon realized that it would be impossible. His brother's network of far-reaching associates would always manage to track him down. Living in solitude, in this isolated place, was, for the most part, a sanctuary for his broken soul, even if it got lonely at times, except that lately, his fur house had become a prison for his brother's enemies all too often. Didn't matter how much he begged his brother to quit bringing captives to his home. His brother didn't care. He did what he wanted. And he liked Chris' fur house because it was in the middle of nowhere.

So, Chris had no choice but to look the other way. After a lifetime of being bullied by his much older sibling, he had learned to obey or be willing to accept the consequences.

But this time, it was different. Sam looked like a nice guy. Someone he could almost have been friends with. He had never felt such a strong urge to rebel. And yet, he knew he didn't have the courage. He would have to allow his brother's men to do what they always did, and Sam would have to die.

He pulled the fur house door behind him, remorse weighting his heart down, and he shut it with a bang. The constant humidity had swelled the wood and distended it, and sometimes it was hard to shut. Then he remembered that he had forgotten to bring little Luna her lunch and groaned with regret. Poor kid. Another victim of his brother's evil ways.

He hurried home and rushed to the kitchen where he found Luna's sandwich and juice bottle still on the table. While he walked back to the fur house, he considered whether he should let her go. Poor little sha, what had she ever done to anyone? But letting her go on her own would be condemning her to certain death. Dangers lurked everywhere in the inhospitable swamps. She was almost safer in her cage. At least he did the best he could to care for her. He walked slowly, trying to figure out whether his brother would be satisfied with just the Sheriff, or if he would demand Luna for himself as well.

Chris Mouton shuddered with horror, refusing to allow into his mind images of what he thought his brother would do to the little girl. His hands shook as he held the juice and the sandwich. He couldn't let him have her. What an unforgivable sin it would be to allow his brother to hurt her. Luna was a sweet, quiet, obedient girl. He had to do something to help her.

His heart was beating funny again, and Chris realized he had forgotten to take his meds again. He looked around for a rock to sit down and rest on until his heart settled down. His breath was coming out unevenly, and he was shivering. He could tell that he was about to have an anxiety attack.

Chris grasped at his chest and fell on his knees, his soul full of despair. How many men had his brother killed? And how much of those men's blood was on his own hands? How many young men, how many scared young women? He prayed to Saint Jude, the Patron Saint of the hopeless and despaired, to give him the strength that he'd never had. He was terrified of his brother the bully, the cruel, evil devil's spawn, and tears of confusion and guilt ran down his face. Then he saw Luna's sandwich and the small bottle of juice lying in the mud where they had fallen, and he put his face in his hands, and he began to cry.

Chapter 16

Freedom!

MEANTIME, LUNA—WHO HAD A PERFECT VIEW of the dirt road through the large window—served as the lookout. Sam had the gut-rending feeling that their captor was on his way back.

"Hurry up, Sam. When he sees that he's forgotten my lunch, he's going to come back with it. I don't think that the house is that far."

"I understand. Now quit talking and let me focus."

He had finally remembered clear as day, exactly what to do. His arms and torso had been tied around and around onto the table. So had his legs, at the height of his ankles. But his hands were also tied. Separately.

First, he had to slip his hands out of the rope around them. He rotated his wrists back and forth to loosen the rope. Bending as far forward as he could, he put his hands up to his mouth and used his teeth to pull on one strand of the rope to make it looser. Within minutes, the ropes were loose enough, and he was able to wriggle his hands out of them.

Luna was as quiet as a mouse, but he could feel her eyes staring at him anxiously.

"It's okay, Luna," he told her lightly. "My hands are free."

"Please hurry up," she said very softly, so softly that he barely heard her.

"Don't worry, kid. We'll be out of here in no time."

Next, Sam kicked off his boots, pushing one off with the other, suddenly grateful for having worn these old, beat-up ones. With his feet bare, it was easier to wiggle, and he managed to turn himself sort of sideways to pull his knees up some, to pull out first one foot and then the other. It sounded easier than it was, and the rope cut into his skin like fire. But after not too much effort, his legs were free.

"I'm almost done, Luna," he told the little girl who hadn't uttered one sound through all his struggles.

"But you're still tied to the table. How are you going to free yourself?"

"I'll slide down and out of them. You'll see." But try as he might, those ropes were tied too tight, and they wouldn't budge. Then, he remembered he always carried a small knife in his pocket, and he got his hopes up.

But the excitement was short-lived. His arms were pinned to his sides, and there was very little space for maneuvering. He had to give up on his knife. So, he continued struggling. He pushed one way and another, but the ropes refused to give. Finally, he had the idea of pulling his right arm closer to his body—as much as he could—giving himself a little bit of leeway, while he pulled the ropes toward his head with his left hand. Millimeter by millimeter, the rope moved higher on his torso, and then higher, to where his body was narrower, and as soon as he could, he slipped down on the table, down toward his feet, until—all of a sudden—the rope was loose, and he was able to slip it off over his head.

Abruptly, he heard Luna take a jagged breath. "I see him," she said, her little voice full of terror. "He's still far, but I see him."

This was too soon. Sam had hoped to plan his moment of escape carefully. He didn't exactly know how he was going to do this, seeing as he now had to worry about the child as well. But planning on running out the door as soon as you were free usually only worked in books and movies. More often than not, you were pursued and shot at, or ran into a trap and were recaptured. And, so on and so forth. The prudent thing was to make a tactical exit. But now, obviously, there was no time for that.

As Sam jumped off the table and put his boots on, his eyes went darting all around the fur house, looking for some sort of weapon to defend himself with, but all he could see was rusty gardening tools. Then he patted his pockets. At least he still had the compass and the serrated knife. They would have to do.

"You're not going to leave me here, are you?" the little voice asked. Sam turned toward Luna and saw her for the very first time, a small, slender, un-showered kid with dirty hair and dark smudges under her big brown eyes. She held onto the bars of her cage quietly, but he could tell she was terrified.

He followed her eyes and looked toward the window, toward the end of the dirt road, where it seemed like their captor had fallen on his knees.

"We might have time to get away," he said. "It seems that our man is busy." Sam looked at the cage, a very well built one, much sturdier than any that he would have built, and got discouraged. But he shook it hard anyway and wasn't surprised that it didn't budge. He needed another idea.

"Do you know how to climb, Luna?"

"Of course, I do. I live in the forest lands."

"Then listen. The cage is a little taller than I am, but it doesn't reach the roof. So, from out here, I'm going to help you climb onto my shoulder. I'll hold you, don't worry. Then you must climb over the edge, just like you were climbing over a fence, and then you'll be free, and I'll catch you, and we'll run away."

"Piece of cake."

"Yes, Luna. Piece of cake."

The child turned out to be a good climber. Her sticky, dirty hands clung well to the bars of her cage. First, she stood on Sam's knee, then his arms and then his shoulders. She was as light as a feather, and Sam was suddenly very grateful that he had managed to find her and would soon see her free.

As Luna crossed over the top of the cage, she gasped again.

"What's wrong," Sam asked her.

"He's up."

"He's up where?"

"He's not on his knees anymore. He's coming this way."

"Okay then, are you ready? Jump. I'll catch you."

Luna fell into his arms, and he wanted to hug and squeeze her because he felt so relieved, but there was no time. They hurried to the door. Sam pushed and pushed, but it was stuck. Then Luna with her slender little body panted with the exertion as she helped to push, and the door creaked a little and budged, and then it creaked a little more, and it budged another couple of inches, and then all of a sudden, the door banged open, and they stumbled forward and stared into the crazy bright sun, and they were free.

Not ten paces away, their captor stood still, staring at them surprised. There was no way to tell if he was armed or not. But there in his hands were the sandwich and the bottle of juice, and there was no feeling of hostility coming from him. Unless the man had a gun—which he didn't seem to have or want to use—there was no reason to fear him anymore.

It was an awkward moment. Sam looked at the man, and the man looked at him. Then Chris looked at Luna and showed her what was in his hands. There was a sad little smile on his face as he walked toward them and put the food in the child's hand. Then he stepped back and let his hands fall to his sides.

"We'll be going then," Sam said as if it was the most natural thing to say in the world. The man just nodded. He looked at Luna and told her he was sorry. And Luna—bless her heart—ran over to him and gave him a hug.

It wasn't until they had left the area and were well on their way to the place where Sam had been attacked, that he asked her about the hug.

"He looked like he needed a hug." It was a simple answer, but one that Sam couldn't understand.

"But he kidnapped you."

"Yes, but he was always nice. And he seemed so sad. I think he needed a hug."

Sam looked down at the child, so wise beyond her years, yet so fragile and kind, and he swore to himself that he would never let her stay anywhere near that Mona ever again.

Chapter 17

Remorse

CHRIS WATCHED THE SHERIFF WALK AWAY, holding Luna's hand, and felt terribly conflicted. This was going to be his downfall. The voices in his head were getting louder and louder telling him how stupid he had been, but he made no effort to stop them or to follow them. Sam being able to free himself and help the girl escape was like a miracle, a personal sign from Saint Jude that perhaps there was salvation for his soul.

Yes. Keeping Luna captive had been his greatest regret, and the most miserable week of his life. And he was glad to see them go, hand in hand, not a whiff of hatred or animosity among them. As if Sam had understood that there was no evil in his heart. Just that dread and that fear of his brother's cruelty that made him do as he was told.

He was free now. But his life was forfeit. As soon as his brother found out, he would set his goons on him, and—after torturing him for information—kill him with as much pain as possible. He knew his brother well enough after all and was well aware of the glee he felt when causing pain to others. He had to disappear.

Chris watched the Sheriff and the little girl until they vanished into the shrubbery at the end of the dirt road, and then he turned toward his house. In his mind, a panicky voice was already telling him what to pack, and shaking with fear, he hurried his steps. The faster he got out of there, the better.

With the TV set blaring in the kitchen, he hurried from room to room, opening drawers and closets, picking up stuff to shove into his backpack. The truck was too obvious. He was going to leave it where it was. But he would take the four-wheeler and ride it as far as he could. Then, he would ditch it.

The shaking wouldn't stop, so he went to the kitchen to get a cold beer from the cooler, and as he opened the can and stood drinking the first foamy, soothing sips, he stared—by habit—at the TV set and watched the news.

There was a lot of the same old, same old stuff: floods in New Orleans, an oil slick covering the sandy beaches of Cypremort Point, two policemen gunned down somewhere in Houma. The usual.

He was about to turn away when he heard the words "murder" and "Half Moon Bay" in the same sentence. That woke him from his zombie-like reverie, and he looked at the screen. A night-time scene showed two paramedics carrying a stretcher to an ambulance, parked in front of his brother's art Gallery. The sirens weren't on, just the strobe lights that turned around and around. The patient's face was covered. He was dead. And someone mentioned that his name was Vinnie.

Chris gasped. So not possible. Could his brother really be dead?

He pulled another beer out of the cooler and sat down at the table. There was much thinking to be done. The newsman was telling the whole story, even interviewing people, and Chris turned the volume higher. Apparently, his brother was indeed dead, and this changed everything.

He needed to clear the voices from his head, and all the fog and the confusion. He reached for the bottle of Chlorpromazine tablets in front of him, the one that sat next to the salt and pepper shakers and swallowed two—an extra one for good measure—and washed them down with a swig of beer. The question now was the following. With his brother dead, was he safe? Or was there still a chance that his associates would come after him?

After sitting at the table for what seemed like hours, he came to the conclusion that there was only one thing to do. He was going to disguise himself as an old vagabond and travel with his four-wheeler through the back roads as close to Half Moon Bay as he could. Then, he would go see Father Armand. The good padre had always been kind to him and had helped him before.

With a clear head, and relieved to have a working plan, Chris got up from the kitchen table and turned the TV off.

Chapter 18
Going Through The Notes

MARGO RE-READ HER NOTES ON THE INTERVIEWS and chewed on her nails with frustration. She either hadn't mastered the art of interrogation yet, or nobody had seen much of anything. She jotted anything interesting in a notepad on her desk, but that first page was almost empty.

Some of the guests had snuck away right after the body was discovered, but in the confusion, it was impossible to know who had done what for sure.

A few people had seen the victim argue with the unknown man out on the balcony. But none of them seemed to know who the stranger was. Nobody remembered what he looked like. Nobody had bothered to take a picture. Yet, everyone who noticed insisted it was a man, but Saffron maintained that she had seen a woman, because of the clues she had uncovered. Saffron hadn't shared her clues yet but was adamant. Manuel too, remembered vaguely a woman coming into the ballroom from the balcony and picking a flute of champagne from his tray. But Manuel wasn't 100% sure. He admitted that he could be thinking of another party.

So, Margo bit off another piece of nail and spit it out. Nasty habit, she thought to herself. She was going to have to quit that. And where was Sam anyway? Was she going to have to run this investigation all by herself? Even Pierre was gone, back to Lafayette, back to work. And all she had left was Maurice.

Trying to focus, she kept reading her notes. According to the lovely Mimi—who usually saw it all and knew it all—Vinnie Chauvin had been leaning on the rails of the balcony, next to the potted pomegranate bushes, holding a champagne flute. That was right before the downpour began.

Then, she saw a stranger approach the balcony door and look around. She knew that look. The stranger wanted to be sure that she wasn't being observed. Yes, she was a woman. She was wearing a black box hat with a veil. She pulled the veil down, and her face wasn't visible anymore. Then, she opened the balcony door and stepped outside. Mimi observed that at that moment, it was raining already.

"Did the two seem to know each other?" Margo had asked.

"Oh, yes. They sure did. The stranger approached Vinnie and gave him a peck on the cheeks. Their body language showed that they got on very well."

Apparently, at least two people had been outside on the balcony, then. A man and a woman. Nobody remembered what the man looked like, but according to Manuel—if this was the woman he was thinking about—she was young and pretty. About Manuel's height, although she must have been wearing high heels. So about 5'8"? And Mimi mentioned slender and elegant. Not much to go on.

Margo kept on reading and making notes for a while. Then, something popped off the page. Harry Broussard, the owner of the Ford dealership said something about a piece of Native Art that he had purchased at the Gallery that—according to the appraisers—had turned out to be a fake. He had planned to have a word with Vinnie at the party because he definitely wanted his money back. He told Margo at the interview that he refused to display a fake among his collection, especially at Vinnie's prices. But the man had died before being confronted. And now Harry Broussard was a very angry man. He wanted to know if the police were going to get his money back.

Margo quickly read through the notes and didn't find any other mention of fake art, but the thought had brought up an imprecise memory of something she had heard a while back. The memory was vague. Maybe it was not even real. Sam would know about it.

She picked up her cell phone and called the police department. As always, Maurice picked up. He had no news for her, nothing about Sam, and he was beginning to be very worried. Sam's phone had now been offline for over 36 hours, which was not like Sam at all. Something must have happened to him, Maurice insisted, and Margo caught the fear in his voice. It was obvious that it was time to do something about the Sheriff's disappearance.

Margo told him not to worry, and that she would get help. But before she hung up, he told her that some new recruits would be arriving that day. Sam hadn't mentioned anything about new recruits to her, but it was good news, although it didn't solve anything. She needed real help immediately and not later, and she knew of only one place where she would get it.

Rob Schexnayder—it turned out—lived in that part of Half Moon Bay that had once embodied the increasing prosperity of the little fishing village, way, way back. Sadly, the prosperity hadn't lasted, and after one hurricane too many, the northern area of the bay had been abandoned to its own resources, and a new and shining and prosperous Half Moon Bay rose further South, at the seashore of the azure waters and gently swaying palm trees where the newly minted rich and famous had built their magnificent antebellum mansions and plantation homes.

It was also the part of town that she had once vowed never to go back to after having been viciously chased and almost murdered during one of her previous cases. She looked around as she drove. Nothing had changed since the last time she had driven this way. If anything, things had gotten worse. Many of the houses were boarded up, and the few that remained were run down, their paint peeling, many a shutter hanging by a nail. And with dismay, she found herself driving toward her secret parking spot, out of sheer habit.

Knowing it would be unavoidable, she simply gave in to the impulse and parked in that same spot where she had done so many times in the past. It was a lovely spot, under a huge shade tree, in a quiet—almost secret spot—on this sad, neglected street. Then she walked.

She enjoyed the walk as it gave her the chance to organize her thoughts, and she breathed in the warm fresh air coming in from the bay. The trees and bushes were overgrown, full of twittering birds and newly budding flowers. Barely any traces of human habitation remained among the decaying houses, but squirrels still chattered when she walked by. But despite the enjoyment, she looked around a few times with that familiar feeling of being watched.

As she got closer to the address she was looking for, she braced herself. She was a little scared. Rob Schexnayder was a legend in South Louisiana. As Sheriff, he had ruled the land with an iron fist, and criminals under his watch had either surrendered, or packed up and left, and he had ushered in a golden era of personal safety and prosperity. There was not a person in town or nearby areas that didn't take their hat off and stood to attention when speaking to the legend.

And so, Margo found herself walking up to the old-fashioned shotgun house painted yellow and white. She stopped at the wrought-iron gate and looked up, wondering if her arrival would be watched from behind the curtains, but nothing stirred behind the windowpanes.

The house was incredibly narrow—as shotgun houses usually are—and looked suffocatingly small compared to her own mansion, but it was cute in a way. It was perfectly renovated, French Quarter style, colorful, freshly painted, and had the most well-organized front yard that she had ever seen. Even the shrubs had been impeccably trimmed to size. Every rock, every pebble, perfectly placed. Not one dead leaf, not one yellowing blade of grass. She walked up to the door with shaking knees. Whoever kept his yard in such perfect order wouldn't be easy to please.

She felt shy as she rang the doorbell. Her hand insisted on shaking, and she swallowed hard. It wasn't every day that one met a living legend. But she stifled her nervousness and stood up straight. She had to cause a good impression. For Sam.

The man himself opened the door, and Margo braced herself, not knowing what to expect. The man was tall, stood ramrod straight, had keen, intelligent eyes and salt-and-pepper hair. In a deep, courteous but no-nonsense voice he invited her in and told her to follow him. She quietly closed the door behind her and followed.

It was cool inside the house, and it was pleasantly dark. She could hear noises coming from the back of the house, but they were very faint. A smell of cookies permeated the air, and she got her hopes up. The living legend, but one that likes cookies.

The house was long, and she followed him through a narrow corridor that barely allowed the man's wide shoulders to fit, to the back, where a large living room with a fireplace and a number of bay windows invited the visitor to relax. Then, she was ordered to sit in an old-fashioned armchair with macassars, and a breathless young woman rushed out of the kitchen with a tray of coffee and cookies. Then she ran back to where she had come from.

Margo sat very properly, her hands in her lap, and she waited. The silence was uncomfortable. Was she supposed to talk first? She was still a newcomer around here and didn't really know how things worked. So, she twitched. The cookies looked good and smelled to die for, and she truly wanted one, but it seemed like bad manners to touch something before her host did. Or was that the other way around? She swallowed tightly and left the cookies alone.

The man in front of her was still handsome. Must have been as gorgeous as a model in his youth. Had to be in his late sixties, maybe early seventies. About 6 feet tall. Probably still worked out. You could tell that his body was taught with muscles and with the willingness to become violent when needed. A dangerous man. But he was smiling encouragingly, almost as if he was having a little fun at her expense. And Margo couldn't help but smile back, and the ice was broken.

Even before the amenities had been gotten through, she found herself pouring her heart out. Things that she wouldn't normally be sharing with strangers came out willingly from her mouth and suddenly, she realized that the clever former Sheriff knew well how to ask questions, and she had willingly told him all about her life without even noticing. She laughed out loud.

"I need to learn how you do that," she said with a grin. "You're a very clever interrogator."

The old Sheriff shrugged. "I shouldn't do that, but I can't help myself. It's the habit of a lifetime. Have a cookie. Sandra makes the best cookies in the world. Go on, no need to be shy." And as he poured coffee for both of them, and they ate their cookies, Margo told Rob Schexnayder about how she had come to be a private detective, how she had lost track of Sam, and how she had this very strong feeling that Sam was in danger. And then, she told him about the murder, and how she didn't know what to do next.

"I've heard of Vinnie Chauvin. He was charming and suave—at least the women say so—but he was a racketeer, and a very clever one. I wouldn't be surprised at all if he'd been selling fake Native Art. His Art Gallery would be the perfect place to transact illegal deals, to launder money, and to run any kind of deals."

"Yes, but I don't even know how to proceed without Sam. Should I just wait for him to get back, or should I try to help Maurice look into this?"

"Normally I would say, you're not a policeman, so you shouldn't even be involved, but you move among these rich people, and they'll tell you things they would never tell Maurice. Since you say that you always help Sam, there's no harm in you doing a little investigating on the side. But that's it. You have to let the police do the rest."

"Then I have to find Sam."

"Yes. And I can help you with that. I know a tracker or two. They should know how to find this house that Sam went looking for. And from there on, they can pick up his trail. Tell Maurice to give me a phone call with all the details he can gather, and let the professionals do the rest. Now go home, and make sure you don't interfere with the investigation. For charges to stick, everything must be official, by the book. You wouldn't want to get in the way of that, now would you?"

Margo shook her head and got up obediently from the armchair. She told Rob Schexnayder that he was right. She said that she was going to go home and mind her own business. She had to practice for Church Choir anyway. She hadn't exercised her voice in ages. She shook hands, said thank you, and headed straight for the police department.

Stay out of it? Yeah, right!

Chapter 19

DAY FOUR: Much Later

THE NEXT MORNING, MARGO HURRIED UP THE FRONT STEPS of the pretty yellow shotgun house with white trim. When Rob Schexnayder called her earlier to tell her that they needed to talk, she knew right away that that was no request. It was an order.

She wondered if she had done something wrong. Had she crossed a line? Had she offended him? Nothing came to mind. But he had sounded so serious that as she rang the doorbell, butterflies did cartwheels in her chest. She was having a premonition. She remembered that fortune teller, what was her name, and her explanation of the symptoms of a true premonition, and Margo knew, without the shadow of a doubt what Rob Schexnayder had wanted to tell her. And with that same certainty, she knew that Rob Schexnayder wasn't ever going to open that door.

Her palms sweated as she waited, and waited, and waited, for someone to open the door. Sandra. She never found out who Sandra was. His daughter? His employee? Well, Sandra didn't seem to be in, and her trip had been wasted. Except for one thing. She knew she had to get into the house.

An impulse stronger than her sense of decorum and self-preservation told her to try the front door. It was locked. She quickly looked to her right and to her left, but the street was empty, and nobody was looking. Sighing at her disappointment in her own self, and knowing very well that what she was about to do was so very wrong, she took the lock picks that Brooks her chauffeur had given her and taught her how to use, and she fumbled with the lock until it popped. Then, quietly, she entered the empty house and gently closed the door behind her.

The foyer looked just as organized as it had done the day before. The curtains were pulled, and the semi-penumbra enhanced the feeling of utter silence and emptiness around her. On one wall in the foyer stood a wooden umbrella stand, one of those tall antique ones that had a mirror and a few hooks for coats and stuff. Nothing was hanging from them. Nothing in its little drawer either.

Other than the eerie silence of emptiness, no unpleasant smell greeted her. She could tell that they had probably had pancakes or waffles for breakfast. Recently. It still smelled a little like maple syrup and coffee. But that was all.

She called out hello a handful of times as a formality, but she could sense that the house was empty. So, she kept on going. A bedroom to her left, with the door ajar. His bedroom. Very masculine. A faint whiff of old spice. He had been a nice-looking older man. Had smelled good too. Why was she thinking of him in the past tense? Because she could tell that something was wrong? Nothing in the drawers but toiletries. His bathroom, which opened from the room, was also empty. Slightly wet. Rob Schexnayder had probably showered not much earlier. Then he had gone to the kitchen to have breakfast, and somewhere in between then and the present, vanished. Even though he had pretty much ordered her to show up because he had something to talk about.

The next bedroom was more generic. Chintz bedspread on the queen-sized bed, matching curtains. Probably a guestroom. So, Sandra lived somewhere else. All the drawers were empty, and the night tables devoid of any traces of habitation. A big black and white cat with a half ear missing sprawling on the bed cover stared at her curiously while she explored, and she made a mental note to call the vet to have him taken care of.

She walked the narrow corridor and looked at the pictures hung on both sides. Many were of Rob Schexnayder down the years. Commendations, press cuttings, group photos with friends, with other officers. It seemed that at one time Half Moon Bay used to have a pretty respectable police force. What had happened that all those had dwindled to just a few? She shrugged and kept going.

Before she entered the sitting room, she braced herself. There was no smell of death, but her feelings of death were so strong that she could almost see him, lying in a pool of his own blood, dead. No. She shook her head. Quit imagining things. He just had to go somewhere suddenly. To run an errand. To take care of something. There's nothing wrong with him.

But she knew in her heart that that wasn't true. The sitting room was empty. In one corner, the remnants of breakfast were indeed pancakes and coffee. There were a small pad and a pen next to the coffee mug. Something illegible was scribbled on it. It was impossible to read. But next to the pad, there was a thick manila folder. And she knew that that was what he had meant to talk to her about. It was her mother's folder. She opened it and saw the crime scene photographs, her dead body with the knife sticking from it, her pretty feet with one shoe missing. All that she didn't want to see.

Her first instinct was to drop the folder back on the table as if it had been on fire, and to run. But she knew that would be a mistake. With shaking hands, she picked the folder up and held it against her chest. This was something she couldn't deal with yet. But one day, maybe, she would be grateful to have picked that folder up. One day she would have the courage to investigate her mother's murder.

She hurried to the front door looking quickly in on the cat. She promised him to get some help, and then she made a beeline to her car and never looked back. For a second, she got the strongest feeling that she was being watched. But she dismissed the feeling and kept hurrying. And now, she really hoped this was the last time she would come to this street. And this time, she was serious.

It wasn't until she was halfway home that she realized that she should have picked up the note pad as well. She almost turned the car around to go get it, but she talked herself out of it. The idea of having to go back was more than she could bear.

Chapter 20

Escape

SAM HELD TIGHT ONTO LITTLE LUNA'S HAND. They followed a well-defined trail for a while. Once Sam felt that they were safe from being followed, they stopped, and he consulted his compass. All he could do was backtrack West, South-West, toward where he assumed John Armentor's house was.

Sam wanted to get away from the fur house as far as possible, as soon as possible. He suspected his captor's brother and his posse wouldn't be too pleased that they had escaped and would come looking for them.

Adjusting for compass readings, they took the most beaten paths with the assumption that they were the most traveled ones. In the wilderness, it took barely a day or two for a path to disappear if it wasn't used. Or so he'd heard.

Every 15 to 20 minutes, Sam tried his cell phone, but still, there was no reception. At this point, the sun was high in the sky, and the heat and the humidity—already oppressive—made breathing harder and harder. It didn't help that water in the puddles, left behind from the rain, was evaporating fast, rising in wet, smoky tendrils from the drenched soil. And he was beginning to fear that either they were lost, or they were walking in circles because they should have arrived already.

Sam was exhausted. He had been carrying Luna on and off on his back because those little legs got tired, but he was wearing out. The humidity was extremely hard on him. He could hardly breathe, he felt like he was inhaling water. The further he went, the more sluggish his movements became. Finally, he had to put Luna down.

After a while, they came across a straight, firm-looking branch—torn off during the last storm—and Sam stopped to clean it up with his knife and fashion it into a walking stick of sorts, not only so that it would help drag his sore, aching body, but so that he could poke the ground as they went so that they wouldn't step into quicksand or some deadly life-sucking mud pond.

They had been walking a good hour and a half when Sam sighted a handful of big black birds circling in the sky.

"They are waiting for someone to die," said Luna, startling Sam.

"Where do you get that from?"

"They're vultures. Look at their naked heads and necks. They found something to eat. Could be dead. Could still be alive."

"Dear Lord, how would you know something like that?" Sam asked, horrified. But sweet looking little Luna just shrugged and held on to his hand.

"Let's go find it," she said. "Maybe it needs our help."

Sam couldn't think of anything to say to that, so when the child pulled him in direction of the circling vultures, he just followed.

But unexpectedly, Luna let go of his hand, took off running, and soon vanished into the bushes. He stopped, confused, thinking, what just happened? It was like dèja-vu, being abandoned in the middle of nowhere again. He yelled out for her to come back, but for a second or two, heard nothing. And then a wild scream, a shriek of panic, pierced the swamp noises, and he realized that Luna must be in danger.

He was sore, hurt, hungry, and thirsty, and had barely been able to drag himself this far, but his mind came wide awake at the sense of danger, and he took off as fast as lightning, forgetting that he could barely move.

Something was making the shrubbery shiver. With the rod, he poked at the bushes and jumped back when he stuck something rubbery and the horrifying image of an alligator's snout wide open appeared in front of him. The gator snapped at him, and out of the bushes sprinted Luna, her slender leg scratched and bleeding. Sam realized that had he been a minute later, the gator would have dragged Luna under the water, and he would have never seen either of them again.

He grabbed Luna's arm and pushed her behind him. He poked at the gator and yelled, hoping the beast would go away, but it grabbed his stick and snapped it in two in those powerful mandibles as if they had been insignificant chopsticks.

Sam jumped back. His mind was going a thousand miles a minute, trying to think of what to do. And then he remembered that he still had the knife in his pocket, and carefully keeping eye contact with the beast, reached for the blade.

But Sam almost laughed, when he realized what a joke his tiny serrated knife was next to a beast that had to be at least eight feet long.

Then, the gator snapped again. Sam tried to walk backward, but there were all those trees behind him. He stumbled and fell, and that gave the gator the chance to approach him and grab him.

He screamed in agony as the gator's teeth connected with his ankle and began dragging him into the oily water. Luna was screaming too, and with panic, Sam realized that Luna would be doomed if he allowed the gator to kill him.

He tried to reach over and around, to stab the beast and at least slow its relentless trek toward the water, but the animal's body was too far. He tried to cling to a sapling, and then another, and tried reaching for the branches of the bushes, but he failed. And the gator continued its death march toward the swamp. He even tried digging his hands into the vegetation beneath him, but everything was slippery with that swampy humid moisture.

At the edge of the water, in a last-ditch effort, he dug his heel, the one that was free into the mud, as if that could have helped, but he knew then— as his feet first, and then his legs were submerged—that he had lost.

He could smell the rotting vegetation around him. He could still hear Luna cry. But a despair without hope began to settle about him as he realized that nothing mattered anymore. Not even his ankle hurt. He wished that drowning wouldn't be too painful a death. The gator would make sure that he was completely submerged and good and dead before it started eating him. The gator was a lazy animal. So much easier to eat a dead man than to struggle with a live one.

Sam closed his eyes and gave himself over to the great silence. And then, all of a sudden, he got it! Play possum. Play dead. He quit twitching and quietened his body, and right before his face was submerged, he took several big breaths of air and a final really big one and prayed.

He wouldn't have much time. How long could he hold his breath? One minute? Two? Supposedly, you could live for three weeks without food, three days without water, and three minutes without air. Or was it two?

As man and beast slid into the water, Sam bid his time. His chest was tight, his lungs screaming for air. He opened his eyes in the murky water and couldn't see his tormentor. Frustrated, he lunged forward at the beast's body with his little serrated knife, but the water was sluggish, and his efforts were being wasted. Sam realized that he had miscalculated. He couldn't see his enemy, and he was about to pass out.

With his last bit of strength, he kicked and connected with the gator's snout, who—surprised—let go for an instant. The need for survival gave Sam enough strength to double down and lunge at the spot where the gator had been a second before. He found himself touching the hard ridge on the back of the beast. He held tight to his ridiculously small knife. If he could go for the eyes! Only the eyes would be vulnerable.

But the great beast realized it was about to lose its dinner and went after him, slow and awkward on land, but a smooth swimmer in the water. With grace, and with all the time in the world, the gator slowly opened its jaw and grabbed Sam by the waist. Then, in a long fluid move, it rose out of the water and up into the air, pulling Sam with him.

Sam's head burst out of the water, and he gulped in the fresh air. But the gator was taking him back down. It was now or never. Staring straight at the eyes of the beast, he lifted the serrated knife and plunged it into the gator's right eye, over, and over, and over again, until the wounded animal let him go.

Sam quickly swam ashore, struggling with the weeds and the mud under his feet, ignoring the pain in his ankle, and the one in his chest. He hurried as much as he could, terrified that the gator would come back for vengeance and drag him away forever.

He crawled out of the fetid water, slipping on the muddy shore, and then crawled over to where Luna stood—petrified, still in shock.

"We have to get out of here, in case it comes back."

"But you're bleeding. Look."

"It's okay. It doesn't hurt. We'll take care of it later. We're not safe here."

Chapter 21

Lost

THE SUN WAS HIGH IN THE SKY. Luna's leg looked ugly, but Sam didn't say anything. What need was there in scaring the little child? His wounds didn't feel that good either, and now, a small cloud of flies—probably attracted by the smell of blood—followed them faithfully as they went.

"I'm so sorry, Luna. Seems like I'm a failure at rescuing little girls. I even lost my cellphone."

"No, you didn't. You dropped it, and I picked it up. I even made sure that it was turned off so that the battery wouldn't die."

"How on earth would you know how to do that? You're just a tiny thing."

Luna shrugged modestly. "That's what my dad always does. Especially when we're out there where we can't plug it in to charge it."

Sam looked around despondently. He had little idea of how to recognize a landmark. To him, all trees, all coulees, all river bends seemed the same. All he had was the compass and a vague idea of which way to go.

But when they reached the clearing, something clicked in his mind. The area looked very familiar. Besides, the vegetation was trampled, with flies buzzing excitedly around small puddles of blackened blood. This had to be it. That meant that they were heading in the right direction.

He put his hand over his eyes like a visor and looked around. The sun was so blindingly bright that he could barely see a thing. But Luna's eyes were great. He heard her scream, Look! And felt his hand being pulled frantically.

They found Armentor under a frondous oak tree, in the cooling shade. Next to him lay the dog, looking quite dead. Sam kneeled down and stared at the man. He showed no signs of being either dead or alive, but as he got closer, he heard a shallow hoarse breath, and Luna screamed.

"He's alive, isn't he? I heard him breathe."

"Yes, Luna. I believe he is alive." Sam turned toward the old man and shook him gently. "Armentor? Wake up."

"Wake up, grandpa," Luna was yelling, jumping up and down from the excitement. Armentor opened his eyes with effort and looked at Luna and smiled. He nodded at Sam and pointed at his throat. Sam didn't know if the man was thirsty, but he bet he was. His throat must be bruised and swollen, but they had nothing to give him.

Then, Sam remembered his regulation backpack. He had taken it off before he was attacked. Maybe it was still around.

Watching out for snakes and gators, Sam carefully poked around the vegetation, trying to remember where he had left his backpack. Then, a vague image of deep pink azaleas came to his mind and he hurried back to the trail, where some sad azalea bushes with withering flowers sat at the foot of some dense foliage. This must be the place. Azalea flowers only last a few days. He was lucky. Had he come this way a few days later, there would have been no trace left of the ephemeral flowers, and without them, he would have never been able to distinguish an azalea bush from any other bush on earth. Much less an army-green canvas backpack that blended in perfectly with the surrounding shrubbery.

He rushed to his backpack—lying right where he had left it—to all his supplies and found the canvas to be moist but intact. He felt an enormous sense of relief. He had a first aid kit in his pack with alcohol, antibiotic creams, and bandages. He had some food and water. He had his map. He cheered up and regained his faith that all would be well.

After tending to Armentor's bruises, he went to check on the dog. The poor animal was hurt, and there were bugs buzzing by its wounds, but when it looked at Sam, its eyes were clear and lively. It was fed a little, given some water, and its wounds bandaged to the best of Sam's ability.

With its leg doctored to and well bandaged, the dog stood up, wobbly but with a wagging tail.

Sam was satisfied. Next, he had to get this crew to safety. He walked to the clearing with his cellphone and turned it on. Expecting no signal, he found none. The clearing was pretty big, and he walked around moving the cellphone one way and the other, refusing to give up, but there was simply no signal. Disheartened, he looked at the little girl and the folks under the tree and wondered what he should do next. Then—suddenly— Luna jumped up from the grandfather's side and came running to him.

"Look," she yelled, pointing to the sky. "A helicopter." She began hopping up and down, screaming for help, waving her little hands over her head.

"Stop, Luna." Sam hated to have to tell her. "That's not a helicopter."

"Yes, it is. It has to be."

"No, sha. It isn't. It's a drone."

"What's that?"

"Well, it's not a helicopter. You can stop yelling and jumping. There's nobody in it. It's like a toy. Go sit with your grandfather."

"And the puppy?"

"Yes, and the puppy. Tell them not to be scared. Tell them Sam will get everyone home safely."

Luna looked at him, her big dark eyes full of questions, and he looked back at her. So small, so frail-looking, but so brave. Her dirty hair shining in the sun. The little girl looked at him with wisdom almost impossible to find in a small child and nodded. Then, she sauntered back to where Armentor and his dog were sitting in the shade.

Chapter 22

Taking Action

"COME ON, MAURICE, WE HAVE TO DO SOMETHING." Margo was on the warpath. "Sam is missing, and now, this old Sheriff, Rob Schexnayder, he's missing too."

"We don't know for sure that the old Sheriff is missing. He could have stepped out to take care of something. He could have been called away on an emergency."

"Oh, you don't really believe that. I can tell that you're just as worried as I am."

"Well, maybe I am worried, Miss Margo, but short of calling in the State Police, I don't know what else to do. The only reason I haven't called them is that you begged me not to. You asked for 48 hours, and I'm hoping Sam shows up. But if he doesn't, I'll have to report it, or else we'll all be in a world of hurt."

"Did you ever contact Rob Schexnayder?"

"Yes. I sent him everything we had on the case of the missing girl, the grandfather's address, and such."

"And did he receive the information?"

"Yes, yes. We talked. He had friends on standby. He was going to give them a call right away."

"I hope he did so before he vanished."

Margo paced back and forth in the frigid police department office, hugging her arms to her chest. It was so cold that she was getting brain freeze. She was about to leave to go outside when the phone rang, and she looked at Maurice with a little burst of hope. But she had no clue what was being said. Maurice lifted a finger and looked at her as if telling her to wait. Then he said a whole litany of "yes, yes, I understand, yes again, of course," and finally an "I'll be right there". Margo's whole body tensed.

"What was that, Maurice?"

"I'll tell you as we walk. Dr. Gabe wants to see me."

"And you're letting me tag along?"

"Why not? This should be interesting."

Margo almost had to run to keep up with Maurice's long strides and brisk walk across the park. They were heading to Saint Hildegard's, the old convent turned hospital.

"So, what did Dr. Gabe say?"

"That a witness who had almost died had regained consciousness and was ready to talk to the police."

"I don't understand."

"I don't either, Miss Margo, but I figured we should go along with it."

They followed directions and found themselves on the third and uppermost floor of the hospital. Delicate patients were kept on this floor, but Saint Hildegard's being sort of a miraculous hospital, where nobody ever died—despite this being the Intensive Care floor—they stepped out of the elevator to a cheerful nurses' station that was decked out in flowers and colorful balloons as if it was the pediatric floor. A nurse stood in front of the desk and cheerfully flirted with handsome Dr. Gabe, who smiled briefly back at her and was making efforts to retreat. But every step he took backward was followed by a brazen step forward by the pretty nurse who stuck her chest out coquettishly.

Maurice coughed discreetly into his fist as they got closer, and when Dr. Gabe turned around and saw them, he gratefully distanced himself from the nurse and approached them.

"Hi, Maurice. Hi, Margo. Didn't expect to see you here," he told her and raised an eyebrow. "Where's Sam?"

Maurice answered quickly before Margo could say anything. "He's out on a job and couldn't come himself. Maybe we can help."

"Yes, well, I don't know if Sam has told you, but the same poison that killed Vinnie Chauvin almost killed this young waiter that would like to talk to you. He mumbled something about a bottle of liqueur, but it was the law that he really wanted to talk to. Come follow me."

The young waiter lying on the hospital bed looked heartbreakingly fragile. He was connected to all kinds of tubes and machines that purred and whizzed quietly, busy keeping the young man alive. When he heard them come into the room, he opened his eyes and tried a smile.

"Maurice, he's still weak. Don't expect too much of him."

"I won't. I promise." He approached the bed and sat down on a chair next to him. Margo stood behind him.

"You don't look good, son. Tell me what happened to you."

"I opened the boss's bottle of *grappa*. He has it imported, just for himself. So, I placed it on the tray and went to get him a small tumbler, a special one that we keep just for him."

The young man fought to catch his breath and closed his eyes. Maurice waited patiently. After a few moments, he opened his eyes again and continued with his story.

"The bottom of the glass was wet. Inside, you know, like it hadn't dried properly. I was about to go back for a kitchen towel, but something distracted me."

"Yes. Go on."

"There were so many strangers in the kitchen. It was a big party. So, I can't be sure."

"Never mind. Tell it as you remember it."

"Well," the young man hesitated and looked at the window as if remembering what had happened. "I thought I saw someone stepping away from the tray. At that moment I could have sworn that the person had touched the tumbler, but later on, I wasn't so sure. Then, it got busy all of a sudden, and I was out of time, so I took the tray with the grappa and the tumbler to the balcony and forgot all about it."

"Thank you for telling me. But how did you get poisoned as well?"

The young man blushed and looked away. He hesitated again.

"It's okay, son. You can say whatever's on your mind. Nobody will be angry at you."

"I'm so ashamed. You see, I've always been curious about the grappa. I wouldn't dare take any from the bottle. I knew Mr. Vinnie knew exactly how much there was left in it. Besides, that would be stealing, and I would never do that. But there was the bottle of grappa on the sideboard in the kitchen, with the tumbler almost full next to it. The boss hadn't drunk much of it. And it was such a shame to let all that expensive liquor go to waste. I had no idea that he had been poisoned, and when nobody was looking, I took a sip."

"A pretty big one, I would think," said Maurice, frowning.

"Yes. It was big." The young man looked exhausted, and Dr. Gabe told Maurice that it was time to go. But there was just one more question that needed to be asked, and Margo couldn't let it go.

"I have just one question. Try to remember. Was there anything distinctive about this person you think you saw by the tray? Anything?"

"Now that you mention it, I could swear he was holding a handkerchief."

"Could it have been a tissue paper?"

"No. It was a handkerchief. My mee-maw uses them, cloth handkerchiefs, and I can recognize them."

"What did it look like? Did you get to see it?"

"Gosh, just for a second, maybe. But I think it had a monogram embroidered on the corner. I know what that is as well. But I didn't see the letter on it. Can't help you with that, I'm sorry."

"You were a great help," Maurice told him. "Get well soon." And after saying their goodbyes, they all stepped out of the room.

"Dr. Gabe, did they test the grappa in the bottle?"

"Yes, they did. The poison was in the glass, not in the bottle."

"So that wet puddle in the bottom of the glass could have been the poison."

"And the person with the handkerchief could have put it there."

"Indeed."

Chapter 23

Contact

BY THE TIME THE DRONE RETURNED SOME 30 MINUTES LATER, Sam had lost all hope of making his cellphone work, and he was instead looking at his map—compass in hand—with the purpose of charting an easy route back to Armentor's house. It was a devilishly impossible task, and Sam cursed his wayward deputy Andy for a thousandth time while he tried to think.

He was about to get up from the rock on which he sat. Armentor lay patiently in the same shady spot where he had been found, and the dog was stretched out faithfully next to him. They had eaten and drunk all his rations. He could tell. He had been watching the old man open the packages and chew for the last half hour. He should have complained, but he couldn't help feeling responsible for his inability to solve the situation, so he let it go.

It was Luna—with her excellent eyesight—who saw the drone first. This time, it came closer to them, and Luna shrieked with excitement and ran over to Sam, pointing at the thing and pulling at his sleeve, telling him to look up.

There was something attached to the drone. It circled downward cautiously, and when it was about 30 feet, it dropped the package and hovered for a second or two before taking off again.

Sam and Luna jumped up and ran to the package. Even Armentor had awakened from his lethargy and was looking at them. The package—about 12 by 14 inches, and as thick as a short stack of magazines, was covered in brown paper, parcel paper, and tied together with string. That was how the drone had held it: by the string. Taped to the package, a white envelope addressed to him.

He tore the envelope open right away and read the words out loud so that Luna could hear them.

Sam, don't worry. We're on the way. We know pretty accurately where you are. But clip the transponder to your belt, to help find you easier. Hang in there. We should be there within the hour.

"Mr. Sheriff, are they sending a helicopter?"

"No, Luna. It wouldn't be able to land with all these trees around. They have to come the same route I did, first by river, and then by land."

"Can we open the box? I need to know what's in there."

Sam laughed. "Need?"

"Yes. I'm hungry. Maybe they sent some food."

"Okay. Let's open it."

They found cookies, and sandwiches, and bottles of water. There was also a basic first aid kit, and at the bottom of the box, the transponder, which Sam turned on and clipped on his belt. Then they got up and took the supplies over to where Armentor and the dog were, and they sat down in the shade to wait.

Chapter 24

Saffron And Margo Talk

MARGO FONTAINE AND SAFFRON SIGUR SAT at one of the tables of the Parrot Joe Shack by a window overlooking the gray, frothy, angry water, and ate their favorite seafood dishes and sipped on some iced tea.

"Who are these people? Do you know any of them?"

Saffron took the photographs out of Margo's hands and looked at them with Margo's magnifying glass.

"Yes. I know most of them, anyway. What exactly do you want to know?"

"I'm trying to figure out which ones of the guests were the dead man's closest friends."

"Let's see. This really elegant woman, the skinny one, is Melba Gaines, manager of the Gallery."

"What do you know about her?"

"Not much. She hasn't lived in Half Moon Bay very long. I've heard that she's related to Vinnie. She's some distant cousin."

"And she's the manager? Lucky girl. She looks very young."

"Actually, you're right. She is very young, like early to mid-twenties. I've met her, and she's perky and friendly. Enjoys living in Half Moon Bay, loves her job. I'm not sure she's that qualified to be a Gallery manager, but suddenly, there she is."

"Look at her in this picture, Saffron. She wasn't expecting this one to be taken. It has caught her by surprise, and she has a funny look on her face."

"That—my dear Margo—is the look of cunning. It tells me that she's up to something. It tells me that she's not as sweet as she appears to be. Hmm, surprising, really. She must be a very good actress."

"You might be right. And I've heard that now, with Vinnie's death, she stands to inherit the Gallery, and everything else Vinnie owned—lock, stock, and barrel."

"But Margo, you're assuming that she's the one to inherit. I've heard that there's a silent partner in there somewhere."

"Do you know who it is?"

"Well, this is just gossip, but it might be this guy, André Daigle, standing close to Mimi." Instead of passing the photograph to Margo, Saffron picked up the magnifying glass again and stuck her nose to it. "More strange business, Margo. The guy is staring at the balcony."

"Let me see. Hmm. Yes. He's looking at Vinnie, who's looking down into the bay. This was taken before it started to rain. Vinnie is alone."

"Could he be the one that went out there to talk to Vinnie?"

"Unless we find a photograph that says so, we'll never know."

Rosalie dried her hands on her waitress uniform apron and cleared the empty plates while Margo and Saffron stared at the restless waters of the bay. A small group of white herons flew by slowly with their necks retracted. Gulls floated on the shallow water of the sandy shore, bobbing for fish. And Margo and Saffron waited for Rosalie to clear the table so they could continue their conversation.

"I read some of the notes from the night of the murder, and one of the witnesses said that Vinnie had sold him a forgery," Margo commented.

"Why am I not surprised? Vinnie was a crook. He was chased out of New Orleans for selling fakes."

"Then why wasn't he in prison? Why was he allowed to set up shop here?"

"Obviously, he had important friends, and plenty of money to buy his way out of whatever jam he would have found himself in."

Rosalie came back from the kitchen, put the cups of espressos in front of the girls and stood behind Margo, one hand on the back of her chair, and leaned into the pile of photographs and pointed.

"That's Josh, my *parrain*."

"Who, the big beefy guy standing by the balcony door?"

"Yes, him. He used to be a wrestler in Texas. He came back after he hurt himself. And now he's Vinnie Chauvin's bodyguard. He looks very mean and all, but he's a softy at heart."

"Haven't you heard that Vinnie Chauvin got himself killed a couple of days ago?"

"Oh yes, the big party at the Gallery. That was him?"

"Yes."

"I'm sorry for my parrain, then. He'll be out of a job. His boss was really good to him."

"Really?" Margo asked. "What I've heard is that he was a cheat and a crook."

"Oh, no. He was really nice to my parrain, and the rest of the family. He got well paid. He traveled all over the world for free, and the boss always sent gifts for weddings, and baptisms, and Christmas, and all that. Everyone in the family loved him. He even showed up when Josh got married, and he paid for his honeymoon to Venice. You know, Venice, Italy. He'll be missed, Vinnie Chauvin."

"Say, Rosalie, do you recognize anyone else?"

"Yes. Manuel. Everyone knows Manuel. And Mimi and her family. They come here a lot. I don't know why since she owns that fabulous Pirate Bay Inn. The food there has to be better than this one. But they're good tippers. And that's Melba Gaines, the cousin. Josh says that she's a piece of work, taking advantage of Vinnie and stringing him along."

"What do you mean, by stringing him along?"

"I don't know. Making promises she had no intentions of keeping? You have to ask Josh. He'll know."

"Anyone else?"

"Matty Daigle. That's Matty Daigle. Short, chubby, eccentric. Always wears those bizarre clothes. I don't know where she gets them."

"How do you know Matty, Rosalie?"

"She used to be in love with my brother. Followed him around, called him day and night. She almost chased my brother out of town. It was a relief when she found someone else to pursue."

Margo and Saffron just stared at Rosalie, who had turned out to be a fountain of information. But Rosalie misunderstood the looks.

"I know what you're thinking. That I'm poor and just a waitress, and she's all rich and glamorous and stuff. I guess she liked the idea of being linked to a working-class guy. Some of these rich girls think it's cool to have a grease monkey for a boyfriend. Except that my brother is very smart. He's in college, and I work to help him pay for his tuition. He's almost done. He'll get a job, and it will be my turn to go to school. Anyway, didn't mean to go off like that."

"Do you know if this Matty is related to André Daigle?"

"Oh, yes. She's his little sister. And if you're looking for a murderer, look no further. Those two did it."

"Who? Matty and André Daigle?"

"Yes. If Vinnie dies, André will inherit the Gallery, that's what everyone used to say. Those two are nasty, greedy people. I wouldn't be surprised if they were broke, the way they've been spending their inheritance."

"And how do you know all this?"

"My parrain. You have to talk to him. He'll tell you all about it." And with that, Rosalie grabbed their espressos—which they never even had a chance to drink—and stormed with them off to the kitchen.

"Why did Rosalie get so angry?"

"Who knows."

"Any news about Sam yet?"

"No. Maurice told me he would call right away."

Saffron sighed. "So, what do we do now?"

"I have an idea if you're up to it."

Chapter 25

Break-in

SAFFRON APPROACHED THE GALLERY FROM EAST ANCHOR, maneuvering the enormous white Mercedes through the narrow back alley with ease. They stopped in an available parking spot across the street and stared.

She usually went along with the crazy plans of her younger protégé, but so far had drawn the line at breaking in. She had complained all along the way but had finally given in. Why? Because it was easier to say yes to Margo than to argue with her.

"So, what do we do now?"

"We look to our right, and we look to our left, and if we're not being watched, we walk up to the building and try the latch."

"You make it sound so easy."

"It is. Remember that we're not doing this to break the law, but to help the law. Maurice has told me that I have 24 hours left before he calls in the state police. And that would break Sam's heart, and you know it."

"Why bother? We don't even know if Sam is still alive."

"Stop talking like that, Saffron. People are on their way to help him as we speak."

"And do you really believe that? Didn't you tell me that the only person who could send him help had disappeared?"

"He disappeared after he sent out the search party. Maybe he's even with them."

"Okay. Let's do it. What's the worst that could happen anyway, right?"

They crossed the empty street after looking both ways. Saffron still remembered when this fancy new amalgam of modern glass and neo-gothic architecture had been just a plain old South Louisiana home: unassuming, mildewy, and crumbling. Then, it had become some kind of theater for half a minute. Now, she looked up at the balcony where Vinnie had died, and she could still hardly believe it.

Whatever she had told everyone, she had carefully omitted one thing. Once upon a time, she had found Vinnie charming, breathtakingly attractive, and unabashedly dangerous, exciting, and powerful. Like so many other women, Saffron had had a torrid affair with him that had lasted only that one summer. And deep down, she was grateful to have been the one who broke it off, keeping her reputation and her self-esteem intact. As if these things were so important anymore.

And now Vinnie was dead. She had many fond memories. She had carefully put her scruples aside concerning her dating someone who even called himself a cheat and a gangster—and laughed about it.

But that charm, she remembered, made it so easy to forgive. All the little lies—and the big ones, all the other women—which infuriated her, and all the dishonest dealings that he didn't bother hiding from her. Still, they were good times. Exciting times. Traveling to far-away lands, cruising the Caribbean in his ridiculously oversized yacht, the private plane, the helicopter. All that, yes, but she couldn't get past the other women, so she broke it off. Regretted it soon enough and went back to him after he begged so nicely, but in the end, she managed to put all that behind her, and get on with her life.

Still, it had bruised her heart. And now Vinnie was dead. Saffron sighed, and Margo looked at her worried. But she brushed it away. These memories had fleeted through her mind as fast as the wind. And she found herself back in the present, standing next to Margo by the front door, waiting for her to use her little tools which—before she could count to one, two, three—managed easily to pop the door open.

Chapter 26
The Cat, Again

MARGO SLID THE DOOR OPEN AN INCH and looked around before opening it wide and letting Saffron pass. They found themselves in a narrow corridor, dark, that led to the kitchen, a storage room, and finally to the main hall. Just a few days earlier, Margo had worn a beautiful ballgown when she had entered the Gallery through the front door. The lights had been on, a huge crowd of beautiful people had mingled happily holding flutes of champagne and canapés. Now, just jeans, unassuming blouse, and flat-heeled shoes.

It was hard to recognize the place in the penumbra. Curtains in golds and reds—she knew because she had seen them before—now were drawn, and little if no light filtered through them. Jamaica Street, usually busy, was about a block away, but occasionally you could hear someone drive by, or honk their horn, and there was this intrusion of life into this silence. No particular sound, but you just knew that there was life out there that moved and bustled even if you couldn't see it, whereas there was nothing within. Nothing left. As if the edifice had already started dying, decaying.

They passed in front of an exhibit of masks—she always thought of funerary masks when she saw them.

"These must be the masks that are supposed to be fake," she whispered to Saffron.

"Don't be naïve, my friend. Knowing Vinnie as well as I did, everything here could be a fake."

"If they are fakes, where are the originals?"

"I think we're getting a little ahead of ourselves assuming that they are, but if they were indeed fakes, if I were in Vinnie's shoes, I would have sold the originals to a very particular, very selective clientele, one that would be happy to keep my secret."

Margo whistled softly. "Meaning that—unless we find records of sales—we'll never know who might have bought them."

"If indeed they are fakes."

"If indeed, yes."

"Wow, no wonder he had so much money."

Margo kept walking around the room, followed by Saffron, who had become suspiciously slow and quiet.

"Anything wrong, Saffron?"

"No, not really. This place brings back memories, that's all. I'll tell you one day."

"You mean, you and Vinnie?"

"Some other time, please," she said. Margo heard the sadness in her voice and linked her arm to Saffron's.

"You don't have to tell me anything, but I'm here if you need me."

They crossed the great expanse of the silent showroom, stopping here and there to admire something of particular beauty. At the end of the great hall, the circular stairway that Margo had ascended for the party shone in diffused white, rose, and gold marble. Saffron told Margo follow me, and they ducked under the sweeping stairway and found themselves behind it, in a dark, quiet little corner, where an unassuming wooden door blended discreetly into the paneling.

Saffron touched the doorknob, about to turn it and enter, when she withdrew her hand suddenly as if she had been burned. She turned toward Margo and grabbed her shoulders.

"There's someone in there," she whispered.

"But how is it possible?"

"I don't know, but I hear music. Come listen."

Margo approached the door and carefully put her ear to it. Then she straightened herself out and said, "Mendelssohn."

"Really? The guy that saved Bach's sheet music from the butcher's shop?"

"Yes. It sounds like one of his *Songs Without Words* for piano. I used to play a lot of Mendelssohn. My mom liked it."

"So, what do we do now?"

"We can only do one of two things: knock and enter and say we found the door open, or go back the way we came, and pretend this never happened."

"Okay. Do you want to go first?"

"Sure. Why not."

Margo cautiously twisted the doorknob and pushed in the door a couple of inches. The music was louder now. It was coming from a gramophone.

"A what?" Saffron asked.

"A record player. We used to have one. After a while, the records get scratched, and they make an annoying grating, popping sound, but my mom swore that was the real way to listen to good music, and that the scratches were like battle scars to be respected and held in awe."

Margo stepped into the office and uttered a startled scream. Saffron bumped right into her as they both crowded into the once-elegant office.

There was nobody there, but the lights were on. Whoever had been listening to the record was now gone, or long gone—who knew. And yet Mendelssohn kept going around and around on the turntable, the sad, moody piano passages providing a perfect background for the horror and the mess in front of them.

Whoever had gone through Vinnie's things—obviously looking for something—had turned the place upside down: the books scattered on the floor like so many dead bodies strewn about. And the papers were everywhere. An open window and a billowing curtain, probably the way in which the intruder had left, and the breeze probably the culprit in all those papers scattered, and the haphazard way in which they had been strewn about. And Mendelssohn's song ran down, and after some mechanical struggles, some grunts and clicks, the mechanism managed to send the arm back to the beginning of the outer loop on the record, and another song began, again.

And Margo stood transfixed, utterly still, horrified, staring at Vinnie Chauvin's desk. She shook her head gently from side to side as if she were going mad.

Finally, Saffron noticed and asked her if she was all right.

"Do you see what I see?" Margo asked.

"What's that?"

"Do you see a cat sitting on the desk?"

There was a terrible jumble of things on the desk and Margo had to point in the direction of the creature that had her so scared.

"There. That black and white cat. Do you see it?"

"Yes, Margo. I do see it. Open window, temptation for cat. Isn't that what they do?"

"Maybe so. But I know that cat. Do you see part of his ear missing? That's the cat I saw on former Sheriff Rob Schexnayder's bed the day I went to see him, the day he vanished."

"Yesterday."

"Yes. What's that cat doing here?"

Chapter 27

Coffee With Dr. Gabe

"AND WHAT HAPPENED NEXT?" Dr. Gabe asked Margo and Saffron who were sipping daintily on their cappuccinos.

"We chased the cat all over the room, but he managed to give us the slip."

"Through the window?"

"No. By then, Saffron had managed to run to the window and close it. We chased him all over the house. But he's still there, somewhere. I called the veterinarian again. Hopefully, he gets to catch the little absconder this time, or else we'll be forced to bring him food every day. Can't let him starve."

"I guess not. Maybe Margo wants to adopt him," he said.

"Margo doesn't want any more cats," Margo retorted. "Margo has her dead friend Jenny's two orphaned cats already who are getting very old and cranky. They don't need their lives stirred up by a new arrival."

"What's going to happen to it?"

"That's not the point right now, Dr. Gabe. We're here because you said you had news."

"And I have to tell someone. I've been calling Maurice and can't find him. Without Sam, and without Andy, there is no police force in Half Moon Bay."

"While that is true, please don't say it in front of Maurice. You're going to hurt his feelings."

"But it's the truth. He's going to have to up his game a notch, or else we'll be left without law enforcement."

"Don't despair, Dr. Gabe. We won't have to resort to vigilante justice. Apparently, we have two new recruits, fresh out of the academy. And we'll find Sam. I bet Maurice is out there somewhere, helping the trackers look for him."

"I don't know how you girls can be so calm, given that God only knows what's happened to him."

"Nobody is calm, Dr. Gabe," Margo said, taking umbrage. "Look at Saffron and those black circles under her eyes. She hasn't slept a wink since he's vanished. They've been friends since Middle School. She's worried sick about him. And me, I'm not calm either. But I've gone for help, and I've prayed, and that's all I can do. The rest, I have to put in God's hands."

"I'm sorry. I didn't mean to be insensitive. I'm worried too. But you're right. There's nothing we can do but wait. So, here's what I wanted to show you." Dr. Gabe took his phone out of his pocket and fiddled with the buttons until he found what he was looking for.

"What are we looking at? It's the lapel of a jacket."

"Yes. It's the jacket worn by Vinnie the night he died. If you'll look closely, you'll see that there's a smudge on it. It's makeup. But we couldn't determine what kind it was. It's the color of skin, but it's very greasy. I was wondering if you two would have any idea of what it could be. I asked the nurses, and they didn't know."

Margo thought about it and didn't know what to say, but after a few seconds, she saw how Saffron's eyes lit up.

"It's stage makeup. It has to be. They use very thick and very oily makeup. Completely different from what we would wear."

"Are you sure? Stage makeup?"

"I'm positive." Saffron swept her glorious mane of red hair off her shoulder and looked straight at Dr. Gabe. "Don't ask me for details. But I'm well acquainted with stage makeup."

"Do you have any? For comparison?"

"Not anymore. But there's this guy who does my hair in the salon next to the Marina. Brad Bijou, I think his name is. He's dating a stage actor. Ask him. I bet he'll be able to help you."

"Then that presents us with another problem." Dr. Gabe said.

"Which is?"

"That at first, I got excited that the killer might be a woman." Margo looked at him horrified, and he quickly corrected himself. "What I meant to say was that we could have narrowed it down by gender. Or at least a woman might have been with him right before his death."

"Yes," said Saffron. "Because Vinnie would have never shown up at a party with a dirty jacket. He got that smudge that night, sometime before he died."

"My thoughts exactly. But here's my problem. If this is a thick stage makeup, it didn't necessarily have to be a woman. It could have just as easily been a man."

"An actor, you mean?"

"Yes. Or someone in heavy disguise."

"I see what you mean."

As Margo followed behind Saffron and Dr. Gabe to the parking lot, she questioned her motivation in keeping her find to herself. For the most part, life had taught her to trust and follow her instincts. So, when she had found the drawing, right where the cat had been sitting on Vinnie's desk, she quickly tucked it in her purse, all the while poor Saffron was chasing the cat, or Saffron was chasing the poor cat. She never even got the chance to take a peek at it. Was she becoming like a magpie—always stealing shiny and interesting objects? Or was her instinct directing her to collect certain things that could later be useful in an investigation? She sighed. She was going to have to discuss that with Father Armand during her next confession. But she patted her purse with satisfaction. She knew it was a clue. And she was very pleased that she had picked it up.

She leaned against one of the palm trees that lined the parking lot and waited for Saffron to be done talking to the doctor. The day was hot and humid, and the air was hard to breathe. She wiped the moisture off the top of her lips and stared at some white herons that flew lazily across the pristine blue sky. She might have sounded brusque when talking about the cat in Vinnie's Gallery. But in truth, she was worried about it. How did it manage to get from the former Sheriff's house to the Gallery? Granted, the two buildings were not far from each other. But had it randomly strolled over to the Gallery? Had it been picked up and brought over? Or had it followed someone?

Suddenly, the light bulb went on in her head. The cat must have followed the former Sheriff. Rob Schexnayder must have been following a lead that took him to Vinnie's Gallery. And the cat followed. Yes. It had to be.

She ran after Saffron and Dr. Gabe.

"I think Rob Schexnayder might be in trouble."

"What kind of trouble?"

"I'll explain on the way. Someone, drive me to the Gallery. Fast."

Dr. Gabe burnt tires as he left the parking lot. He knew Margo well enough by now to trust her instincts. The pebbles and oyster shells that topped the dirt at the parking lot popped and crackled under the car. Margo—worried sick—blamed herself for not thinking straight. She was distracted, chatting with Saffron when they had gone to the Gallery. That was why she had not given thought to much of anything.

She berated herself. She had the feeling that they were going to be too late. She was out of the car even before it stopped, and she ran across the street without looking to one side or the other.

The door was unlocked. Just as they had left it. As soon as she stepped into the house, she began calling for the former Sheriff. She went from room to room, calling out his name, searching for him systematically. Everything was dead quiet. Everything exactly the way they had left it.

At the bottom of the circular stairway, the cat jumped out of nowhere, and with an anguished little cry rubbed its silky body against her legs. She had the most horrible premonition. And when the cat started going up the steps, she followed, with a dread in her heart.

The ballroom was a mess. Nobody had picked up after the party. Chairs had been upended, soiled tablecloths, half hanging off tables, with champagne flutes overturned, and rotting canapés on the silver platters. The smells of humidity, spoiled food, and champagne turned to vinegar couldn't mask an underlying smell of vomit and decay.

Margo had stopped in her tracks, horrified at the desolation in front of her. But the little cat hadn't forgotten. It rubbed itself against her legs and cried, waking her from her reverie, so she followed it to the back, where several white silk sofas covered with modern, multicolored throw pillows were strewn about strategically for style and comfort.

Next to one of the sofas, the little cat stopped and turned to look at her. She stepped closer very slowly, wishing she didn't have to look. But the little cat cried and cried, and she picked it up, and together they went to take a peek at what was behind it.

She heard Saffron and Dr. Gabe coming up the stairs. But there was no point in waiting for them. Eventually, she was going to have to look, to identify him. So, she took one step, and then another, and holding the shaking little cat in her arms, she leaned over.

There he was, of course, lying in a pool of coagulated blood. It was him, the former Sheriff. She had taken an instant liking to him and would never forgive herself for having left the first time without checking upstairs.

She whimpered as she watched Dr. Gabe lean over Rob Schexnayder's body and held some tears of regret behind. Saffron was standing next to her, an arm around her shoulder, comforting her with soothing words.

"Now, I know what you're thinking, Margo," she said, "but it wasn't your fault."

"But we shouldn't have left without checking upstairs. When I saw the cat, I should have known he might be here."

"Now, now, there's a good girl. You need to quit crying. He died in the line of fire, so to speak."

"Stop blabbing girls and call 911. Rob Schexnayder isn't dead."

Chapter 28

Looking For Father Armand

CHRIS MOUTON LOOKED UP AT THE SKY and told himself it wasn't going to rain. Good. The roads would be passable, the waters navigable. He regretted not having a dog, a companion. He had always wanted a puppy, but time never seemed right. He remembered that poor hurt dog he had found next to the old man. Pretty hurt they were, both of them. Would probably be dead by now.

But in hindsight, it was better not to be responsible for any other creature. As he walked around the house unplugging appliances—except the freezer of course—and shuttering windows, he was grateful not to have to leave a four-legged friend behind.

A backpack and a duffel bag were all he'd packed. It was all he'd be able to carry once he'd ditched the four-wheeler. But the most important stuff was in his backpack so that if they came after him, he could drop the duffel and run.

He walked around the property. Locked the house, checked the back door. Then he hurried over to the fur house. There were too many traces of Sam the Sheriff and the little girl Luna in there, but there was no time to clean up. He had to put his hopes in Father Armand's ability to protect him in as much as possible.

Giving his home a last wistful goodbye, Chris Mouton hopped on his Yamaha Grizzly ATV and hit the road.

The going was good, the weather pleasantly warm. He traveled the back roads, the muddy dirt roads, grateful for the modifications he had put his ATV through the new self-cleaning deep lug tires, the deep waffle pattern handlebar grips, and the cleated footpegs. Mud flew in his wake as he crossed shallow ponds and muddy ditches, and by nightfall, he had reached the river. And he was covered in mud and swamp slime.

Behind a wild clump of giant pampas grass, he stopped in front of the small boathouse/fishing camp that had been in his family for ages. He needed some rest. He would stay the night. He knew the shelves were stocked with canned food and beer, and what else did an exhausted man need but that, and any old camping bed to sleep on?

After cleaning up, he sat in a rocking chair in the front porch and rocked himself gently back and forth as the wooden boards creaked underneath him. He sipped his warm beer and leaned his head against the back of the chair. What a night. The stars were out, and the sky was clear. He stared at the moon and wondered how man had been able to travel so far and manage to find his way back home.

Back inside, he stumbled around in the dark until he made himself comfortable on the camping bed. The pillow wasn't too bad, and the blanket was dry enough to keep him warm. Outside, the frogs chirped and bellowed with enthusiasm, looking for company, or singing to the moon—who knew. Point was that it didn't take long for the body to relax, and within minutes, Chris Mouton was blissfully asleep.

Chapter 29

The New Cat

MARGO SAT ON THE SOFA IN HER BEDROOM, holding the new cat. She didn't want to give it a name. He already had one. She had faith in Saint Hildegard's power to heal everyone under her roof, and soon former Sheriff Rob Schexnayder would be well enough to come collect his cat and take him home.

It was late, but for the people partying on the beach, it wasn't. There had been a beach volleyball tournament in Half Moon Bay, and the town was full of tourists. Cars drove back and forth under her window, with their ugly music blaring from their boomboxes. No window was thick enough to block the racket. Down on the beach, the tourists were getting drunk, squealing with delight, making noise, making the local dogs bark.

Ice and Fenway—Jenny's cats—refused to be friends with the new cat, but were curious, so they sat on Margo's bed, staring malevolently at Margo, and watching her pet the newcomer as if they wanted to chase him away.

Several motorcycles zoomed by, popping their exhaust pipes, broom-broom, making her hair stand up. Why so much noise? Why? Was it really necessary?

She tossed in her bed restlessly. Ice and Fenway were chasing the new cat. She turned her bed lamp on and grabbed Ice and Fenway and put them outside in the hallway. It was the little newcomer who needed the most comforting until his daddy got well. And she and the little cat had barely settled down finally when the other two started howling outside the bedroom door. It was going to be a long night.

She stared at the ceiling. Her eyes followed the reflection of the headlamps that traveled across the dark walls and ceilings as they passed and shone into her room. She wanted to get up to close the curtains, but she was starting to get sleepy. So, she rolled away from the window and snuggled with the little cat. She was beginning to doze off when she realized that nobody had bothered to let Sandra know that her boss had been found and was alive in the hospital.

First thing in the morning, that was what she was going to do. Go see Sandra and tell her what had happened. Or at least go and leave her a note.

She closed her eyes, thankful to put a long and tough day behind her, and she dozed off into oblivion. But she had barely had time to get to her first dream when there was a banging at her bedroom door. She opened an eye and saw Lucy standing at the door. The light streaming in from the hallway woke her up and made the cat jump off the bed.

"What on earth is going on, Lucy? If I don't get some sleep, I'm probably going to die."

"I'm so sorry Miss Margo. You know I wouldn't bother you if this wasn't an emergency?"

"So? Out with it. What's wrong?"

"It's Sam."

"Is he on the phone?"

"No, Miss Margo. He's just been admitted to Saint Hildegard. That was Dr. Gabe on the phone. He told me to tell you that Sam wants to see you. Right away."

"Oh, okay. I have to call Saffron."

"No. Dr. Gabe said no Saffron. Just you."

Chapter 30

DAY FIVE: Saint Hildegard

AFTER BROOKS DROPPED MARGO OFF at the front door of the hospital, she stared sleepily at the long, empty hallway. The automatic door whizzed closed behind her. It was freezing in there, and she pulled the sides of her sweater tighter around her chest.

She walked to the reception desk, where one lonely nurse slept on her arm making bubbly snoring noises. She looked up at the clock and saw it had just turned midnight. The witching hour. The hour in which all supernatural creatures come to life.

Margo shivered in her flimsy sweater and wondered what to do. The poor nurse looked like she needed that sleep, and she hated having to wake her up. Maybe she could find the patient on her own.

She walked quietly around the reception desk and looked at the computer on the table from behind the sleeping nurse's shoulders. She should have known. A screensaver had filled the dormant computer screen with swimming koi, graciously moving from one side to another of the virtual aquarium. She moved the mouse an inch to see what would happen, and the password page came up. No luck there. Without the password, the computer would remain silent. She was going to have to find Sam on her own.

There is no place lonelier in the world than a rural hospital at midnight. All the visitors gone, all the patients sleeping, most of the nurses and doctors, home with their families. Occasionally, there was a reason for activity in the middle of the night, but mostly, Saint Hildegard's was like a haunted house, it's colonial architecture intact, its corridors with their antique stone tile flooring, echoing under her feet like the footsteps of a ghost.

She passed the cafeteria. Closed and gloomy. One lugubrious light was still on at the back by the counter, and an old man with a sad face was wiping the counter with a checkered rag, wiping and wiping the same spot repeatedly. He looked up and nodded at Margo as she passed by. Then he lowered his head again and went about his business.

She continued walking. She passed a large room behind glass doors, and she saw people, so she approached and stuck her head to the window. Perhaps the emergency room. Rows and rows of plastic chairs, and a few of them occupied by sick looking people. But Sam wasn't among them. He had to be on the third floor then, where the important cases were. Whatever those were called.

Finally, she got to the elevators and punched the call button. In the hollow silence, the whirring of the moving box, and the ping as the doors opened, startled her. Should she wonder why she had been asked to come alone? Or was it too late in the night to even care?

At least, on the third floor, there was some action. Two nurses at the reception were gossiping, and Margo recognized one of them—the one that had been flirting with Dr. Gabe.

The nurses smiled at her when she approached, and the perky one told Margo to follow.

"Is Rob Schexnayder on this floor?"

"Our old Sheriff? Yes. He's much better. He's out of danger."

"What exactly happened to him?"

"Sorry, can't say. You'll have to ask the doctor. Here we are."

Margo stared at the closed door, indecisively. Then, at the encouragement from the nurse, she knocked, and then, she opened the door.

Chapter 31

Sam's Alive

MARGO FOUND HERSELF IN A FUTURISTIC ROOM of electronic wonders. Machines whirred around her. And things went bleep-bleep softly, barely heard above the sound of the air conditioning. If anything, it was even colder in here. But she was the only one shivering. Dr. Gabe, in a Hawaiian shirt and light-colored linen pants, didn't seem to feel the cold. Nor did the patient—sleeping deeply—whose upper body was bandaged but naked.

"Margo, nice to see you. I'm sorry that we had to drag you out of bed, but this is an emergency."

"It's okay, Dr. Gabe. What's wrong with Sam?"

"The specialist just left. He thinks Sam will be fine, but it's a bit too early to tell."

"What happened to Sam?"

"He wrestled an alligator and lived to tell us about it."

"Is he hurt? He's all bandaged up."

"Yes. The alligator grabbed him and dragged him underwater. He was wearing heavy hunting clothes, and that's what saved him. Otherwise, the bites would have been fatal, as they usually are."

"And the bandages?"

"Nurse Nancy cleaned his wounds and applied her special salve. Then, she bandaged him."

"A special salve?"

"I know what you're thinking, Margo. There was a showdown between her and the specialist, but she won. As unconventional as it is, her salve has so many healing properties, that the specialist gave in."

"Is that it?"

"Not at all. There's no sign of infection so far, but there's always the risk of Burkholderia pseudomallei, which are usually due to contamination from the environment. Multiple microorganisms, especially aerobic Gram-negatives, have been isolated from wounds after alligator attacks."

Margo stared with an open mouth at this string of what had just sounded like gibberish, and Dr. Gabe laughed.

"What this means—in plain English—is that a study of the mouth of alligators has shown that the flora of its mouth might actually consist of the flora of the feces of its previous preys."

Margo felt that rise of bile in her larynx signaling a need to throw up, and Dr. Gabe quickly grabbed her shoulders and told her to look at him.

"It's okay, Margo. I know its gross, but it's a good thing we know how this works because Sam's already been given a broad spectrum set of Ceftriaxone + Doxycycline + Metronidazole."

"Huh?"

"Antibiotics."

"Oh, good. So why am I here?"

"Follow me."

Chapter 32

Luna

THE NURSES LOOKED UP AND SMILED AT THEM, and the perky one even waved shamelessly at Dr. Gabe. But he didn't smile back and kept on walking instead.

The room they entered was smaller and emptier than Sam's. The room was dark, but the light from the corridor shone diagonally into the room and illuminated a tiny patient, barely visible in the enormous bed.

The little girl, covered in blankets up to her chin, wasn't hooked up to any machine and slept peacefully despite the bright light shining in on her.

"This is Luna. She's the little girl that Sam rescued. He thinks she's in danger and needs to be taken somewhere safe."

"Are you thinking about my house?"

"Yes."

"But it's not safe."

"It has to be at your house. According to Sam, we're dealing with some type of mafia organization. He doesn't know who to trust, and this can't get out. So far, only you and I know about her."

"And the nurses?"

Dr. Gabe blushed. "One of them knows, but she won't say anything."

"The younger one?" Dr. Gabe nodded.

"Are you sure you can trust her?"

"I have to. I needed help."

Margo sighed. Her house was big enough to house ten little girls, and Lucy and Brooks were loyal to the death. And she looked so innocent and vulnerable under that pile of blankets that how could she refuse? How could she?"

"All right then. What do we do?"

"Take her down in the service elevator, put her in your car, and take her home. She won't wake up until tomorrow. She's heavily sedated."

Dr. Gabe deftly picked up the sleeping child, blankets and all, and Margo held the door open for them. She closed it quietly behind her and followed them.

Anyone who has seen a horror movie knows how hauntingly disturbing the unseen side of a hospital can be. Doors with red danger signs, one large laboratory with a glass wall that housed hundreds of body parts or specimens in glass jars on the shelves, rooms lined up side by side with bars like prison cells, with padded walls and utilitarian-looking built-in beds, all the more terrifying in the penumbra of an empty, poorly lit hospital wing.

Almost before they got to the service entrance, they passed an isolated corridor from where whimpers and cries seemed to emanate. Margo gasped, horrified, her imagination running wild. Dr. Gabe looked back at her and chuckled.

"It's not what you think, Margo. There's a narrow channel under the hospital that connects to the sea. It moans when the tides change. Call Brooks and ask him to bring the car to the service entrance. We're almost there."

"Are you going to follow us or something?"

"Better not. Too many cars at this time of the night in front of your house could make someone curious."

"Then what do I do?"

"Settle her in a nice little room away from possible roaming eyes, and nothing. Wait till she wakes up in the morning and tell her what's going on."

"But not even I know what's going on."

"She's a very bright child. She probably knows already she's in danger. She was held captive for over a week. Tell her you're Sam's friend, and you'll keep her safe. Call me only if you need me. We have to act as if none of this would have happened."

Luna moaned a little as they positioned her on the back seat, but she never woke up. As they crossed the empty streets with flickering stoplights, she told Brooks what all she had just learned, and they decided that they would leave making plans till the morrow, because everyone was too tired to think.

Luna slept through her being carried upstairs to a guest room, and Lucy—always the protecting type—chirped with excitement like a mother hen as she told Margo a hundred miles an hour how well she was going to take care of the child.

But Margo was beyond caring. It was almost three in the morning, and the world had been sleeping already for hours. She entered her room like a zombie and changed to the pajamas she had strewn in a hurry on her bed. It wasn't until she began climbing in the bed that she noticed that the cats had finally made peace with each other. All three of them were bundled in a furry pile, keeping each other warm. And then maybe, Ice and Fenway knew the little newcomer needed to be comforted, and in her absence decided to step in.

Sam was safe, the old Sheriff was alive and Lucy, who loved having guests in the house, had a little girl to soothe her unfulfilled mothering instinct. And—at least temporarily—they had a new cat.

All was well with the world.

Chapter 33

The Vermillion

CHRIS WOKE TO THE SUN SHINING IN HIS EYES. For a second, he was surprised. He had slept deep and long. Better than he had in a very long time. He felt his freedom in the sound of blue jays chattering, the morning breeze whistling in the shrubbery, making the flimsy, thin windows of the fishing camp shake. And then there was the sound of waves, slapping against the wooden stilts after a speed boat flew by.

In the self-made prison he had been living in due to his brother and his associates, he had forgotten the true value of living off-grid: the quiet contemplation, the peace within when you sat for hours holding a fishing rod, the joy of being one with nature, rocking in a chair by the water, sipping on a beer.

He gave thanks to his namesake, the one his mother had named him after, St. Christopher, Patron Saint of travelers, as if she'd known at his birth how much protection he would need. He remembered very little about her. She must have been a saint herself to put up with the overbearing bully who also spawned his half-brother Vinnie.

His mother, small, dark, very French, so kind and patient, gone so soon. Almost the only thing he remembered about her was the time he had run away from home after a beating from the bully, and later found because he had gotten hurt. The room where he slept with his mother—in the house in which he still lived—had the curtains drawn. His leg was broken, but that didn't hurt as much as his wounded pride.

He saw again his mother's gentle face, leaning over him and giving him a kiss. *Here's a St. Christopher medal,* she had said. *I'll put it around your neck, mon fils, and it will always protect you on your travels. St.*

Christopher will never let you get hurt again. He still had that medal, and it was still around his neck.

Well, he decided to quit moping and get on with it. He knew the flat bottom boat was in good condition. He kept it up himself. He ate a can of baked beans with a pack of saltine crackers and washed them down with a warm beer. Then, he gathered his things and shut the door behind him.

There seemed to be a finality to everything he had been doing in the last couple of days and wondered if that was a premonition of death. And he sighed. But whatever. Sooner or later, everybody had to say goodbye.

He took one last look at the fishing camp, just a small bit sad that he had never had that dog, or a wife and a family. No point in wishing for one now, but it would have been so nice to have someone to wave goodbye to.

After he was far enough from the vegetation growing at the edge of the mighty Vermillion, he turned the motor on, and followed the wind south, to this one place where he could hide his boat and find that shortcut to Half Moon Bay. By lunchtime, he should be there, sitting next to Father Armand, begging for help.

Nothing else he could do.

Chapter 34

Luna's Story

LUNA PUT HER CROISSANT BACK ON THE PLATE and repeated patiently. "They chased me because I seen them feed the alligator."

"Wait, hold on a sec. What exactly do you mean by that?"

"I mean that maybe I was snooping, and I shouldn't, but they have this *masticated* alligator and I was curious. I seen him before."

Margo, Lucy, and Brooks all stood around Luna in the kitchen, watching her eat three times more than any small child should. Luna picked up her croissant and munched on it, with all the look of someone who's decided to ignore her audience.

"So, Luna," Margo tried again. "You saw a group of men feeding a masticated alligator?"

"I won't be saying any more. You don't believe me."

"No, dear, it's not that I don't believe you. It's just that I'm surprised, is all."

Appeased, Luna nodded. "Oh, all right." She stuffed the last piece of croissant in her mouth and looked expectantly at Margo. It had taken many assurances that "I'm Sam's friend," for the little girl to relax and be willing to tell her story. "So how did it happen?"

"I ran away from home again because Mona was being so mean. She yelled at me because I let the dog inside the house. She was very angry, and I missed my dad, and I was tired of all the yelling. I have a secret place."

"Is that where you always go?"

"Yes. Sometimes I stay for days."

"And you're not scared?"

"A little, sometimes, at night. But I'm more scared of Mona."

"And you don't get hungry, or thirsty?"

"No. When I can, I bring food for a *mergentsy*. I have water, and cookies, and chips. I even have a blanket."

"And where did you learn to do that?"

Luna laughed. It was the innocent mirthful laughter of an innocent child. And for a second, that was what she appeared to be. Someone who had been kidnapped, who had had to run away from home several times, a six-year-old who knew how to take care of herself. Margo shook her head in amazement. In clean clothes, with freshly washed hair, she didn't even look that old.

"So, tell me, Luna, how did all that happen?"

"Um, I was running away, you know. There is a big, big house in the woods. It's pretty, and I sometimes go by and look at it. I'm going to live in a house like that one day."

"I'm sure you will. Go on."

"The men were there, outside by the pond, so I hid behind a fat tree and snooped."

"Did you hear what they were saying?"

"A little bit. But they were bad words. I'm not allowed to say."

"Okay. So, what were they doing again?"

"Ugh. I told you already. They were feeding the alligator. They threw the man in the pond and told the alligator to go eat."

"Lord have mercy. Was the man moving?"

"Not so much."

"And then what happened? They saw you?"

"Yes. And one of them called me a *welding bench* and said to go get her."

"A meddling wench?"

"Well, a meddling something. And they all started running after me."

"You poor dear."

"And the man said 'nuff is enough, and one of them caught me and took me away."

"You said his name was Chris, right?"

"No. That came later. He locked me in a cage and apologized. He said his brother was very mean, and that he was scared of him. I told him that I understood. He was always kind. I felt sorry for him."

Margo nodded. "Okay. And the masticated alligator?"

"Yes, that one. It was really big. I thought they were going to throw me in the pond too."

"You poor child. You must have been so afraid."

"I don't know. Not so much. But I didn't want them to throw me in the pond."

"And then?"

"And then, after some days, Chris brought Sam the Sheriff and tied him to the table. He tied him with a lot of ropes, but the Sheriff squeezed out of them, and he rescued me. And on the way, another alligator attacked me, but Sam rescued me again, and he got hurt for saving me. I'm tired of talking now. May I have another croissant? And another juice, please?"

Chapter 35

The Best Stop Holiday Motel

SHORTLY BEFORE NOON, Chris touched port at the *Quai des Pêcheurs* and tied his flat-bottomed boat to a pole sticking out of the water, by the pier. He got out, stretched his legs, grabbed his stuff, and looked around. It had been a couple of years since, but nothing had changed. Except for his own self. He felt alive, with a purpose, and breathed in the salty air with pleasure.

He walked through a gathering of gulls which—refusing to move out of his way—were eating chopped up fish heads someone had thrown out to them. Damned birds. There were too many of them. And they got more aggressive as the years went by, stealing food out of people's hands, even snatching a bite out of someone's mouth. Didn't these idiots know that the more they fed them, the more they would breed?

He rushed through the fish market and waved hello here and there to some people he knew from way back. He got excited when he saw his tante Marie's ramshackle establishment from afar and almost sprinted the last few steps.

He chuckled when he got to the door and saw that The Best Stop Holiday Motel sign now hung by a thread. If he ever had the chance in this lifetime, he would come back and fix that, and maybe paint those peeling shutters, and stuff.

He pushed the squeaky front door open, and, as if he had stepped into the past, he looked around and saw that nothing, but absolutely nothing had changed. The wallpaper, the same, just a little dirtier. The furniture—he chuckled—he remembered the furniture he used to climb on, and it was exactly the same.

He saw the owner hurry to greet him. He watched her fondly, hands on hips, wondering what she was going to say, that dear, sweet, short, overweight, dark-skinned Cajun woman with wiry white hair and chatty attitude, who had helped raise him.

She came closer, and still, she hadn't recognized him. By now she probably needed glasses, the old dear. She wiped her hands on her dirty apron and approached Chris with a friendly smile.

"*Bonjour, monsieur*. Oh, *mon Dieu*, is that you, Chris? *Ç'est pas possible!*" Her eyes lit up, and she opened her arms and enveloped him in them, and he smelled on her that familiar aroma of good home-cooked food and other fond memories and hugged her back.

"Bonjour, *tante* Marie. Long time, *einh?*"

"Oh, *mais* why didn't you tell me you were coming?"

"Nah, I wanted to surprise you. *Ça va?* You look well."

"I am well, I suppose. It hurts a little bit here and there. And sometimes lonely, mais well. You should come and stay with me for a while. Keep an old woman some company."

"Did you hear about Vinnie?"

"That *bon-rien?* I sure did." Marie sighed sadly. "I saw it on the news the other day. My poor Vinnie. What a terrible way to die. The world will be a better place without him, mais I will miss him so much. Come with me to *ze* kitchen, sha. My food is going to burn."

Chris followed his tante Marie through the warren of dusty hallways and dark, shady corners where he had played so often as a child. The peeling paint and the tattered wallpaper depressed him. The place was dark and claustrophobic and smelled of mildew. Maybe he shouldn't promise to stay too long. He had just arrived, and already he felt trapped.

He walked behind Marie, taking his steps slowly, sunk in years of sad memories of his mom and a mean, nasty father, but soon the depression lifted when he was assaulted by the enticing smells of his childhood, and he realized that he didn't remember the last time he had had a good home-cooked meal.

He loved this kitchen, enormous, open, with wall to wall opaque windows that allowed in a cascade of cheerful light and brightened the otherwise run-down room. His tante—as was customary with her—had several pots of foods bubbling cheerfully on the stove at once. Chris salivated. While his tante stirred the foods in the pots vigorously, he sat down at the table, at his favorite spot. She plopped a large plate of piping hot boudin and a cold beer in front of him, and she sat down.

"So, where's Marcel?" Chris asked, eating between words. "He always used to be in the kitchen, *non?*"

"Sha, poor *cher* Marcel, he's no more. He got so old, so run down. One morning he didn't wake up. Ze place is so quiet without him."

"You should get another puppy."

"I'm not sure it's a good idea. I'm too old now. I don't want to die and leave him behind. Who would take care of him?"

Chris nodded. "I always wanted a puppy."

"I remember."

Chris ate and drank in silence for a while, not used to human companionship much anymore. Marie, too, seemed lost in her own thoughts. Then suddenly, she asked.

"Why are you here, Chris? I can tell there's something on your mind."

"I'm in trouble, Marie, and I'm in town to see Father Armand, the priest who helped me that last time when I got in trouble, remember?"

"Ze time you stole that car?"

"No, tante. The time Vinnie stole that car and put the blame on me."

Marie nodded sadly, absentmindedly. "Poor Vinnie."

"You're not going to start being sorry for him, are you? Not after all the grief he's caused us?"

"No, sha, of course not. Mais death is so final. Is all."

"So, I was telling you. Vinnie was involved in some nasty stuff. Someone was bringing him Native American artifacts, he was making copies, and selling them as originals."

"Everybody knows that."

"Really? Does everybody know about the murders as well? The kidnappings?"

"Maybe."

"Marie, if you know something, you should go to the police and tell them. Keeping secrets could put you in danger."

"Mais Vinnie is dead. Who would want to kill an old woman?"

"His associates. They would cheerfully cut your throat to keep you quiet. And me, I'm sure they want to kill me. I must go into hiding. These people have long arms. You have to be very well hidden to remain safe."

"And why do they want to kill you?"

"Because I was supposed to keep a little girl called Luna, and Sam the Half Moon Bay Sheriff prisoners in my fur house, but I let them escape."

"Sam? I know Sam. Nice young man. Trustworthy. He was investigating the death of an old man on the beach. Last year, that was. And you were keeping him prisoner, you say? Have you gone mad?" Marie got up from the bench and walked slowly over to the stove, where she poured herself some coffee from the percolator bubbling on the burner. She looked upset.

"Your mother will be turning in her grave," she told him when she sat back down.

Chris looked down at his hands sadly. "I know. But Vinnie beat me up so many times, I got tired of saying no. Was easier doing what he wanted."

"He wanted you to do that?"

"Yes. He said he had a plan."

"*Quel surprise*. Vinnie always had a plan. Last time he was here, he left a box—locked—and said to keep it safe for him and he would be back."

"Do you know what's in it?"

"Mais non. I didn't open it. Vinnie carried it up into the attic, and there it is, still. Then he gave me the key and told me to keep it safe for him until he came back. He was very secretive about it."

"Can't be anything good."

"Maybe treasure. Maybe enough to get this place fixed up."

"Can you really imagine Vinnie leaving treasure behind? That's almost funny."

"Mais, a person can dream, non?" While Chris wolfed down two more boudins and another beer, Marie enumerated all the repairs she could do to her hotel with just a little money. She did love this fleabag hotel to pieces.

"Vinnie was fond of you, Marie, so maybe you're in the will."

"Oui, oui. I'm so sure of that."

"Then why don't we find out what's in that box? Who knows? You might just be right."

Tante Marie climbed the stairs slowly. She complained about her knees and her hips. And Chris followed her slowly, thinking that she was too old for this.

The higher they climbed, the more demoralizing the place looked. Peeling wallpaper and burned-out lightbulbs were the least of it. What she needed was not a refurbished hotel, but a nice, well equipped little house in a quiet spot of Half Moon Bay, close to the seashore, close to Father Armand who would make sure that she would be taken good care of. And maybe a stray cat or a puppy adopted from a homeless shelter. Someone to love, and someone who would love her in return.

At the top of the last floor, he pulled the attic ladder down and told his tante to wait. He climbed the dusty wooden planks carefully. They looked like they were rotting away. What would he tell her if there was no money in that chest? No treasure, nothing interesting? It would break her heart. He had already given her something to hope about. What would he say if there was nothing?

He looked around in the darkness. Everything shoved into corners was trash. Piles and piles of it. He sat on a footstool with his hands in his lap and waited for his eyes to adjust to the darkness. Everywhere he looked, he saw mountains of magazines, other mountains of newspapers. Why had she kept this stuff, anyway? And those were rats scurrying in the dark corners, waiting for him to leave, he was sure. Next time he came, he would bring a cat. Should there ever be a next time.

His tante was pacing. He could hear her, walking back and forth, muttering to herself. He got up from the footstool and walked around. A tiny ventilation window near the rafters provided a minimum of light, and as he walked the perimeter of the attic, he saw a chest. It was small, really more a box than a chest. But it was newer than anything else up there, and it was nicely carved. Probably the only nice-looking thing among all the discards of who knew how many discarded lives. And it was locked. This had to be it.

He grabbed the chest and slowly walked down. The wooden planks under his feet were wobbly, crumbling already. He had to talk Marie into leaving this place. Those were termite holes he saw wherever he stepped. But they would have to see. This box was like the lottery. They would either win, or they would lose. All they had to do was open the box.

"Did you find it? Yes," she was all excited. "That's the one. Let's open it."

"First, I have to close the attic door. Then, let's go to the kitchen, and you go get the key. But let's have a shot of something strong. To brace ourselves in case of disappointment."

"All right, Chris. You bring the box along."

Marie couldn't stop talking. "Vinnie wouldn't have left the box up there if there hadn't been something important in it, right?"

"No, tante Marie. He wouldn't have. But don't get your hopes up."

At the kitchen table, Marie poured out some Aguardiente—probably a gift from a guest—two generous helpings, one for her, one for Chris. He shook the box and declared that it wasn't empty. So, they sat down, side by side, and Marie, with shaking, rheumatic hands, inserted the key and opened the box.

Her hands went up to her face and she squealed. Chris leaned toward the box to see for himself. It was packed tight with wads of money, all sitting in thick plastic bags. And on top of the money, a white envelope addressed to her.

"Oh, dear Lord, it's a treasure, Chris. Look."

"Are you sure?" Chris took the box out of her hands and pulled it toward him. "And there is a letter."

"You read it. My reading glasses are in the bedroom."

"Okay." Chris opened the envelope and smoothed the letter out on the table. "It's addressed to you, and this is what it says."

'Dear Tante Marie,

'By now, I'm probably dead, and you've told that little bastard Chris about the box I left in the attic. He's the one who fetched it for you, isn't he? Never mind. He doesn't know it, but I've always been fond of him. I'm sure he thought I was mean and cruel, but I just wanted to do what my father had failed to accomplish: make a man out of him.

'It didn't work. He was always too soft, too scared of the world. But if I'm dead, it's not my problem anymore. What's in the box is for you. How many times have I tried to give you money, and you've refused? Well, now that I'm dead, you have no choice but to keep it.

'Get out of there. Go buy yourself a cute little house somewhere and get yourself another dog. No more excuses. Now you have the money to do whatever you want. Don't complain. Enjoy it. And don't go running to the police with it. They'll take it away from you, and you'll never see a penny of it ever again.

'I love you, old girl. I wish I had spent more time with you sitting at that kitchen table like you must be sitting with Chris right now. Life got so complicated. Some of it I regret, the rest of it was okay. I have this terrible feeling that my days are numbered. I'm surrounded by too many greedy people.

'I might have forgotten to tell you whenever I saw you last, that the best times of my life were spent in your hotel, eating your wonderful cooking, and enjoying the family stories you know so many of. I remember running down the dusty hallways raising a ruckus, and you running after me with a wooden spoon, trying to stop me. What fond memories.

'I hope you have a long and happy life, tante Marie. And tell Chris I'm sorry if I was ever mean to him because I've always loved him too. After all, he's my little brother.

'*Au revoir,* you two.

Agnes Makóczy

'Vinnie.'

Chapter 36

DAY SIX: Sam's Back

MAURICE FOLLOWED SAM AROUND THE OFFICE like a worried mother hen. Finally, annoyed, Sam turned around and told him to go away. He hated being so blunt with Maurice, who had such a good heart and was so sensitive. But he didn't like to be mollycoddled. Besides, he had to think. Get back to work. He couldn't do that with Maurice underfoot.

If Chris Mouton didn't attack the old man, and his dog, and him, then who did? Not Vinnie. Vinnie was dead already. It must have been some of his goons, following orders given before their boss' death. It kind of surprised him that Vinnie should have wanted him dead. He had never given the man a second thought.

He called Maurice to bring in the new kids and while he waited, he looked at the sheet of suspects that Margo and Maurice had put together for him. But he wasn't paying too much attention. He wasn't too excited to meet the new recruits. The alligator bites on his arm and leg were throbbing. And there was a scratch on his neck. A nasty one. That one he got when the alligator was dragging him into the swamp.

Overall, the driving force of his life at that moment was the relentless pain. And the alligator. The monster's huge dead eyes. The smile full of hungry teeth. He just couldn't forget fighting the alligator. He could barely think of anything else. When he closed his eyes at night, hoping to sleep, he was back in the swamplands, being dragged under the murky water, fighting for oxygen, fighting for his life. He smelled the humidity of the swamp and the fetid breath of the monster's open maw. And that was all he could focus on.

You had to wonder what kind of luck had kept him alive. He wanted to be by himself and think all that through. Over and over again. He wanted to understand. Like a masochist, he needed to suffer in silence, and revisit the near-death experience, and not have to deal with two policemen he had never met before. Strangers. Yes, and all because of Andy's fault.

Suddenly, the anger welled up inside him and he flung his coffee mug against the wall. Then—ashamed of himself—he tried to get up and go clean up the mess, but he was in too much pain. He should have listened to the doctor and stayed in the hospital. But he couldn't stand being stuck in that narrow bed another day. It was worse than sleeping on a sofa.

"Those records, where are they already?" he yelled out at the poor Maurice, who came in with some folders, followed by two identical-looking young men in police uniform. They looked startled to meet their angry boss like this, but Sam took no pity.

"What is this? A joke? Identical twins? How am I going to tell you two apart?"

"Hey, Sam," said Maurice trying to appease him. "I don't think you should be getting angry like that. We'll figure it out. They can wear nametags, or different colored shirts, or something. At least there are two of them. We won't be so shorthanded."

"All right then, you know-it-all. Put them to work on these files and give me those records. And tell Margo to come straight in when she gets here."

"Sure, boss."

Sam opened the folders and tried to read, but the headache was brutal, so he leaned back in his swivel chair and closed his eyes. He was trying to remember the faces on the photographs pinned to the corkboard in the fur house. Some were blurry with age. One particular one had caught his attention. It was bigger than the others, the figures more visible. He could almost recall their faces: six men in hunting gear, with big, nasty rifles, wearing camouflage, and at their feet, their kill. A black bear, some alligators, some big cats. He hated the grins of satisfaction on the men's faces. He hated people who killed for sport. Who killed for pleasure. Nasty looking guys, all of them.

But he had barely had a chance to look. There had been no time. He was hurrying to get Luna away from there. So, he glanced at the photograph as it caught his eye, but briefly. And yet, for some reason, the image stayed with him. He had a feeling that—if he met these guys on the street—he would recognize them. And there was something odd about the picture. What was it? He would have to give that some thought.

Next thing he knew, the door was being opened, and there was Margo, annoyingly cheerful as usual, followed by a cloud of cloying perfume scent. All ready to go. Always ready to go.

"Where should we start?" She was in a chatty mood, all bushy-tailed, and Sam grunted with annoyance, but too fond of her to tell her to knock it off. He put up with the chatter patiently until they got to the parking lot and he climbed into the police truck. For once, it was Margo who would be doing the driving. Sam's leg was so sore that he wanted to scream. He bit the pain down.

"I'm hungry. Let's go to Chez Toussaint," he said, "on the way out of town. We can kill two birds with one stone. I want to meet this musician. Do you know where it is?"

"I think so. About ten miles after the Country Club?"

"Yes. That's the one. Now tell me about this Zac Benoit guy."

"He's kind of a local celebrity. He's the bandleader of Benoit Rocks. They play Wednesdays and weekends at Chez Toussaint. Surely you've heard of him."

"Maybe. I'm not sure."

"So, Zac plays the accordion and sings. But he also moves with the local it crowd."

"How come?"

"He's interested in Matty Daigle, one of the suspects."

"I've heard that name."

"I'm sure you have, Sam. Her brother is the deceased's business partner. And here we are."

Sam watched Margo park his oversized truck with ease, and then come around and help him out. She seemed to enjoy being in charge.

The going wasn't easy. The uneven ground was covered in pebbles and oyster shells, turning every step into an agonizing undertaking. He leaned heavily on Margo, who never flinched under his weight, and they walked laboriously toward the front door.

Fake palm trees lined the parking lot, their garish bright neon lights—pinks, blues, and purples—flickering on and off brightly in the midafternoon sun. By the time they made it to the front door, Sam was out of breath and they had to stop. A giant wooden alligator, an eight-footer, stood guard over the entrance with its maw wide open, showing rows of sharp carved teeth.

The animal had been beautifully hewn out of a single giant log. Every detail was carved with lifelike precision. It sat among a clump of Pampas Grass as if it were in the swamps. It gave the impression of being alive, and ready to attack. In a moment of delayed PTSD, Sam got the shakes, and a wave of panic washed over him.

"Come on, Margo," he said breathing heavily, quickly, grabbing her by the elbow. "Let's get out of here."

The inside of the establishment was cooler, much cooler than the humid outdoor heat, and Margo shivered. A girl at the door asked Sam if they had a reservation, and Sam pointed to the badge on his crisply ironed uniform shirt and said, "We sure do". The girl looked startled for a second as if she had a guilty conscience, but then forced a smile and asked them to follow her.

Margo had never been to Chez Toussaint and was surprised to see that the interior was bigger than it looked from the outside. A huge dance floor sat empty in the middle of the big room. To one side, a fairly large stage was populated by a handful of musicians who seemed to be getting their instruments ready for the concert. On the other side, several tables were occupied by bored-looking people—mostly men hugging beer mugs—who looked up vacantly at the waitress as she passed by them.

Sam picked the empty table closest to the stage, asked for two cokes and the menu, and they sat down.

"No beer today?"

"Taking too many meds. I don't want to die of an embolism or something."

"Do you know which one is Zac Benoit?" Margo asked him.

"You said he plays the accordion, right?"

"Right. That's him. He used to play with Wayne Toups' band. Then, he met Matty Daigle and became more ambitious. Now, he has his own band."

Sam smirked. "Because that earns him more money, right?"

"I have no idea. Classical musicians always live on the edge of starvation, but maybe Cajun Music pays better."

As if on cue, the band started playing L'anse Aux Pailles, and a handful of couples got up to dance. Margo and Sam worked through some pretty awesome seafood platters and some bread pudding, and by the time they were done, Zac Benoit and his band had stopped for a break.

"My leg's killing me," Sam said. "Would you be kind enough to invite Zac Benoit to sit with us for a couple of questions?"

Sam was really suffering, and the thought of having to stand up felt like hell. Margo got up grumbling, but not complaining loudly, and walked toward the stage, where Zac had just placed his accordion carefully on a chair. Sam chuckled. Margo didn't like to be told what to do. She must have mentioned a free beer because the musician followed her happily to their table.

When Zac sat down, he whistled to the waitress. "Hey, Sally, bring me a cold one, will you?" Then he turned toward Sam.

"How can I help you?"

"I'm investigating a murder in Half Moon Bay," Sam said.

"That must be Vinnie Chauvin's murder, right?"

"Yes."

"Good riddance. A lot of people are sleeping better now that he's dead." Zac Benoit sat back and relaxed, a big grin on his face.

"That's a bit harsh. What did you have against him?"

"Well, for one, he was always hitting on my girl."

"Matty Daigle?"

"Yup."

"I thought Matty Daigle was going out with Artur Petrov."

"That pompous Russian? He's no friend of Matty's."

"That's not what I hear, Zac. The Maestro is young, hip, handsome, famous, and very rich. He's the visiting conductor for the Symphony, in charge of the new Opera Season. He has that aura of celebrity that young women tend to admire."

"And he has an ugly gash on his face that he got in a bar fight. He has to use heavy makeup to cover it up." Zac made an ugly leering face. "He's despicable."

"And yet he's been seen out and about with the lovely Matty."

Zac got angry and stood up, pushing over the beer mug, and spilling the contents that splashed on the floor.

"Sit down, Zac. I'm not done."

Zac sat down but looked very unhappy.

"So, tell me about Vinnie Chauvin."

"What do you want me to tell you? He was a jerk. Always trying to corner Matty and kiss her or grope her."

"So, is it true that you punched him at a restaurant? Broke his nose?"

"I did no such thing. I mean, I didn't break his nose."

"What happened?"

"What happened was that Matty went to the restroom, out by the phone booths. When she didn't come back after a while, I went to look for her. The bastard had cornered her by one of the booths and was groping her. What was I supposed to do?"

"What did Vinnie do after that?"

"He sent some Chinese dudes to beat me up a couple of days later. They almost broke my arm."

"Why did Matty put up with all of that?"

"Because her brother André and Vinnie were business partners, that's why. Well, their dad was the partner, originally. But he died, so André took his place."

"Was there a lot of money involved?"

"I think so, yes. But I don't know the details. Matty and I don't talk business."

Sam looked at Zac Benoit with one eyebrow raised up for a few seconds. Then he asked the question.

"Where were you on the night of the murder?"

Zac looked confused and tried to think. He had become visibly agitated. His hands shook as he held onto the empty beer mug.

"I don't know. I can't remember. Probably here. I'm always here."

"So, is this thing between you and Matty Daigle serious?"

Zac looked even more startled but answered with a steady voice. "You bet. I'm going to ask her to marry me."

"And her money?"

This time Zac got up, offended, and left. He headed back to the stage and climbed the three, four steps, and picked up his accordion from the chair. He never looked back.

Sam chuckled. "Time to go," he said.

"He did say that Master Petrov wears heavy makeup."

"He sure did."

Chapter 37
The Maestro

INDEED, ARTUR PETROV WAS EVERYTHING EVERYONE HAD DESCRIBED HIM TO BE. Margo's heart skipped a beat when she saw him—as it always did—from afar. She loved her Pierre to pieces, but she was still human. Petrov was a gorgeous looking creature, with raven black hair worn rather long, which contrasted extravagantly with his piercing blue eyes. No wonder the lovely Matty Daigle might have had a soft spot for him.

Margo parked the truck at its designated spot by the courthouse and went around to help Sam out. He was wearing his cynical smile, but she could tell that the Sheriff was hurting. Those painkillers Dr. Menard had given him were near worthless.

They slowly walked across Independence Park and skirted the singing fountain which was surrounded by moms and children as usual. Even the sounds around him—the giggles, the barks of the dogs, the crowd-pleasing circus loop music of the fountain—seemed to grate on Sam's nerves. He looked like a man on the edge. After walking a few feet, he took Margo's arm and leaned on it.

"What else do we know about this Artur Petrov?"

"This is his second year conducting the Opera Season. People seem to like him."

"Why exactly? Because he's handsome and debonair, or because he's so good at what he does?"

"Well, he's a good musician. As I might have mentioned before, Sam, I sing in the opera choir, and I can confirm that he's a pretty good conductor. He's Russian, you know. In Russia, they take musical education very seriously."

"Nothing but the best?"

"Exactly."

"So, why isn't he in Russia, or in Europe, where—as you always remind me—Opera is very popular?"

"Good question. Since you ask, I must tell you. There have been rumors."

Sam stopped walking and looked at her. His eyebrow went up.

"I'm listening," he said.

"Okay, so what happened was that they got tired of his attitude and they courteously sent him away. They called it 'a world tour', but I was left with the impression that they were trying to get rid of him."

"And why's that?"

"They considered him an enfant terrible. He has a temper. The musicians are scared of him. Or rather, scared of displeasing him."

"Does that apply to female musicians as well?"

"No, I don't think so. What's more, I believe they're all in love with him."

"Is that so?" Sam turned back toward the Opera House and dragged Margo along, leaning heavily on her. "I can hardly wait to meet him."

"Sam, we should have those wounds looked at."

"Let's have a chat with Petrov first. Then, we'll see."

The musicians were on break. Several of them stood by the back entrance, close to the cigarette kiosk. Some of them sat on benches, huddled together, laughing. Others had walked away from the crowd and were smoking. Margo spotted the conductor right away, and she pointed him out to Sam.

Artur Petrov did stand out from the others. He was taller and slender to the point of gauntness. He wore a gothic, tight-fitting Chesterfield coat in charcoal that reached down to his knees, and a white shirt with ruffles at the wrist. He was a showman, a man who went to great lengths to look like an artist. But Margo had to admit that he wore it well. He looked like some young hero from a Victorian gothic romance novel.

The women who surrounded him enthusiastically—musicians and singers—seemed to agree with this point of view, and they elbowed each other out of the way so that they could get closer to the Maestro. And by his beaming, self-satisfied smile, you could tell that the Maestro loved it. He was basking in the glory of being himself.

Sam scoffed loudly, and the little group turned around to look at the newcomers, surprised to see them standing there.

"Off you go, girls," Sam told them, and waved them away with his hand. "I need to talk to Master Petrov."

The girls scattered, and Petrov looked at Sam with a cynical, but a rather friendly smile.

"They love you, don't they?" Sam asked.

"They appear to. But it's a tradition that musicians fall in love with their conductor du jour. Then, another will come, and I will be forgotten." Petrov chuckled. Then he looked at Margo and smiled, showing magnificently perfect teeth.

"Nice to see you again, Miss Fontaine. Are you friends with this limping lawman?" He laughed at his own joke and moved to hug Margo, who took the advantage to lean in and give him a kiss on one cheek, and then the other.

The conductor realized he was wearing his makeup and pulled back stiffly, and he looked suddenly apologetic.

"I'm sorry, Miss Fontaine. The scar, you know." His eyes looked distressed as he patted his pockets and extracted from one of them a snow-white, pristine, handkerchief.

"Oh, don't worry about it, Maestro," she said quickly, and her hand reached out to his arm in a kindly gesture. "I got it." Margo pulled out her own handkerchief from her purse and wiped her face, where some of the makeup had been smeared on her cheek. Then, she carefully folded the piece of dainty cloth and put it away.

Artur Petrov then turned toward Sam. "I have this scar on my cheek," he said. "It's not that visible, but it makes me feel self-conscious, you know."

"Yes, I've heard. That's why we're here. Is there any place where we can talk?"

"Of course. We can go to my office." The Maestro approached a young man sitting on one of the benches, told him a few words, then walked back to Sam and Margo.

"I told him to make sure that we're not disturbed. Let's see if we can find some tea."

They followed Petrov into the building, and into the dark, deep silence of the storeroom. Odds and ends filled the cavernous room, in big, messy heaps. Props, baroque furniture, gilded statues, and everything else that was essential to a well-presented performance.

A lush red carpet covered the floor as far as Margo's eyes could see, and she inhaled happily the aroma of antique furniture, freshly sawed wood, oriental costumes, of perfumes and incense, that pervaded the back of the stage.

Petrov stopped at an unimportant door to his left, and they followed him in. The room was small, but it looked more like Ali Baba's cave than a utilitarian office. The furniture looked extravagantly expensive. A few priceless portraits, a couple of landscapes in gilded frames, and the Maestro's desk, which could have competed with any museum's masterpiece, so beautifully it was carved. And in one corner, on a side table in the lovely office, a real Russian Samovar.

"My weakness," Petrov said, and he grinned. "I couldn't take those little electric kettles any longer. Please, sit."

Sam and Margo sat on a leather sofa, of a deep grayish-blue color that was as soft as butter, and as shiny as silk. And Petrov pushed over an armchair and sat down, facing them.

Within seconds, they heard a polite knock on the door, and Petrov bellowed out an Entrez with a heavy French accent. A young woman waltzed in—giggling—and proceeded to serve tea and tiny cakes, arranged on a silver platter, all the time never allowing her eyes to leave Petrov for long. All that was missing from the surreal scene was that the young woman should be wearing a Japanese kimono, and should take the Maestro's shoes off, and place embroidered slippers on his feet.

Sam looked on admiringly. It was so obvious that he had just experienced a fleeting moment of jealousy. A pretty young woman, treating her Master like a king. Margo thought, ugh, just like any man, with his fantasies.

Then, the young woman vanished to a small dismissive hand signal from the Maestro, and they all settled down to enjoy their tea.

"You seem quite popular," Sam said. "And, contrary to what you told me, they do seem to admire you."

"I suppose I can't help it. I am quite charming. And I have to confess that I do enjoy being popular."

"Especially after what happened in Saint Petersburg."

"What do you mean, exactly, Sheriff?"

"That we've heard you were sent away from your previous engagement."

Petrov looked at Margo. There were reproach and betrayal written all over his handsome face. "Was it you who told?" he asked her.

"Maestro, you should know that I admire you every bit as much as everyone else," Margo said quickly, "but we're investigating a murder. I felt it my duty. I apologize."

"I didn't know you investigated crimes, Miss Fontaine. You're a musician, nyet?"

"Yes, but I'm also a private detective. So, I sometimes help Sam."

"I see." He looked at Margo coldly. His friendliness had vanished. "Well, I'm rather disappointed. But I'll allow you to ask your question."

"It's about Vinnie Chauvin. You were at the Gallery the night he was murdered."

"Yes. And so were many other people. And I can tell you categorically that I didn't kill him if that's what you want to know. He was a toad, but I had no interest in killing him. I'm a famous musician, not a murderer. And I had no motive."

"Are you sure, Maestro? You have a temper, and both Vinnie and you were interested in Matty Daigle."

"The flirting heiress? That was just a bit of fun."

"People saw someone arguing with Vinnie outside, on the balcony. Someone tall and slender, someone like yourself."

"Am I the only tall and slender man in Half Moon Bay? Is that all you have?"

"No. There was also some thick makeup on his lapel. At first, we thought it was the regular kind, but it's heavier, thicker than that. It's like yours."

Petrov jumped up. "How dare you?" He looked accusingly at Margo. "Now I understand the kisses too. You knew about the scar. You knew about the makeup. So, you kissed me on purpose so that the makeup on my scar would rub off on your skin, so you could clean it off and send it away for testing."

"Maestro, please."

"Don't you 'Maestro, please' me. This is betrayal. This is a dirty trick. Go. Send your little handkerchief and have it tested. You will be so disappointed. Because you will find that it was not I who killed him."

"Please sit back down, Maestro," she implored. But Petrov—looking very offended—crossed his arms and refused, until Sam barked at him an angry sit, and he sat back down in his armchair without another word.

"I have one more question for you, Artur Petrov." Sam looked at him to convey the seriousness of the situation. "Think carefully. Is there any way that the makeup on Vinnie's lapel could be yours?"

The conductor looked like he was about to blow up again. But then he put his hands together in his lap and looked at his shoes. After a couple of minutes, he looked up, straight at Sam.

"Actually, perhaps it was my makeup after all. You see, sometimes it gets on my hands if I touch my face."

Sam and Margo nodded, encouragingly, but Petrov hesitated.

"Go on," Sam said.

"Well, maybe, just maybe, I wiped some dirt or fuzz off his lapel, and there was a tiny bit of makeup on my hand."

"That's pretty farfetched, Maestro."

"Yes. I understand. It is hard to believe. But I tell you that I didn't kill the man. And maybe that makeup isn't even mine."

"But you went outside on the balcony to talk to him?"

"I don't recall."

"Come on, Maestro. Surely you recall."

"I tell you I don't. I might have been drinking a little bit too much." Petrov looked down at his open hands. They were shaking, all right. "Sometimes I drink too much. And then, I forget what happened. But I'm incapable of killing. Of that I am sure."

Sam and Margo got up from the sofa and walked to the door. Margo looked back. Petrov was leaning forward. His head was in his hands.

"That went well," Sam said facetiously. "We got us another suspect."

"Yes. It sure seems like it."

Chapter 38

Two Crows

ODETTE SAT IN HER MOTHER'S KITCHEN, sipping on a piping-hot cup of chicory coffee while her mom cooked—and gossiped—and watched the news on the TV, all at the same time.

The day had dawned pretty, with clear skies, and Odette looked toward the window from time to time, enjoying the splash of colors in the flower and vegetable garden, and the chickens running around, followed by their baby chicks. As always, she was grateful that their treasure finds had allowed Two Crows to prosper. The handful of houses that belonged to the settlement had been quickly renovated, upgraded, running water and electricity installed, and everyone now owned a TV set. What an accomplishment that had been.

But now, Vinnie had vanished, and there had been not a word from him. If anything ever happened to Vinnie, it would all be over. The world of contraband was too dangerous for her to navigate on her own. She listened to her mom's chatter and even answered her comments from time to time, but all she could think of was the future: hers, and that of her people. What a mess.

Odette looked at her busy, busy mom, and smiled. They had already discussed Odette's siblings, the neighbors, and the man who wanted to marry her blissfully widowed mother, when the newsman on TV cut to a scene in Half Moon Bay, the front of the Gallery, and pointed to a gurney being rolled out, its passenger unmoving, completely covered by a white sheet. One hand—bare and stiff—stuck out from under the sheet and hung over the side, a thick gold ring and a fancy watch clearly visible, as the cameraman ghoulishly zoomed in on it.

Odette's mom turned up the volume. "Hey, isn't that your boyfriend Vinnie Chauvin that they're talking about? That's his Gallery, look."

"I don't know, mom," she said and got up from the table to get closer to the TV. The mom was still talking, and Odette had to tell her to shush so she could listen.

"You see? Autopsy results have been released today in the death of prominent Half Moon Bay businessman Vinnie Chauvin."

"Yes, mom. Please let me hear what he's saying." A terrible stone plunked down on her heart. And she wanted to think, and she wanted to hear what the newsman was saying, but her mom just wouldn't stop talking.

"So that's why you never heard from him."

"I realize that. But I had a bad feeling. He would have called me. He always does—did."

"What's going to happen now? The police will find out."

"Maybe not. We were always very careful."

"But we lost our contact. Could you still deal with his business partners?"

"No, mom. I would never dare. They aren't the kind of people it is safe to deal with."

"What should we do?"

"For now, nothing. Maybe the whole thing will die down, and they'll forget us."

"At least you're safe here. I'll gather the others and let them know."

Odette listened to hear mom telephone her friends one by one, and soon her mind drifted off to times past, to happy times, traveling with Vinnie, lying on the beach with margaritas in hand, or sitting in a gondola in Venice, with the gondoliere singing O Sole Mio. Such happy times. Who would ever fill that void?

Oh, Vinnie, she thought sadly, I feel so lost. She put her head on the pillow of the reclining chair, trying to find solace in the good memories, and she closed her eyes. She tuned her mom's voice out, and the sound of the TV that her mom forgot to turn back down, and crawled into her quiet place within, where she could mourn in private.

The beeping of the cell phone startled her awake. She looked around, disoriented. She must have fallen asleep. The TV was off, and her mother had left, turning the kitchen light off.

She looked around for the phone, but by the time she found it, it had stopped beeping. She had a ton of messages, all from Chris, Vinnie's young brother. Half-brother, actually.

Well, she was surprised by the urgency. Chris never called. She ran through the messages, and they were all pretty much carbon copies of each other. She read them with dread.

"The cat's out of the bag, Odette. You must come to Half Moon Bay immediately. The police know about you and Vinnie, and they need our help to get his killers."

Odette called Chris back right away. "I'm not going anywhere. Sorry."

"You have to. If you don't, the law will hunt you down. I know you think you're safe where you are, but don't bet on it. They will scour the swamps with their satellites. They will use thermal signature technology to find out where the heat emitting humans are. Satellites can even bounce laser lights off your windows and—by measuring distance differences between a vibrating window and the satellite—they can reconstruct your speech from orbit. So, don't for a minute think that you can hide."

"I can't do it."

"Listen, Odette. They don't care about your side business. What they do care about is the smugglers, and the people who are selling the forgeries."

"And the people who killed Vinnie?"

"Of course. And the people who killed Vinnie."

"But it's a long trip, Chris. I don't want to go. I want a few days of peace and quiet with my family."

"Neither you nor your people will be safe until we do this."

Odette remained silent for a few seconds. Deep down she understood the dangers. Vinnie worked for a ruthless crowd. His life was constantly under threat. She sighed heavily into the phone.

"I'm sorry, Odette."

"Thank you. You're right. I'll do it. I'll be there by nightfall."

"No. Not my place, Odette. Not safe. Come to Half Moon Bay. Come to St. Quintian's. Side entrance, where the priest lives. Knock. We'll be here."

"I'll have to drive all night."

"Whatever it takes, Odette. Let's do this, and then get back to our lives."

"All right, then. Maybe at 5 a.m. That's as fast as I can make it."

"Side entrance. Drive safely. And bring your expedition pack. We'll be leaving as soon as you get here. Don't ask. I'll fill you in later."

Odette went to her bedroom and began packing. The sky was getting dark on the horizon, ruining what had started off as such a lovely, sunny day. Within minutes, the storm was above her, and the rumbling began. She heard her mom rushing from room to room, closing windows. A set of spectacular lightning flashes lit up the sky all across the horizon. Thunder shook the windowpanes. Then, the lights flickered. Oh no, she thought, this was not good.

Chapter 39

DAY SEVEN: Margo, 4 a.m.

MARGO OPENED ONE EYE UNHAPPILY and looked at the alarm clock. 4 a.m. What an ungodly hour. Maybe she could snooze another half hour. She wouldn't need that much time to get ready.

She gathered all three purring cats around her: Ice and Fenway, and the one without a name, and tried to get back to sleep. But she could hear Brooks and Lucy moving around downstairs, and she felt guilty.

Grumbling with displeasure, she moved carefully away from the lump of cats and got out of bed. She padded barefoot to the open window and looked down on the dark waters of the bay. The angry froth illuminated by the rolling thunderstorm crept back and forth on the sand. The Walkway was empty for the most part, except for a couple of stray dogs, running for cover against the incoming storm.

She inhaled the smell of ozone and rain that rushed in with the breeze. The storm was going to be bad. She wondered if Sam could be persuaded to cancel the trip. But she knew—deep down—that it would be impossible to deter Sam. Once he got an idea in his head, that was it.

Sam had been very mysterious about the plan. So far, all she knew was that there was only one woman in the expedition, and she was going with them to ensure that this woman—who was very important, apparently—didn't feel uncomfortable among all the men.

She took one last look at the churning sea, and at the cloud of rising fog. The dogs had reached the far end of the road and had vanished. The street was empty again, the boulevard, the walkway, everything deserted, like buildings in a ghost story.

She walked into the kitchen, where Lucy in her pajamas and robe forced a cheesy croissant into her hand and placed a cup of coffee in front of her. She ate and talked quickly, giving Lucy instructions about the little girl Luna's care, and all the other things that worried her, and finally made it to the front door, where Brooks was already sitting in the car, waiting for her.

She turned around and looked up at her bedroom window and saw Ice and Fenway looking down at her. Ice, with his beautiful white fur shining by the light of the streetlamp against the dark room, and Fenway, so tiny, stuck close to her brother, looking down at her with that worried little look.

Suddenly, she got an awful feeling that something was going to go horribly wrong and she should go nowhere but stay home. She even hesitated. She almost turned back toward the door. But she had already promised, and people were counting on her. There was no turning back.

She waved at them and blew them a kiss. They drove to St. Quintian's Church in silence. The town was slumbering quietly. There is just something so mysterious about driving through a town when it's sleeping. In a couple of houses, the lights were on, but for the most part, everything was dark.

As Brooks turned into the church parking lot, Margo saw the first hint of the early dawn.

"I wish I was going with you, Miss Margo," he said.

"I'll be fine, Brooks. You know that I'm quite capable of taking care of myself."

"But you would be safer with me."

"I would probably feel safer as well, but you're needed here. You must keep Luna safe. Whatever she saw in the swamps has put her life in danger. You're the only one I trust to keep her alive."

Margo listened patiently to Brooks complain. Life as a simple chauffeur was too boring for an adventure-loving young man like Brooks. And he never did finish saying his piece until he was good and parked, and Margo got out of the car and promised for the gazillionth time to be careful.

There were numerous cars in the parking lot already. Sam's huge, oversized, souped-up pickup truck, another one she had never seen before, then a bright yellow jeep, and another—older—jeep of a disturbing greenish, yellowish, puke color with enormous headlights mounted on the top. And at the back, Father Armand's antique Bentley, that old, spit-polished, shiny treasure that he had recently acquired at an auction. And behind all the cars, the walls of St. Quintian's, the pride and joy of Half Moon Bay, and the solace of the faint of heart.

Brooks walked with Margo. It would probably get really hot later in the day, but this early, at 5 a.m., a cool wind blew in from the sea, and Margo shivered in her jacket. She was thankful that she had thought to pack a light blanket, a sun hat, a change of clothes, and plenty of food and water. She had no idea what awaited her. Her backpack was heavy, but she was heading out well prepared.

Margo stepped into the refectory and shyly noticed that she was late. The meeting had already begun. Everyone looked at her with some degree of hostility. The only one that smiled was Father Armand, who walked over to her and put an arm around her shoulder. His handsome face looked drawn, tired as if he hadn't gotten any sleep.

Madame Mouton—Father Armand's devoted housekeeper—was also there, clucking like a mother hen over pots of coffee and biscuits—probably her cheese and bacon biscuits, which she was famous for. She too looked tired but determined that everyone should get their share of coffee and biscuits.

"You're late as usual, Miss Fontaine."

"Five minutes, Sam. That's all."

"I suppose I better start at the beginning, then."

Wow, Sam sure was in a foul mood. Margo thought to herself that he had probably not recovered completely and was still in pain. But boy, could he get mean. She wished again that she had stayed home.

"Well, don't just stand there. Come sit with the others so I can explain."

Margo looked helplessly at Brooks who just shrugged and followed her to the pews.

"We're heading northeast to Houma, and then north to Thibodeaux. From there, we'll get on Highway 1 and continue on into the deep forest lands beyond the swamps, although I'm not sure yet how far we need to go beyond the bayou. At some point, we'll be crossing the Mississippi. We'll know more about that when we get there. After that, we're going to follow Chris and my cousin Brett, who both know the area well.

"This is Josh. Stand up, Josh, so everyone can meet you. Josh used to be a bonafide wrestler. Did a stint in the army. Was Vinnie's bodyguard. Josh, you're going to stick to Odette like her shadow. You know your way around swamp and forest land. It's your job to keep her alive whatever it takes."

"Margo is here to keep Odette company. Men, watch your language. Be respectful of the ladies. And make sure you keep them safe. And you two," he told the new recruits, pointing at them, "stay armed and stay alert. We don't know what we're getting into.

"And now, your blessing, Father."

Margo watched everyone lower their heads. This was the kind of moment Father Armand lived for. He called for all the saints, angels, and archangels, for the Virgin Mary and all her family, and—in one word—everyone in Heaven to their protection. He rambled on for a few minutes, taking little breaks to yawn, and then—probably suspecting that he had overdone it—he stopped abruptly and said, "And now, you better go."

Chapter 40

The Expedition

SAM'S COUSIN BRETT RODE WITH HER AND THE SHERIFF. While the two men conversed about family and friends, and the recent horror story of the moonshine party gone bad, Margo—riding shotgun in the front passenger seat—looked out of the window and watched the sun come up on her right. Fog blanketed the thriving rice paddies and the free-roaming cows sleeping under outcrops of trees. A typical South Louisiana morning. That, and the bad roads full of potholes, and the slow-moving trucks, and impatient drivers like Sam, who always pushed on to get ahead of them.

But the morning was full of excitement and hope, as always before an adventure. There was nothing on earth like hitting the road before dawn, a good coffee in hand, and the open road ahead.

Eventually, the men stopped talking, and Sam turned the radio on. Within seconds, the first few drops of rain fell on the windshield, and Margo sat up straight.

"That reminds me, Sam, that you still haven't told me why we're even venturing out in this weather."

"I've been meaning to tell you. Governor Touchet's wife and daughter have been kidnapped."

"You're kidding, right? I haven't heard of any such thing," she said.

"Well, that's the point. The kidnappers said no police, nothing on the news. We're going to deliver the ransom money and bring his wife and kid home."

"Aren't there like Special Forces people who can do this?" Margo turned and looked at Sam suspiciously, feeling betrayed, and thinking that this was not the adventure that she had hoped for.

"Not any who know the area well. Who know how to get around in the swamps and forest lands."

"But we're just a bunch of amateurs. We're not trained for this."

"Listen, Margo. Governor Touchet called me yesterday. He's a friend of my uncle's, you know, the politician?"

Margo nodded.

"So, I owe my uncle too many favors. I couldn't say no. Unfortunately, I don't have Andy anymore, so I had to improvise. Andy grew up in that area, knew it like the back of his hand. And me, I don't have Andy anymore."

"How about Rob Schexnayder, the old Sheriff?"

"He knows the swamps too, but he's still in the hospital."

"Well, I don't want to be responsible for saving the world."

"Please don't be grumpy, Margo. I must do this, and I need you here with me. Especially now that I don't have Andy."

"Oh yes, Andy again."

"It won't be too bad. You'll see. I promise." Margo crossed her arms in front of her chest. She didn't like the plan one bit. What had started as a simple adventure—part of which was to take this Odette home to her tribal lands—sounded like it was morphing into one of Sam's secret missions. And she hadn't signed up for that. Would he take her back home if she asked? No. She was pretty sure that he wouldn't. Once Sam decided on something, it was almost impossible to make him change his mind.

A steady drizzle now alternated with gusts of heavier walls of rainwater. They slammed violently against the truck, making it shudder. Margo tried to ignore her growing unease. Did this trip have something to do with the kid Sam had rescued, the one that was hiding in her home? Why wouldn't he just tell her? Why?

Through the foggy windowpane that she kept wiping with her sleeve, Margo gazed at the waters of Bayou Terrebonne roiling gray and frothy in the angry weather. Tiny pleasure boats rocked from side to side, moored next to tiny docks. Beyond the river, the gently renovated antebellum homes of Houma lined the shores, standing elegant and immortal on West

Park Avenue, as a snippet of colonial history that refused to die. Then, they left the lovely town behind, and the road became tedious and monotonous again.

Swoosh-swoosh went the windshield wipers and Margo closed her eyes. She would have dozed off had it not been for the annoying cacophony coming from the radio. Sam turned it off, and Margo sighed with relief. They definitely didn't share a taste in music. She glanced at Brett in the back seat. He seemed to have fallen asleep. His mouth was open a bit, and a gentle snoring made his lips quiver.

Sam broke the silence. "We're going to try to make it to Luna's grandfather's house first."

"Why's that? Why not go straight to the rendezvous point?"

"Because we can rest there. I can find out how he's doing, let him know that we found Luna, and ask him if he's seen or heard anything."

"Sam, why do I have the impression that you're hiding something from me?"

"Don't be silly. There's nothing to hide." Then, Sam discreetly put a finger on his mouth and looked quickly at her. Margo nodded. So, Sam was hiding something but didn't want to say in front of his cousin. He would probably tell her later, whatever it was.

Chapter 41

The House On Stilts

MEANTIME, THE WEATHER CONTINUED DETERIORATING. The road became slippery, and the truck skidded as Sam made sudden moves to avoid dark, deep puddles on the road. Soon the water had accumulated to such extent, that the edge of the road—like a lake—became one with the vegetation to the sides, blending with the fields of sugarcane and the rice paddies until only the vanishing white line in the center of the road remained visible, sloshing under the rising water.

Wherever Margo looked, all she could see was water. Copses of trees, their roots sitting in water, flooded fields empty of cattle, houses, barns, and garages, all locked down. The wind—seeming to get stronger and more violent—blew leaves and small twigs against them, and kept shaking the truck, threatening to push it off the road. Behind them, the yellow jeep which carried Chris, Odette, and Josh, was barely visible in the downpour. The other pickup had completely vanished into the storm.

Finally, after what seemed like hours and hours, Sam turned onto a feeder road. "We're almost there," he said. They turned right again, followed a narrow road on the top of a packed-earth dam that separated water from land. "There it is," Sam said, and he pointed in direction of the river.

A last few bouts of thunder at the edge of the horizon signaled the end of the storm, and the clouds separated, and a little wedge of blue among the dark rain clouds allowed a few rays of sunshine through.

Margo looked toward where Sam was pointing. At first, all she could see was an impenetrable wall of trees and bushes, everything looking wet and soggy. She lowered her window and stuck her head out. A wet drizzle moistened her face and her neck, and the cool, fresh air blew in the scent of Cyprus and wildflowers.

Soon the trees became sparser, and she sighted the place: a largish wooden one-story building with a long porch facing the river, sitting on stilts.

"It's called Bo's Landing and Catfish Shack," Sam told her.

"Bo's?"

"Yes. Bo is the owner. He's expecting us."

"Are we planning to cross the river in one of those?" Margo pointed at a run-down cruise boat that came into view as they approached the Shack. The decrepit boat—with the name Cajun Cruises painted in peeling red paint on its starboard—was leaning ferociously to the side under the onslaught of the mighty Mississippi.

"You'll have to ask Bo, but my guess is not that one. It doesn't look very safe."

"Those other ones, then, you think?" she asked. Several smaller boats had been pulled up on the muddy shore and had been tied to trees and poles. But two of them were in the water, slapping from side to side, bumping into each other, and Margo's heart sunk. "I've changed my mind, Sam. I think I'd rather go back home. Look at how fast the river is flowing. And those boats are tiny. We're going to get killed. This whole mission sounds like suicide."

"It will be okay. The guys who work at the Shack will take us. They're used to crossing the river in this weather. It's probably nothing to them."

"Oh, Sam, I don't think I can do it. Why don't I wait for you guys here?"

Sam didn't say a word. He stopped the truck on a bed of pebbles and sand behind the Shack and hobbled around to Margo's door and opened it. When Margo stepped down from the truck, Sam leaned in toward her as if he was going to kiss her in the ear and whispered. "Please stay with me. You're the only one that I can trust. Smile. Pretend. I'll explain when I can."

Within minutes, all three vehicles were parked side by side, and the group walked up the steps to the river-facing porch, where three middle-aged scruffy guys sat on chairs, drinking beer and looking curiously at the newcomers.

Sam lifted a hand, making his group stop while he approached the men in the shack and talked to them. One of them, one thin, sinewy guy who chewed tobacco, got up from his chair and shook hands with Sam, and they exchanged a few words. Sam nodded, and then he called for the others to come to join them.

They all sat down at the long rustic camping table and wooden benches on the porch, and a waitress with wiry white hair that looked like someone's granny brought out cold beers and bowls of unshelled peanuts for them. The two guys who were not the ones chewing tobacco pretty much ignored them and kept talking about another sighting of the alligator's ghost. Margo sharpened her ears and listened.

"Just this week, two people vanished from Mudville. Locals said that they had seen the white gator drag one of them away. And he was still alive. He was screaming, kicking, begging for help."

"Yeah, I heard about that. Some of the people watching got close. I guess they were trying to help. But it was too late. The poor man was so mangled that it was a merciful death to drown. The gator dragged him into the bayou, and that was that."

"Was the gator actually white?" Margo asked, feeling shy to interrupt the men but really wanting to know.

"Yes. At least that's what the girl on the 6 o'clock news said. White as a ghost. There were some who wanted to go to the rescue, but they were too afraid to follow, on account of what they said was an alligator's ghost."

"That's nothing, man. You shoulda seen what I seen." The guy called Tim moved closer to the newcomers and downed the last of his beer, ready to tell his story. But Bo—the owner of the Shack—just laughed. He moved the lump of tobacco around in his mouth and spit some black saliva into the river. "Hold on, is this one of your tall tales, Timmy?"

"First, don't go calling me Timmy. My name is Tim. Second, this is not a tall tale. Hey, Susie, bring me another one," he told the granny when she passed by, showing her his empty beer bottle. Margo, who got excited at any possibility of hearing a local story, got up from her seat and sat down at the edge of the bench so she could hear better.

"You've been to Mirabeau, haven't you?"

"That's that old plantation right on the edge of the river, right?"

"Yes. That one." The group fell quiet. When Tim realized that he had captured his audience, he began telling his story in a grandiose fashion. Embellishing as he went.

"There was a murder at a country estate recently. I had heard it from someone. Then Sheriff Henderson sent for me and Buddy here with the boat. It sounded mysterious, so we hurried up and went." Susie plonked down a fresh bottle of beer in front of Tim and took the empty one with her. The group held their breath while he had a healthy swig of the cold one, and then—turning around to face the group—he continued.

"We brought the boat to where we'd been told. The house is enormous. You can go see it for yourselves. It sits right on the edge of the water. So much so that Buddy here jumped out and landed on one of the front steps, and we tied the boat to the column proper. Yes, the plantation's column." Tim scratched his head.

"It's enormous. You have to look way up to see how tall those columns really are. Anyway, the place looks very impressive as you travel that way. You can see it from all the way downriver, but once you get close, you realize that it's just old and sad, and it's sinking into the mud.

"So, anyway, they say it's been empty ever since the river began rising, like a hundred years ago. The front door was almost rotted away, and the inside of the house was all dark. No electricity. What little you could see, there was some furniture left, and the curtains, well, what was left of them, hanging in strips, and some mirrors and paintings on the walls, but everything so damaged as to be near worthless.

"So, anyway, Buddy here whistled real loud, and the sound just echoed all over the silence, like a boom. And we heard someone whistle back from upstairs, and there we went.

"Just so to give you an idea, how scary the whole thing was, the steps going upstairs were all rotted. I stepped through one of them, and I thought my leg had broken off, and Buddy had to pull me out. If I had been all by myself in that place, I would have probably died, you know? Like stuck there forever.

"But we made it upstairs and looked for the doctor, and there he was, standing at the end of this super-long corridor-like. As you got closer to him, you started smelling the dead people."

"Yes, and the smell of mildew and rotting stuff was horrible too. We had to cover our mouths with bandannas, it was so bad."

"Okay, Buddy. Who's telling the story?"

"Sorry, Timmy. Go ahead."

"So, we got to the end of the corridor," he said. "It was like a family room. There were some magazines and books on tables, and some dried-out plants in pots, and little much of anything else."

"Except for the dead people."

"Yes, except the dead people. They were sitting kind of lopsided in rocking chairs. They had been dead a long time. The smell could tell you that. And that was why we had been asked to bring the boat. There are no roads to speak of anymore behind Mirabeau. It's all overgrown. The dead have to be carried by boat or left where they are to rot in peace."

"You had said it was murder, right?" Margo asked.

"Oh, yes. Clear as day. Even from where we stood, quite a few steps away, you could tell that their throats had been ripped out."

"Oh my God, that's terrible. Did you ever find out who they were?" Margo asked.

"Yes. There used to be a caretaker, but he was old already, so he didn't work anymore. He lives in a house behind Mirabeau. He must be at least a hundred years old. He said that they used to have kids—the old couple—he didn't quite remember how many, but that one day the kids up and left, and nobody knew what had happened to them, because nobody ever saw them again."

"Poor things," Margo said.

"Yes. Now the old caretaker said that maybe they had ventured too far into the bayou and were snapped up by some gators. Or they found a nicer place to live. The point is, they never came back, and the old folks were left on their own."

"What a sad story."

"Yes. Imagine getting to be that old and being abandoned like that. There were a couple of maids that did for them for years. Kept an eye on them after the young ones disappeared. But they were old too. The caretaker seemed to remember that the maids had died a while back. No telling how those two survived on their own."

"How were they discovered?"

"Kids playing. They had dared each other to go upstairs. You know kids. They thought it was cool, as they put it, to roam in a haunted house and find some dead bodies. They told the parents, and the parents called the police."

"Is Mirabeau haunted?"

"That's what they say. It certainly looks it."

Chapter 42
The Spy

MARGO WAS AFRAID. Too many stories of death before a death-defying adventure. She looked at the others. Sam, his cousin Brett, Josh—the parrain—and the young policemen were fine. But Chris was as pale as the alligator in the story, and Odette looked like she had stepped into her worst nightmare. Margo looked despondently at Bo, who must have felt her fear.

"You can still back out, Miss," he told her. "No shame in wanting to stay alive."

Margo felt a slender ray of hope, but Sam spoke up. "We can't," he said, and he waved the idea away. "We have to keep going."

"Fine with me," Bo said and spit some more black saliva into the river. "Tim and Buddy will take you across. But it'll have to be tomorrow. The storm's passed, but the river flows too wild. Better wait for it to crest and then calm down."

Margo watched Chris and Odette pensively. After the haunted house story, they had moved down to the steps and were sitting on the last rung, the water almost lapping their feet. Their heads were close to each other, and they spoke so quietly that it was impossible to hear what they were talking about. But their body language said a lot.

They knew each other well. And—even though Odette had told her a couple of times that they weren't friends—Vinnie's death seemed to have brought them closer. They sat with their knees touching, and at times, Chris put an arm around her shoulder. Even Chris—who had mentioned being terrified of his older brother—appeared to be mourning his passing.

Josh—who should have been watching Odette like a hawk—stepped out of the bushes by the Shack and walked toward the steps where Chris and Odette were chatting. He saw Margo watch him and waved. She waved back but remembered that she hadn't seen him in a while. Where had he been? How long had he been gone?

She looked around her. The twins—the young policemen—had also vanished. Maybe they were out back scouting the terrain. Maybe they had to go to the bathroom. Together? Hmm.

And where was Brett Stark, Sam's cousin? Her eyes moved around casually, like she wasn't that curious, and saw him by the door, in a dark corner, sitting on a chair with a broken backrest. He was doing like he was drinking a beer, but after watching him for a few minutes, Margo decided that he was just pretending. That beer was never raised to his lips in all that while. He wasn't drinking beer. He was eavesdropping. His head was slightly inclined in direction of Sam, who was laughing at something the Shack guys were telling him. Brett wasn't laughing, though. He was as still as a moment in time, his face tilted toward the group. No wonder Sam didn't want to talk in front of him. Brett Start—his cousin—was a spy.

The afternoon crawled by at an exasperatingly slow pace. Margo watched idly the Mighty Mississippi River—that even at the best of times was of a dirty chocolate color—because there was nothing else to do. The river had way overflowed its banks, carrying in its powerful stream empty milk gallon containers and other floating plastic trash. It looked dangerous and threatening, and too much of a challenge for those tiny boats tossed about by its relentless flow.

Slowly, finally, the afternoon wound down. The sun went down beyond the trees, and a soft haze descended over the river, bringing the swamps into life with the twittering of nightlife. Frogs sang to their girlfriends, cicadas chittered for more rain, and a cloud of mosquitos descended on them all, getting inside sleeves and necklines, inside ears, nose holes, even trying to get into their eyes.

The whole camp jumped up and ran indoors for cover. Margo—who always lathered herself with anti-bite lotion—was snickered at by the skeeters, who laughed at her and bit her anyway.

Bo, chewing the same lump of tobacco he had been working on all afternoon, closed the door behind them and made sure all the windows were tight. Then, he grabbed a wet towel from the bar and began swatting the bugs.

Sam didn't look good. There was a greenish, yellowish tinge to his skin and dark shadows under his eyes. She would have liked to touch his forehead to see if his fever was back, but she didn't dare. He wouldn't appreciate being treated like a child in front of strangers. So perhaps it was a good thing after all that they had to rest. He had refused numerous times to have his wounds checked so there was nothing else Margo could do except hand him a couple of Ibuprofens from her stash.

The smells coming from the kitchen were enticing. The granny waitress and another younger woman were busy, moving around, frying and chopping stuff. She remembered that she hadn't eaten anything all day. When the fried catfish po'boys came, she wolfed hers down like everyone else. They chased that down with a beer and set up camp in the restaurant. Buddy and Tim apologized and brought mats out, and a couple of sleeping bags. Then, the granny waitress and the young woman said good night and left, and everyone settled down to rest.

Margo sat with Odette on the couch they had been assigned for the night, and they got to chatting. It was too early and too uncomfortable to fall asleep yet, but Sam had already settled himself into one of the sleeping bags and was snoring away. The others sat at a table and drank beers and smoked, talking softly.

Vinnie had been nice to her, Odette told her sadly.

"He was gentle and kind, but at the same time so exciting. He showed me a world beyond anything I had ever imagined. He took me to the symphony, and to museums, and we went on all those wonderful trips around the world."

"Maybe he was truly in love with you."

"Yes. Maybe. I know I had fallen in love, but it was so complicated."

"At least you have those wonderful memories."

"I don't think I'll ever meet another man like him." Odette sighed and leaned back on the sofa. "I wonder who killed him."

"Yes, me too."

"You know, I never liked his cousin, Melba Gaines. Of all the nasty, hateful people. Maybe she's the one."

"Why would she want to kill him?"

"To inherit the Gallery, of course. And all his money. She told me one time that she had gotten Vinnie to change his will, and she said it in a way that implied that she was sleeping with him."

"Did you believe her?"

"I did at the time."

"What made you change your mind?"

"I watched Vinnie like a hawk after that, but he never showed any signs of being interested in her that way. He was nice to her. He called her cousine, and bantered with her, but never in a sexual way. She was just being spiteful."

"I suppose it could have been anyone at the party. Though usually, most poisoners tend to be women." Odette nodded and then fell quiet, looking like she had gotten lost in her thoughts. Then—after a few minutes—she asked, "Have you met James Lee Reeshard?"

"The James Lee Reeshard?"

"Yes, the famous sculptor, and the scariest man I've ever encountered in my life."

Margo sat up straight. "No, I haven't. Not personally, anyway. Tell me about him."

"It was one of those weekend parties Vinnie liked to throw. I was spending a few days with him. It was a pool party at the Country Club. We were having lots of fun, Vinnie, his friends, and me. Then—out of the blue—everyone fell silent. It was so weird. They were all looking in the direction of this very tall, strange-looking man heading our way. He always dresses like a vampire. He even wears a top hat, and one of those long black coats that reach him to the knees. Anyway, nobody said anything else. They just watched him. That was the end of the fun."

"How so?"

"People just got up, gave excuses, and left."

"But why?"

"I don't know. There's something so malevolent about him. It's like an evil aura that surrounds him. He looks at you like he could read your thoughts. And he never smiles, even when people are telling jokes. So, people usually end up all depressed and go home. Maybe he killed Vinnie."

"Was he friends with Vinnie?"

"They were best friends, from way back. He was the guy that copied the artifacts I brought from Two Crows."

"Have you told Sam?"

"No. What's the point?"

"As you said, he could be the murderer."

"That's what I thought. But why would he kill him? Vinnie was his meal ticket."

"True. Maybe they had a falling out."

Odette shook her head. "I don't know. I saw him many times after that party, and they always seemed to be very close."

"Well, I guess an artist of his caliber would be quite capable of making fakes of your artifacts."

"Yes. Clay masks, pottery, all that? Piece of cake."

The heat and the humidity had become unbearable in the enclosed space, but opening a window was out of the question. And there were still too many mosquitos inside the restaurant. Every time that Margo felt like she was about to drift off to sleep, they would begin buzzing in her ear, trying to get under the blanket to bite her. It didn't matter how many times she shooed them away. They always came back. A large, slow, overhead fan moved the hot air around but provided little relief.

Outside, the storm was back, lashing the restaurant. Someone had turned the last light out, and the big space was pitch black. Tables and chairs stood out like silent ghosts wherever she looked. Odette had curled up on her side of the sofa and fallen asleep under her blanket. Margo lay there in her corner, restless, unable to sleep. From time to time, walls of water smashed at the windows and startled her, made her wonder if they were going to be washed away into the river. All these years in Half Moon Bay and the storms still intimidated her.

She must have fallen asleep, because, suddenly, someone was shaking her awake.

"Margo, wake up." It was Odette whispering. "I heard something." Margo sat up and listened. She put a finger on her lips so Odette would be quiet. The room was silent except for the men snoring and breathing heavily. A slim ray of moonlight had reached the couch, and she saw Odette, that familiar panic in her eyes. Poor Odette was on the brink of a nervous breakdown.

"I don't hear anything. It could have been the wind."

"No, Margo. I know what I heard. I was sleeping, and it awakened me. Then it stopped."

"What was it like, the noise? Do you remember?"

"I don't know. Like someone was walking around shuffling their feet."

"It's okay. Whatever it was, it's gone. Now go back to sleep. I'll stay up for a while, to make sure."

"Please be careful."

"I will. Don't worry. Now close your eyes. That's a good girl. Go to sleep."

Margo sat quietly for a few minutes in the darkness, and soon Odette's rhythmic breathing told her that she had fallen asleep again. She was convinced she had heard something. Yet everything was all right in the room. But now, she was wide awake. She tried to settle back into her spot, but it was pointless. A strange room in a strange place, full of strangers. Had it been Odette's imagination? Or a dream? Probably that and nothing else.

She was restless. She padded barefoot to the window and stood there for a few minutes looking out into the pitch-dark night, illuminated by nothing except the haze of the clouds, and the silver cattails on the shore. She was surrounded by people, but she was alone in this vast, dark night. The wind whistled through the bushes, and the two flat-bottom boats tied to the pier banged against each other with a thud, thud. The river was still angry. She couldn't see it, but she knew it. She thought about the comforts of home, and about Ice and Fenway sleeping in her big empty bed.

She was about to turn back to her spot on the sofa when a huge flash of lightning zigzagged through the sky, followed within seconds by a threatening roll of thunder. The windows shook, and Margo shivered, but not because of the thunder. She thought she saw a white alligator slip into the frothing river, right by the boats, and she stuck her nose to the windowpane to see it better, but the ghostly gator was gone. Her hand went to her mouth, stifling quickly the scream that almost poured out of her mouth. It was carrying something big in its maw. And it was still alive. For a second, she thought she could do something to help, but even before she blinked again, the apparition was gone. Just like that, it had vanished.

Chapter 43
Turn Of Events

THE MAN SAW THE SHADOW AND WATCHED IT as it approached closer to him, and his hand went to his holster. Young, tall, slender, wasn't enough to describe someone you had never met before—in the dark. Hiding behind a tree trunk as he watched the stranger, he waited for the pre-arranged sign, the tweet of the Paruline hochequeue or Louisiana Waterthrush. He knew well what the Waterthrush sounded like. He just hoped his contact figured it out as well.

When he finally heard the twittering his contact thought was the Paruline, he laughed out loud. It sounded nothing like it was supposed to. He stepped into the light and whistled the proper sound back, and he stuck his hand out.

"Hi there," he said amicably. "Nice to meet you."

"I'm glad you could make it. We have to hurry up if we want to catch up with them."

"Word is they're traveling slowly. Shouldn't be too hard."

"What do we know about them?"

"Not much, except that a lot of money will be changing hands. I bet we can help them with that." He laughed, thinking about those amateurs. "And I've found out where they are meeting."

"Are we expecting a bloodbath?"

"I am," the man said, and he chuckled, patting his holster and the gun that was slung on his shoulder. "Don't worry, I have more ammo in my backpack."

"Not worried. I've got plenty of that too."

"I'm almost sorry for them," the man said.

"Why's that?"

"Well, they don't know the area. Swamps, alligators, snakes, quicksand, no workable maps, an overhead canopy of trees so thick that your GPS and your cell phone will be useless. That enough of a reason?" He laughed.

The shadow felt a little uncertain. This wasn't anything like what he had ever undertaken before. But the man punched him softly on the arm. "Listen," he told the shadow. "With your military training and my knowledge of the area, we'll do just fine."

Chapter 44

DAY EIGHT: Death By Murder

MARGO WOKE UP TO SCREAMS. At first, she thought she was having a nightmare, but when she threw off her blanket and a vigorous early-morning sun blinded her temporarily, she knew she had slept through the night, and this was no nightmare.

Odette was standing a couple of feet from the sofa—just by the counter—and it was she who was doing the screaming. There was a dead man lying at her feet, a big kitchen knife sticking out of his chest. Odette stood in shock, in a puddle of his blood, her face in her hands, her eyes gone wild.

The men were slowly waking up, looking around, disoriented. Margo hurried over to Odette and shook her to calm her down.

"I can't calm down. He's dead. He's dead. Look, someone killed him. It's Buddy, isn't it? He was the one who was going to take us across the river."

"You need to quit screaming, Odette. Breathe. It will be okay. I'm going to check on him. He might still be alive."

Odette nodded. She was as white as a sheet of paper, and a few beads of sweat shone on her upper lip. Margo patted her shoulder and bent down next to the man. She knew he was dead. His eyes were wide open, and he wasn't blinking, but she checked anyway, more for Odette's sake than anything.

There was a lot of blood. Buddy's shirt was soaked, and there was a big coagulating puddle of it on the floor. Some of it looked like it had dripped away in between the planks of the wooden floor.

Tim approached Margo. "That's one of our kitchen knives," he said. "The one missing from the set, look."

Margo turned around and looked at what Tim was pointing at. She nodded. One of the carving knives was missing for sure. It could be then that Buddy had been killed by someone inside the Shack—during the night.

She looked at Odette. The poor woman was still in shock. Couldn't have been her. She would have had to be an excellent actress to pull off that look of abject panic and the shaking of her hands.

Then, she looked around, at the men. It was obvious that they were all trying to look as innocent as possible. It wasn't Sam, of course. It could have been Tim, or Bo himself, but that was absurd. They worked together day in and day out, the three of them. Besides, Buddy's friends looked forlorn, heartbroken. Why would either of them have picked to murder their friend the day that a Sheriff and his two lieutenants were visiting? No way.

How about Chris? He could have known Buddy from before. All these rural people seemed to be related to each other, or at least know each other. Chris did seem a bit of a recluse, eccentric, too nervous. Perhaps he had it in him. After all, he had kidnapped Sam and kept little Luna a prisoner. Was he a psychopath? He almost fit the bill: a person who exhibits amoral and antisocial behavior, who lacks the ability to love or to establish meaningful personal relationships—well she didn't know about that one—and shows extreme egocentricity, even failure to learn from experience, as in having allowed his brother to bully him even as an adult.

So that left Brett—Sam's cousin, Josh who was Odette's parrain, and the two young policemen. Now that was a thought. Were they really policemen? Events had been precipitated at such speed that there had been no chance to run checks on them.

Margo tried to remember what she had read about stabbings. They were messy affairs—spurts of blood that would leave visible traces on the murderer. Not one of the men had any blood on their shirts or arms, but by then, everyone—it seemed—had approached the dead man and had touched him. Feet had also stepped into the bloody puddle, leaving a mess of bloody footprints all over the room.

Sam seemed to be in an agony of pain. It should have been up to him to check things out and interrogate everyone, but it was obvious that he wasn't up to the task. While he got himself together, maybe took some medicine, Margo hurried to the front door to check the bolt. It was just as they had left it last night, tightly shut.

Windows were tightly shut as well in the main room of the restaurant. She unbolted the front door and turned the knob. The door screeched when it opened, and she tried to remember whether she had heard any screeching sounds during the night. But just as dreams vanish quickly after you wake up, so do sounds that disturb you through the night. Therefore, she couldn't say if she had heard anything in her sleep.

Margo stepped outside onto the covered porch. She inhaled the clean, fishy damp smell of the river. The sun was rising beyond the line of trees on the other side of the river, tinting everything pink and yellow. The water was still flowing swiftly, rushing by, carrying the remnants of the storm, but it either didn't look as threatening as it had last night, or she had gotten used to the idea.

An exultation of Cattle Egrets approached the Shack with slow elegance and settled carefully on the leaning Cajun Cruise ship. Others continued their flight, and she watched them for a while until they disappeared into the horizon. And the sky, that rare, perfectly blue sky, of that particularly pure color so distinctive to South Louisiana, and the perfection of it all, kind of tamped the shock she was feeling. She had almost forgotten that there was a dead man inside.

Quickly she looked down, not sure of what to expect. The floor on the deck was wood. A late rain had washed away their footprints when they retired, and there seemed to be no new ones. No muddy ones, anyway. So, in theory—accounting for the locked door and windows, and the lack of muddy footprints—the killer must have come in another way.

By now, everyone was on their feet, awake, smoothing out wrinkled shirts and finger combing mussed up hair. Bo was already chewing a lump of tobacco, or maybe, it was still the one from last night. He looked very distressed, he and Tim both.

Suddenly, the expedition had developed a big glitch. The body needed tending to, and the group needed to cross the river. Surrounded by stressed-out men, she decided to withhold her opinion, and she went and sat down next to Odette, who was huddled in a corner of the sofa, hugging her knees that she had pulled up to her chest. She was no longer in shock, but she still looked bewildered, her eyes wide open with fear, with horror.

"What's going to happen now?"

"I don't know," Margo answered. "But I don't think the plans will change. Sam is the most driven man I've ever met. He'll push through, regardless."

"Poor Buddy. He was a nice guy."

"He sure seemed to be."

"I don't understand why anyone would have wanted to kill him. Do you think it was one of us?"

"Well, Odette, it wouldn't have been too hard for one of us to kill him. We all had the opportunity. It wasn't Sam, though. He's a very decent man. Chris—if you don't mind me saying this—is too shy and too weak looking. Buddy was a big guy. It wasn't one of us either, for sure."

Odette looked at Margo, bewildered. "That leaves Tim and Bo, the two young policemen, Josh, and Sam's cousin Brett. One of them is a murderer, and we have to travel into the forest lands with him."

"Let's not jump to conclusions."

"Then it was the person I heard walking about in the night."

"I already checked. No stranger came in through the front door, or the windows, but I haven't checked out back. Stay here and don't panic. I'll be right back."

The men were still standing pointlessly around the dead body, and Margo quietly slipped to the back of the bar, from where a narrow door led to a fairly large room. She quietly closed the door behind her. She found herself in some sort of a storage room, one end of which was piled up high with trash bags and discarded boxes. On the other side of the room stood a surprisingly lovely—and completely out of place—beautifully carved antique wooden desk, with a table-top computer, a stack of papers, and some office odds and ends. To one side of the computer, a small aquarium broke the dead monotony with a dozen or so tiny, colorful fish, swimming cheerfully, oblivious to the drama unfolding in the other room.

She walked to the end of the room and opened the back door to a clearing, at the end of which stood a tight, overgrown, wall of centenarian trees.

The air was cooler back here. Margo stepped outside, and a world of sounds assaulted her. The world behind the Shack was alive with the sounds of nature, and the movement of birds and butterflies, of rustling leaves, of little critters hopping out of her way as she walked. The pleasant breeze carried the clean, piney scent of shrubbery, and soon dried the sweat on her neck and her forehead.

There was mud everywhere. She noticed right away that a line of large footprints led to the back of the clearing, and she turned around. They continued on to the back door that she had just left, becoming less and less visible as the individual walked on the concrete. She stared at the prints. They must have been a pair of boots. Large. But impossible to tell what kind or size precisely, as the prints were so distorted in the squishy ground as to be worthless. What you could tell for sure was that the prints came and went. The person had exited the forest line, entered the house, and then left the same way.

It was a good discovery, but a sobering thought. And Margo couldn't help but extrapolate. Was Buddy the intended victim? Was he even visible enough in the dark restaurant for the killer to pick him out and kill him? Or was it random? If it was random, that opened a whole new can of worms.

Margo followed the footsteps, careful to land on clumps of weeds or pebbles, to avoid sinking in the mud. Had the intruder intended to steal something, and was surprised by Buddy? Buddy could have been going to the bar to get a glass of water, or he could have been visiting the toilet, surprised the intruder, and confronted him. It was a more comforting thought that having to think that one of those men inside the Shack was a killer, especially since they were being forced to spend the next few days traveling in the wilderness together.

She poked around the shrubbery for a possible clue, but just half-heartedly. This whole expedition stunk. They had barely left town, and already there was a dead body. She thought of her comfy bed and her cats, Jenny's cats, and she wished she had never consented to come.

She noticed a scrap of paper, glaringly white against the green foliage, and she picked it up. It was small, wrinkled, like when you crumple a piece of paper before discarding it. She smoothed it out and realized with horror that it was a roughly drawn map of the Shack, the river, the boat dock. There you go, that's it, she told herself. The murderer had come with a purpose, and with directions. He had been told where they would be spending the night. Where to find them. Or was it a coincidence? She folded the small map and shoved it into her jeans pocket. Sam might be interested, and he could decide what to do about it.

By the time she made it back, the group was already getting ready to leave. Sam, standing by the open front door, was busy on the phone. She heard the words 'ambulance' and 'police' and assumed that he was making arrangements for the body. With Sam and the rest of them on assignment requested explicitly by a Governor, there would be no delay for them. Sam hung up the phone, came back in, and grabbed his backpack. He looked grim and feverish, but as determined as ever. He certainly didn't look like he was getting better. At the first chance, she would have to ask to see his wounds. In an environment like this one, wounds tended to fester fast.

While everyone finished packing backpacks and folding blankets, they ate the sandwiches that Tim was passing out. Coffee came next in disposable Styrofoam cups. It tasted vile to Margo, who was used to her morning cappuccino, but at least it was coffee. Sam stood by the window, drinking his coffee by himself, and Margo approached him.

"Everything okay, Sam?"

"Everything's fine. Why are you asking?"

"Because you look kind of droopy and quiet. Even more than usual. Is something bothering you?"

Sam looked out the window with sad eyes. "Not really. My wounds hurt some, but that's about it."

"Someone should look at those, you know. You don't want them infected."

"At Armentor's house. Right now, I have other problems." Sam looked away, and Margo knew she had been dismissed.

The group was told to pile into the two flat-bottom riverboats. She pulled Odette's arm and told her to sit with her, and she noticed that Chris quickly followed Odette to the back of the line. Even though it was Josh who was supposed to guard her, it was, in the end, Chris, who never left her side.

Margo watched the water with suspicious distrust. She stood last in line purposefully, waiting for the others to climb into the boat so that she could observe how they did it. Bo had originally planned to stay behind— she had heard—but now, with Buddy dead, had no choice but to take the other boat across. First, they had to walk yards of mud and ankle-deep dirty water and then—one by one—step into the very wobbly, rickety boats, the ones that she had been suspicious of the day before. She swallowed hard when it was her turn, but Bo smiled at her encouragingly and extended his hand.

Margo clung to Bo's hand as long as she could, terrified that the thing was going to keel over to the side and throw them all in the water. Everyone in the other boat was already sitting in position, and they all watched her struggle—grinning—probably waiting for her to fall. She felt humiliated at failing a test that everyone else had passed with flying colors. She sat down in her assigned seat and waited for the boat to quit wobbling with her eyes down. And then, they were off.

Chapter 45

Another Death

MARGO HAD DONE MANY THINGS IN HER YOUNG LIFE but had never crossed such a wide river in such a tiny boat, especially after such a vicious storm. She watched Bo deftly push away from the shore with an oar, and then drop the outboard motor into the water. After a couple of pulls on the mysterious starter rope, the engine came to life, and Bo sat back at ease, one hand on the edge of his seat, the other on the throttle arm.

Once the initial fear wore off, Margo realized that this was quite the adventure, and she settled down to admire the scenery in front of her and quickly forgot about the dead man.

The shack soon became smaller and smaller. They were not only going straight across to the opposite shore but were going to travel some miles along the river. Bo worked hard to keep the boat stable. In front of them, the other boat, driven by Tim, was trying to break away from the middle stream and head for the coastline, but the current was very strong and kept pushing his boat back.

The river looked so much wider and so much more threatening from where she sat than previously, from the shore. Occasionally, big rotten tree trunks hit the side of the boat, making it rock and threatening to capsize it, but Bo was good at this and kept them safe.

Then, suddenly, Bo stopped the boat and whistled. The other boat stopped as well and Tim turned to look at Bo, who let out a string of urgent archaic French that Margo didn't understand, and he pointed at the opposite side, where an enormous alligator was just easing itself into the water.

Margo gasped. As it entered the water, the gigantic beast began swimming in slow, gracious strokes, taking is time, its eyes always above water level, staring intently at the boat in which she was sitting, staring right at her, coming straight for her. She willed Bo to go faster. To get out of the way. Surely, they were in no danger. The boat was small but much bigger than the creature, and it was made sturdy and strong. She wrung her hands, trying to control her angst. Everyone was so silent that it exacerbated her anxiety. Was she the only one horrified? Wasn't anyone going to do something?

Her eyes searched for Sam in the other boat. He looked feverish and bewildered. He too was staring at the alligator as if hypnotized, as it smoothly swam toward them. She felt tormented by fear. Didn't someone have a plan? Shouldn't someone be doing something? Were they all going to just sit there helplessly until the alligator attacked them and ate them all?

Finally, she called out to Bo. "Can we shoot it? Does anyone have a gun?"

Bo looked at her, his weather-beaten face in a big frown. He chewed on his tobacco and spit the fetid black saliva into the water. "No, we can't," he said. "If I shoot, we capsize because of the knockback. And that would be worse. We would all fall in. There are other alligators in the water. I can sense them waiting. Besides, an alligator's skin is like armor. Bullet-proof armor. If I get it in the tail, or the back, or the head, it won't do anything to it but make it angrier. No, we won't shoot."

"Can we turn around?"

"We could try, but it will probably catch up with us anyway."

"What are we going to do?"

"Sit down and let me think."

Bo chewed his tobacco vigorously for a few seconds, and then he whistled to Tim again, and they talked some more in French. She did recognize one word: femmes, women, and she deduced that Bo and Tim had come up with a plan.

She watched anxiously, her heart thumping so hard that it felt like it was going to burst her eardrums. She clung to the wooden plank she was sitting on, and she waited, holding her breath. The alligator dove under the water. In the murky, frothing, chocolate liquid, it soon became almost impossible to see.

Bo repositioned himself in his seat and held the throttle, moving it so that the prow of the boat pointed toward the spot where the alligator's body had just disappeared. Odette and Chris held each other, not saying anything, not making the slightest sound.

Then, the other boat made a move. The alligator's eyes were barely above the rush of water, the enormous beast gracefully swimming against the current, taking its time, as if it was taunting them. It was in no hurry. It knew that they were at its mercy. Margo wanted to scream that they were all going to die.

As the gator got closer and closer, Tim—with his boat—moved to intercept. The distraction worked, and the gator seemed to hesitate for a fraction of a moment, and then it changed course.

"Oh, no," Margo cried out, too loud, and Bo looked at her sternly and shook his head. She was distraught. She understood now what the plan was. The two boats now were so close to each other that Margo could see the panic in Sam's eyes. His cousin Brett, and one of the young policemen—the two men closest to the gator—quickly picked up oars, and Margo waited, chewing on her knuckles. This had been Bo and Tim's plan, and they were all trapped in it, and not one of them had a choice. Whatever she would have preferred to do—or not do—had no meaning whatsoever. They would either be saved or doomed, by the decision of these two strangers.

Then, Bo took off. With the other boat intercepting, offering their lives to save the lives of the two women, they easily navigated the wild waters and had almost made it safely across, when a terrible scream pierced the air.

Margo looked on horrified, holding her breath, as the gator leaped out of the water, and, in an impossibly gravity-defying move, grabbed one of the twins by the arm—oar and all—and dragged him away. Brett never hesitated. He beat the water where the gator sank, as if it would have made a difference, trying to hurt the enormous beast. But it was futile. The young policeman's screams continued to pierce the air for a second or two. Birds and monkeys came alive on the shore, fluttering on the tree branches, screeching, screaming out their own fears, but the poor young man's earsplitting howling drowned out the sounds of nature.

As in a freezeframe, the image remained burned into Margo's mind, Brett—confused—staring at the water with the oar still in his hands, and the young policeman, reaching for his brother's hand, gaping, frozen in time. And the look on Sam's face. Poor Sam, who knew better than any of them what that must have felt like, who was still suffering from a similar attack, and whose infected gator bites might still kill him.

Overwhelmed with emotion, Margo prayed to Saint Gertrude, the Patron Saint of the dead, and begged her to give the poor young man a swift and painless death. It had all been so quick. Within seconds, the disturbance in the water had vanished, and the birds and monkeys in the trees quietened back down, and all was as if nothing had ever happened.

They reached the shore without talking. Bo and Tim each jumped out and pulled the boats partway up the weedy shore. There was a rotting, make-shift pier, and the boats were tied to it.

Margo felt like a zombie. In a trance—shaking with feverish horror— she took Bo's hand and struggled herself out of the boat. She missed her footing and stepped into squishy mud, and Bo pulled and pulled, and then she was safe. But something had broken inside her. Inconvenient and embarrassing tears flowed down her cheeks, and there was Bo—so kind— awkwardly trying to dry them. He held her by the shoulders as they walked over to where the other boat had been pulled up, and he let her go. There was so much sadness in his eyes.

This whole adventure had begun almost as a lark for her, but now, there were two dead men, and who knew what other dangers ahead. She wished she had listened to Brooks, and Lucy, and Father Armand, and stayed home. Now, there was no choice but to continue, unless she wanted to go back to where she had just come from. But she couldn't face the river, not so soon, so she put her backpack on, thanked Bo for his kindness, and followed the others into the woods.

Chapter 46

The Swamp Lands

THE GROUP WALKED SILENTLY, everyone sunk in their own misery. The sun was shining, but there was nothing to be cheerful about. The mosquitoes—that in town only attacked as the night approaches—buzzed around them in hungry and restless circles. The rains had led them to a breeding frenzy. It was pointless to swat them away, or to put your jacket on despite the sweltering heat, or to even cover your head with a scarf and a hat because the mosquito always found a way to its favorite food supply.

Odette slowed down her pace so that Margo could catch up with her.

"All a male mosquito needs to survive is a drop of flower nectar," she said. "But the females are like vampires. Sugars are not enough for them. They require the nutrition of human or animal blood. Without it, they can't reproduce properly. They need the protein to produce their eggs."

"Well, they don't seem to bite you much, but look at the cloud of skeeters following me. I can't get rid of them."

"Oh, I can fix that for you. Wait here."

Margo stopped, while Odette hurried into the bushes and came back after a minute or so with a clump of long, ordinary-looking grass.

"This is called Sweetgrass. It's what my people use as a bug repellant. Look at mine," she said, and she pulled out a small cheesecloth bag full of dried herbs. "It would be better if we could burn it, or dry it, but this will have to do. Scrunch it, squeeze it as much as you can to break the juice out, and then rub it on your skin, you know, arms, neck, ears. The skeeters hate the smell. I promise you that they won't bother you anymore."

"Wow, thanks." Margo rubbed the rough, sticky leaves on her skin, and right away saw the skeeters fly away. "This is marvelous."

"I know. It's a trick I learned from my mom."

"Thank you so much."

"Sure thing. Listen, I better run ahead to catch up with Chris. He's kind of lost without me." Odette giggled and disappeared.

The group had divided into pairs. The trail was narrow, perfectly suited for two people walking side by side. Odette had caught up with Chris, and they were now at the head—leading—since Chris knew the area the best. They seemed to have forgotten their sorrows, and chatted amiably, Chris pointing things out to Odette, and the girl, laughing. They were full of life. Young. They shared the memory of someone who had been a great presence in their lives. They had that in common. Margo was surprised at how fast they had become friends.

Brett and the surviving twin walked behind them, together in their sorrow. They walked with their heads down, for the most part, looking at the ground. They said very little to each other. Once or twice Brett gave the young man a consoling pat on the back. Then, they would continue walking in silence. They followed Chris without showing any interest in the landmarks he pointed out, the sets of trees, or the formations of rocks that guided his way.

Josh—the parrain—had completely forgotten that he was supposed to stick to Odette to protect her. He walked behind Brett, more or less next to Sam, but not interacting with him at all. Not that Sam looked like he would have liked to chat with anyone. He seemed to be dragging himself with great effort, mopping his brow with his arm, and stopping for brief seconds to catch his breath. Margo hurried on to catch up with him and hooked his arm around hers, so he could lean on her. Sam smiled at her and gave her a quick thanks and then continued his slow, lethargic advance forward.

With Josh right in front of her, it was unavoidable that she should watch him. After a while, she realized that he looked oddly nervous, glancing at his watch time and again. Something was not right with Josh, and her suspicions of traveling with a killer came back to her. Because there was something fishy about Josh. Of that, she was sure.

The canopy of leaves and branches above them soon turned the trail into a walking sauna, trapping the rising heat and humidity as the rainwater puddles evaporated.

Sam was struggling more and more now, and at some point, Margo began dragging him. His skin was burning hot, and yet he shivered as if he were cold, but the temperature was surely in the high nineties, at the least. She was ever so grateful when Chris stopped at a clearing and lifted his arm.

"We stop here for a break," he said, and he took his backpack off and threw it on the dusty ground.

"How long?" Brett asked.

"Oh, maybe a half-hour should do."

"Are we far?"

"No more than a couple of hours. We should be there by noon."

It was the perfect spot for a break. They were close to the water, and a mild meager breeze rustled through the vegetation, cooling their skin as it helped their sweat evaporate. To one side of the clearing, and close to the water, a couple of flat-bottom riverboats sat forgotten, upturned, their paint peeling. Margo helped Sam over to one of them, under a shade tree, and checked the wood and the aluminum for safety, and they sat down.

"Thank God for the shade, right?" Margo said, trying to sound cheerful. "Are you feeling okay?"

"Yes, for the most part. I'm in pain, but nothing we can do about that."

"Would you let me check your wounds? They might need to be cleaned."

"Margo, I have no intention of pulling my pants down in front of everyone."

"Come on, Sam. If they get infected, your leg might gangrene, and you'll lose it."

"Okay, okay. We're not far from Armentor's swamp house. You heard what Chris said: two hours tops. There was a bedroom, I think. I'll take my pants off there. Maybe I can ask you to take a look and clean the bites if you think you must."

"Oh, Sam, maybe this wasn't such a good idea. Maybe we shouldn't have come."

"You know I had no choice. I must try to get the Governor's wife and daughter back. Before they kill them."

"Do you actually think they'll give them back for the ransom money?"

"I have to hope so."

"That is, if they're still alive."

"They have to be. Listen, Margo. I have to tell you something. You're not going to like it."

"Oh God, what?"

"The kidnappers want Odette and Chris to deliver the ransom money."

"Did they specify them by name?"

"Yes. Odette Alves and Chris Mouton."

"But Sam, that sounds like more than a simple ransom."

"That's what I was thinking. They want to apprehend Chris and Odette. They baited their trap with the Governor's wife and kid to get those two."

"This is so wrong. Isn't there anything we can do?"

"There isn't much. The kidnappers specified civilians. If they saw anyone in uniform, they said that they would shoot the hostages."

"But you're the Half Moon Bay Sheriff. You don't think they will recognize you?"

"Right now, I just look like a wounded civilian. Maybe that'll fool them. The thing is that it all sounded like such a doable idea, that I allowed my uncle to talk me into it. But now I regret that I brought you along, and indirectly, caused the death of two innocent people."

"Don't say that, Sam. I'm not glad to be here, but it is what it is. Maybe I can help somehow."

"Remember. You're the only one I can trust."

"But what are we going to do?"

"We'll see. For now, we keep going. I have a plan, at least the beginning of one. Maybe luck will be on our side, and we can get out of this alive."

Sam lay down on the flat bottom of the boat and covered his face with his hat. Within a few seconds, he was fast asleep, and Margo sat down on a clump of grass next to him. Without a book to read to pass the time, Margo's troubled mind kept going back to what Sam had said about the kidnappers wanting to get a hold of Chris and Odette. They looked like such an ordinary pair of young people, friendly, innocent, without an apparent bad bone in their bodies. What on earth did the kidnappers want with them? And had they really orchestrated the abduction just to get to them? But why?

Chapter 47

Confessions

EVERYONE HAD SETTLED DOWN TO REST, the men, except for Chris, leaning against tree trunks. The minutes ticked by slowly for Margo, pulling the length of time like chewing gum, endlessly longer and longer, until Margo thought that she would scream.

She tried to entertain herself. She watched some ants carrying a dead bug in a long, tortuous procession. They disappeared into the shrubbery. Then she saw a couple of lizards inflating and deflating their necks, which had turned red. They seemed ready to fight. She hated violence, so she stopped watching them. She didn't spot any snakes or squirrels. There was nothing else to see.

Tired of the idleness, she got up and walked over to where Chris and Odette were sitting on a bed of pebbles, their shoulders touching, talking very softly with very serious faces. Whatever drama they were going through, they were living it in private.

She waved as she approached and said hi. Then, encouraged by their welcoming smiles, she sat down with them.

"Is Sam doing all right?" Chris asked.

"I don't think so. That alligator that dragged him under the water did a number on him."

"I am so sorry. You probably know it was my fault."

"Sam doesn't see it that way. He told me you had no choice."

"Odette here knows a lot about natural medicine. Maybe she can help." The girl nodded and looked up. Margo noticed for the first time that Odette had the most impenetrable dark eyes. You couldn't even see the cornea, just a big, mysterious, dark puddle. It startled her and gave her an uncomfortable feeling. She had never met anyone with black eyes before.

"Pardon me for asking. But where did you learn about natural medicine?"

Odette laughed. There was something charming about her laughter, though, and it put Margo at ease.

"I'm what they call a Native American. I belong to the Two Crows tribe, a distant offshoot of the Houma. We, women, begin to learn about plants and medicinal herbs as soon as we learn to walk. If your Sam lets me, I bet I can help."

"Well, I'm not sure he'll be willing to take his pants off in front of you, but if the pain becomes unbearable, he might change his mind."

Chris chuckled, but then he became very serious.

"I'm so sorry," he said.

"We've been through this," Odette said and patted his hand. "I'm the one responsible for this mess." Then she turned toward Margo and explained.

"You see, I met Vinnie when I was very young, when he was still a nice person, fun, decent, and honest."

Chris coughed into his fist.

"He was," she affirmed, and nudged him with her elbow. "He was. It was after I started bringing him the artifacts that we found on our land that he became greedier, harder. And as the money came in, he slowly changed."

"I've heard some of that," Margo said. "Apparently, he was buying the real stuff from you, having them copied, selling the copies as authentic in the Gallery, and the real pieces for small fortunes to private collectors."

"Yes. It was very lucrative."

"So, what happened?"

"He became too successful," Chris said. "Some criminal gang contacted him, and they offered him protection."

"Protection from what?"

"From nothing. But that's how the Mafia operates. He said 'no' a few times, but they beat him up, they burned his car and stuff like that. Eventually, he realized there was no way out, so he said 'yes' since it was obvious that the hoodlums were never going to back off."

"And where do you fit in, Chris? If you don't mind me asking?"

"Until recently, I had no idea what was going on. From time to time they borrowed the fur house, paid me well for it, and forbade me to come near it. They had me terrified. I lost all interest in the fur house. I never went close to it again."

"What changed?"

"They brought the little girl Luna. I didn't even know they had built a cage."

"How could you not know?"

"Because—believe me—from then on, I pretended that the fur house didn't exist."

"So, they brought Luna. What then?"

"They put the fear of God in me. They told me she needed to be fed and to be kept an eye on. It wasn't me who they threatened to hurt, but the child. And such a sweet, polite girl she is. I took care of her until they brought Sam in. By then, I knew that I couldn't accept what was going on, so—as soon as I had a chance—I got out of there."

Both Odette and Chris fell silent. Margo nodded and sat in silence with them. She understood.

Everyone around them was resting with their eyes closed. She could hear Sam snore.

"What's going to happen?" Odette asked.

"I don't know. I'm assuming the kidnappers will get their ransom money and let the hostages go."

"You don't actually believe that Margo, do you?"

"No. Not really."

"They want Chris and me. The rest is just a charade."

"Yes. Sam suggested something of the sort. But why would they want you?"

"They want Chris because he knows the swamps like the back of his hand. With Chris, they can move around Louisiana as they please, and nobody will be able to capture them."

"Makes sense, I guess. But you, Odette? Why do they want you as well?"

Odette sighed. "I'll tell you why. Two Crows is in a hidden area of the forest lands. It's surrounded by impenetrable swamps. It's completely isolated from the rest of the country. They have no contact with the outside world, and they want to keep it that way."

"And?"

"And we're the only ones who know where the artifacts are. They contain incalculable treasures. Imagine that we found a hidden city, like the ones built by the Aztecs and the Mayans."

Margo looked incredulously at Odette. This was something too far out.

"I know it's hard to believe. But these hidden cities are everywhere in Central America and the south of the country, all the way to the tip of Florida. Read your History."

Margo nodded, remembering the article she had recently read about drones that had revealed a hidden ancient village buried under dirt and vegetation in New Mexico.

"Margo, Two Crows is sitting on a treasure trove. No telling what else there is yet to be found."

"Wouldn't you want some archeological society to excavate the city?"

"Absolutely not. Imagine what havoc they would bring. The dwellers of Two Crows would never have another peaceful day. The news vans would show up, then, the conservation societies, the scientists, the looters… No, thank you."

"And that's what the bad guys want?"

"Yes. Imagine if they had me to tell them where the treasure is."

"And Chris to tell them how to get away safely with it." Margo nodded and finished the sentence for her. "Does Sam know? The treasure, I mean."

"Nobody does. And it's best if we keep it that way. Safer."

"Yes. I can see that. So why tell me?"

"We had to trust someone. I guess we used our better judgment. And I'm glad we did."

"Thanks. I swear I will never tell."

"Good. Or else, we'll have to kill you."

Chris and Odette laughed at that with a clear and friendly laughter, as if it had been a joke. But a frisson ran up Margo's spine. Would they be willing to kill to keep safe such a dangerous secret? What's more, had Vinnie been indiscreet, disclosing their secret? And had they felt threatened and found it necessary to silence him? Those two, for all that they were supposed to have been strangers when they had first gotten together for this trip, they were surprisingly chummy as if they had known each other a lifetime. Margo understood Sam's unwillingness to trust others. They looked so innocent and vulnerable, these two. But were they, really?

Margo got up from the pebbly floor and waved goodbye. As she stepped away, she heard her name mentioned, and she sharpened her ears.

"Shouldn't we tell her the truth?" Odette was asking.

"Not yet," he answered. "I want to make sure we can trust her."

Chapter 48
The Trek

SAM WAS SHIVERING AND MUMBLING IN HIS SLEEP. Margo touched his forehead. It was burning. She rummaged among Sam's belongings but found nothing to help him with. All she came up with was a very basic First Aid kit, a bottle of some stinky salve, and one of painkillers. She could give him that for the fever but hated to wake him up.

She looked around. Everyone was resting. Who to bother? Then, she remembered Chris mentioning that Odette knew about natural medicine and that she, herself had offered to help. She walked back to where they were sitting.

"Sam's not doing well," she told them. "He's burning up with fever. The wounds must be infected."

"I'm surprised that he's even alive."

"Odette, didn't you know some natural medicine? Something we can give him now to help him get to the house?"

Odette stood up and quickly looked around. Margo waited anxiously.

"Yes, maybe. Chris," she turned toward the young man. "Go make Sam a walking stick. Something he can lean on, with a crossbar that he can place under his armpit. But first, I need a small fire close to Sam. Don't you usually carry around a small aluminum pot to make coffee? I need boiling water."

Margo followed Chris and Odette across the clearing and chewed on her nails while Chris gathered a few sticks dry enough to burn and lit a fire under them.

Meantime, Odette had gone her own way. She walked around the bushes, stopped in front of one or the other—pensively—and then continued walking. As she went, she gathered clumps of foliage. By the time she got to the fire, the water was boiling. Sam, oblivious and deeply asleep, seemed to be having a nightmare. His head whipped from side to side angrily, and he muttered something you couldn't understand. He seemed to be getting worse.

Odette crushed some leaves into the pot and stirred.

"What is that?" Margo asked, pointing to the foliage in Odette's hand.

"I didn't find much, but one of them is Red Clover, which is a sedative and an anti-inflammatory, and this other one is Goldenrod or Solidago Ludoviciana, the Louisiana goldenrod. It's part of the sunflower family. It's good for everything. It's what my mom calls a panacea. But basically, it fights inflammation and can be used as an antiseptic for cuts and abrasions. It would be better to apply this in a salve to the bites and scratches themselves, but for now, drinking it will do."

"Do you think it will work fast enough to get him on his feet?"

"I hope so. Anyway, let's give it a few minutes to seep. Once it cools down, we can give it to Sam to drink. It should lower his fever long enough to get him to the house. I'll be able to do a lot more for him there."

While Margo sat silently with Odette close to Sam, Chris kept busy whittling a branch into an acceptable walking stick or a crutch. Eventually, Sam stirred, and Margo ran to him. He looked feverish and miserable. He stared at Margo and grabbed her arm. He told her something unintelligible and repeated it many times, but all Margo could do was shake her head.

"I'm sorry, Sam," she told him. "I can't understand." Sam closed his eyes and sighed. It seemed like he had fallen asleep again. "Sam, wake up. Please wake up. Odette made you some medicine that will make you feel better."

"No, no. We mustn't," he said deliriously, shaking his head.

"We mustn't what, Sam?" Margo asked, trying to wake him up. But Sam just kept talking to himself in his fever.

Chris came over and helped Margo sit him up, while Odette did her best to make him swallow some of her potion. Some of it spilled down his chin and onto his shirt, but he managed to swallow most of it. Then, Chris eased him back down.

"Now, we wait," Odette said.

"This is a disaster. What are we supposed to do now?"

"I have no idea," Margo answered. "Sam was very secretive with his plans."

"That's because he probably suspects that there's a spy among us."

"But why would there be a spy? And who could it be?"

"Don't look at me," Chris said belligerently. "I'm not the one. And I can vouch for Odette as well. Actually, we're the victims here. We're the ones being forced to put our lives at risk for the success of this operation."

"But what operation?" Margo asked, insisting. "Nobody tells me anything."

"Be grateful. The less you know, the safer you are."

"I don't want to be safe. I want to know what's going on."

"Margo," Odette said. "Listen to me. Let's get Sam on his feet and into a bed. That's our priority right now. We can talk semantics later."

"I guess you're right. Look, Sam is stirring, and he seems to look a little better."

Margo and Chris helped Sam stand and try out his walking stick. And Chris put Sam's backpack on his own shoulder, and after getting everyone to get moving, they hit the road again.

They fell into a slow but steady rhythm. Brett walked ahead with the young policeman, leading the group. Josh, who had all but forgotten his obligation to guard Odette, followed them at a short distance, lost in his own universe.

Margo wondered how Brett knew which way to go, but he had picked up Sam's map and compass, so she assumed there was enough information on it. Occasionally, Brett stopped to consult the map and the compass, and then they would keep going.

Chris was doing a great job helping Sam walk. It was obvious that Odette's concoction had given him a respite. Sam hobbled, held up by his crutch on one side, and Chris's supporting arm on the other.

Margo and Odette soon fell behind the others. The day had turned viciously hot and humid, making the going very hard. Margo felt like she was walking inside a swimming pool full of scalding hot water. She had never experienced such humid air. And her feet—her poor dogs—were barking. They felt swollen in her boots and were by now probably covered in blisters. She had heard that explorers had been known to take their boots off after a long trek, to find that their feet were soaked in blood. She sighed. At least the mosquitoes weren't biting.

By and by, they left the lower shrubs and the occasional standing cypress trees of the bayou, and they entered what Odette called the forest lands. Margo looked at her watch and realized with a shock that it wasn't even noon yet. Time had stopped running in an ordinary fluid direction and had stalled somewhere, making the passing of time stretch like chewing gum. How could it be so early still? She felt like she had walked miles and miles of roads and obstacles, and her body ached, and her feet were crying. How she wished again that she had stayed home.

She looked at the others. They too all seemed to be struggling. Not to even mention Chris, who was now carrying not only his own backpack and Sam's but pretty much Sam himself. He was no weakling, as she had initially surmised. This was one tough young man.

She had been taking layers of clothing off as they went. First her jacket, then her sweater, and her extra shirt, and when there was nothing else to take off, she wished for a pond, even if it was infested with gators and water moccasins. She would have braved them all to get some relief from the heat. Then, someone yelled, "Look, we're here."

As one, the group woke up from their lethargy. Everyone looked toward the pointing finger. An old cottage about a hundred feet ahead had just appeared from behind a wall of trees and bushes. In front of the house, a stream meandered in a bed of pebbles large and small. Once everyone stopped on their heels and stood quietly, Margo could hear clearly the little stream gurgle away down the incline. It put everyone in a cheerful mode. Even Sam looked alive again.

"That's the one," he said and hobbled ahead of them with Chris's help. "Y'all wait here."

Margo marveled at the first swamp house she had ever seen. It was a one-story house on short stilts. It had rained so much recently that the ground hadn't quite dried up yet. Puddles the size of car tires dotted the area, and there was a pleasing scent of cypress and honeysuckle in the air. The house was completely covered by a canopy of trees, so it was much cooler than the path that they had come from.

As Sam walked up to the house, a disreputable-looking dog began barking his heart out. The thing was on chains, and it pulled against them violently. But as Sam approached, the frenzy of anger turned into a frenzy of joy. The dog had recognized him and was hopping on its hind legs like a circus dog, and Sam walked straight to it and let it off the chain.

They hugged. Yes, they sure did. Margo had never seen this side of Sam, and it surprised her. Dog and Sheriff were happy to see each other. And despite there being so many strangers, the dog ignored them all. Then, she remembered that Sam had saved the dog's life, and it was probably smart enough to know. And that was the cause of its tremendous joy: gratefulness.

A burly man opened the door and looked at the group. He seemed mighty put out, but he did greet Sam with a bear hug. Margo was too far to see him, but she imagined Sam wincing from the pain. It was Sam who had saved this man's life as well. This was Luna's grandfather.

Sam and the burly man talked for a few minutes and Armentor nodded. He gave Sam a vigorous pat on the back and waved for the others to come in. The dog stuck by Sam like a shadow and licked his hand whenever it had a chance.

Everyone hurried up the steps and entered, but Margo lingered, so she could savor the loveliness of the house, the trees around it, the wooden swing chair hanging by chains from a tree to her left, and the carefully planted flowers in pretty pots. The quiet was surprising. Now that the dog had stopped barking, you could hear the bugs chirping in the bushes, and the cruel little blue jays taunting the squirrels.

She walked up the steps to the porch. Two rocking chairs sat side by side, with a table in between them. Empty beer bottles on the table, dog food in a bowl next to one of the chairs, and an old hunting magazine. It was a different world out here.

She heard laughter and loud conversation, and she pushed the front door open. The penumbra within the house gave the illusion of coolness.

But it was just a fleeting impression. Fans—several of them—gyrated from side to side, providing very little relief from the heat.

The living room was large, larger than it appeared from the outside. It was an all-purpose room. A patchwork sofa, a love chair, some random mismatching armchairs, and a coffee table, occupied the center of this room. To her left, a china cabinet with some porcelain plates and mugs, a washbasin like the ones you usually see in bathrooms, a candelabra with three lighted candles, and a chalkboard behind it full of notes in tiny, tight handwriting. And to her right, the dining table, behind which was a kitchen, quite similar to the one she had seen at Bo's restaurant.

They all took seats as instructed, while an angry-looking middle-aged woman slapped things around in the kitchen making a fresh pot of coffee—why coffee in this heat, for Heaven's sake?—and throwing together sandwiches, looking put out, every bit as if she hated every second of it.

Sam disappeared through a door pointed out by Armentor together with Chris, and Margo and Odette sat down side by side on the loveseat, which at close inspection turned out to be covered in dog hair.

"I thought they wouldn't let the dog in, with the way he was chained outside."

"I know. That woman in the kitchen does not look like an animal lover."

Margo chuckled. "Maybe the husband lets it in when she's not around."

They both laughed. At least Odette didn't look so unhappy anymore. But wouldn't she, herself feel unhappy if she knew that she was the designated cheese in the mousetrap?

"I'm sorry," Margo told her. "It must be terrifying to have to expose yourself like this. I don't exactly know what the plan is, but I don't like it. And I sure wouldn't like to be in your shoes."

"Well, I guess in some way, I deserve it. I could find excuses by telling you that I was too young when I took up with Vinnie, but I knew very well what I was doing."

"But you didn't know that Vinnie was a racketeer, though, did you?"

"That would be a tough question to answer. You see, everyone has this preconception of Vinnie that doesn't truly fit him. He was tough and ruthless, yes. But at the same time, he had this gentle side, the caring side, the one I fell in love with. After that, I found it easy to overlook his foibles."

"Is it true that he was a womanizer? I know I shouldn't ask. I don't want to hurt your feelings. But rumor has it that he had a thing for Matty Daigle."

"Maybe he did, but from what I saw, it was more like Matty Daigle was looking for a sugar daddy, if you know what I mean."

"But Zac Benoit told Sam that he had found him groping Matty behind some phone booth at a restaurant. And when Zac punched him to defend Matty, Vinnie sent some Chinese goons to beat him up and break his arm."

"Oh, I hadn't heard that one. I remember Vinnie was friends with this Chinese family. They own a chain of restaurants. They have a son called Tiger Lee, I think. He's really into martial arts. Maybe Vinnie asked him to pay this Zac a visit and scare him a little. Did he definitely break Zac's arm?"

"No, I don't believe he did."

"Oh, good. Tiger Lee is a nice kid. Can't really imagine him becoming violent."

"Look, Chris is coming."

"He's probably ready for me to check on Sam's wounds. I'll be right back."

With Odette gone, Margo had now time to look around at leisure. Brett, Josh, and the young policeman had settled close to Armentor, who was rubbing his dog between his knees. They were talking about hunting, and about what had happened when they crossed the river and lost the young policeman's twin, and Armentor told them about a white albino gator that ruled the swamps further up north, absconding from time to time with people's pets or their young children. Many had tried to hunt it down, but the crafty old gator had so far resisted capture.

Chris approached her and sat down next to her. "Sam's not getting any better," he said. "Odette is going to apply her salves and do for him what she can, but he would be better off in a hospital."

Margo gasped, horrified. All sorts of things ran through her mind. Sam was going to die. She had never known him to be sick. And even if he didn't die, he was abandoning her with all these strangers. She watched Chris walk over to the other men and tell them the news. He didn't seem to be bothered by losing Sam. Nor did anyone else. They just went on chatting as if nothing had happened.

She walked over to where the guys were downing beers and sandwiches, and she tried hard not to feel intimidated. These were all big, burly men, outdoorsy men, hunters, fighters, tough guys, much older than she was. She tried to disguise the fear from her voice.

"What are we going to do?"

"I vote that we continue on, with or without Sam," Josh said. "The Governor is counting on us. Otherwise, they might kill his wife and daughter."

"But I don't feel confident going on, not without Sam's expertise. Didn't he say he had a plan he wasn't ready to share?"

"He did say that," Chris said. "But he's feverish, and nothing he says makes any sense. I say we have two choices. Either we keep going, and give it a try, or we go back to where we came from, and let the kidnappers deal with the situation as they see fit."

"They'll kill the wife and the kid," Margo said.

"They probably will."

"Well, if you put it that way," said Brett, "give me another beer, Armentor, and I'll do some thinking."

Everyone nodded in agreement, and Margo looked on horrified as the men began drinking as if nothing had transpired, while her own soul was so tormented. How could they drink at a time like this? She grabbed Chris's arm and pulled him to the side.

"When is the rendezvous? Do you at least know that?"

"Yes. It was going to be before nightfall tonight. We were going to shoot for 5 pm., but now I don't know."

"Could we get there on time?"

"Technically, yes. It's only 2 p.m."

"So, if we left Sam behind, we could still go, exchange the money for the hostages, and get away before complete darkness."

"Again, technically yes, if nothing goes wrong. My house isn't far from the meeting place. If the exchange went smoothly, we could spend the night there."

"What are the odds of pulling this off?"

"Almost none."

"And what will happen to you and Odette?"

"They won't kill us because they need us. Question is, could we talk them into letting us go?"

"Doesn't sound like they would be willing."

"Maybe we can strike a deal with them."

"I don't understand. What kind of plan is this? Who came up with it? It's absolutely ridiculous."

"Sam and the Governor. Listen, it can work, if we assure them that we shall continue dealing with them."

"They won't believe you."

"What would you have us do? I don't want to have the death of a woman and a child on my conscience."

"So, you would offer your life in exchange for theirs?"

"I don't know. Maybe. It's a tough choice. The guy who runs to rescue people out of a burning car knows he could die. He does it anyway."

Chris looked sadly at Margo and shook his head.

"What are we going to do?"

"I have no idea, Margo. I'm terrified. How did Sam ever talk us into this?"

"How indeed?"

Chapter 49

The Invalid

BRETT PUT HIS EMPTY BEER BOTTLE on the kitchen counter and burped. Then, he approached the love seat where Margo sat with Chris. At that same moment, Odette came out of the room and closed the door behind her.

"Sam's not going anywhere," she said. "He's in really bad shape. I've done everything I could, but it won't be enough to save him. What he needs is a good hospital with real doctors."

"Then it's decided," Brett said defiantly. "We go on without him. We'll have us a nice shootout and bag us some kidnappers." The others in the kitchen laughed loudly at this, and Margo cringed.

"I better go tell him good-bye then." She got up from the loveseat with a heavy heart. Her knees were wobbly. Sam was going to die. She was going to lose another loved one like she had lost Jenny and her mom.

She pushed the bedroom open and entered the quiet room. It was as hot as an oven in there although the windows were open. The breeze made the sheer curtains billow and blew in an aroma of salty, mildewy, fishy swamp smell. But above that was the more pleasant, more pungent one of herbs, and the scary one of a very sick man.

She approached the bed. It was a roughly made wooden double bed under which a large colorful tribal rug contrasted in color with the deep red blanked that covered Sam to his neck. On a night table to the side, a primitive candelabra with three lighted candles tried—and failed—to make the room less dark. Next to it, a collection of pots with salves and bottles of painkillers juggled for space with a jug of water and an empty glass.

Margo hesitated by the bed, hating to bother Sam in his sleep. The room was dark, and the bed almost not big enough for him. In one corner, an armchair was covered with discarded clothes and a backpack. Sam's things. The rest of the room was messy. That angry woman in the kitchen didn't like to clean house.

There was a small aluminum foldable chair next to the bed, and Margo sat down. A naked Sam lay under the red blanket, covered to his neck with bandages. He opened his eyes weakly and frowned.

"Is that you, Margo?"

"Yes. Me. How are you, Sam?"

"I'm not sure. There's not much pain. Odette gave me enough medicine to put down an elephant."

"But you feel okay?"

"I have no plans to die if that's what's worrying you."

"We should have never come. The others are saying that they will go on without you. They're looking forward to shooting the kidnappers. And I'm terrified that it will all turn into a bloodbath."

Sam's burning hot hand grabbed hers and squeezed. "We're in too deep to quit now, Margo. I could tell you to stay here with me, to go back to Half Moon Bay with me, but I know Odette won't back down, and she won't be safe as the only woman, not even with Chris protecting her."

"But I'm scared."

"Then don't go. Stay. You should have that choice."

"Oh, Sam." Her voice came out small and vulnerable. She gave it some thought, but she already knew what her answer would be. Like the man who runs to the burning car to save someone at the cost of his or her own life, she would stay with Odette.

"I have to go," she finally told him. "My conscience allows me no choice." She sighed.

"Be brave, young Margo. You'll do fine. You won't be harmed. I can tell everyone respects you. They will protect you. And think about all the people whose life depends on this."

"I'll do my best," she sniffled.

"And if I don't come out of this alive, I want you to do me a favor."

"Don't talk like that, Sam."

"Just listen. Tell Saffron that I saw her."

"Tell Saffron?"

"Yes. Tell her I saw her the night of the murder. She was in the alley with some other man."

Margo nodded but didn't know what to say.

"Tell her." Sam looked toward the window.

"What, Sam?"

"Tell her I was so disappointed." Sam closed his eyes. He seemed to have fallen asleep. Margo let go of Sam's hand and got up carefully from the foldable aluminum chair.

When she got to the door, she looked back at Sam, already sleeping quietly in the dark hot room, and tried to imagine a life without him. Then it dawned on her that Sam was in love with Saffron. Was it possible? It sure explained his moodiness of the last couple of weeks. Sam had seen Saffron with another man. And now, he was going to die without ever seeing her again.

She sighed sadly and closed the door behind her. The others were already at the door, chomping at the bit, their backpacks on, their guns on their shoulders. To one side, Odette stood looking out of place, small, scared, young like her, holding her stuff, looking like she wished she was somewhere else. She gave Margo a huge smile when she saw her.

"I thought you had changed your mind to stay behind with Sam."

"No way. I promised Sam to keep an eye on you."

Somebody said, on va, and someone else answered, oui oui, on va, and everyone headed out. Armentor and the dog told them good-bye at the door. The angry woman—Mona—was nowhere to be seen.

Chapter 50

The Forest Lands

THERE WAS A TRAIL, LEADING AWAY FROM THE MARSHES. Within a half-hour, they had left behind the bald cypress trees, with their easily identifiable buttressed trunks, knobby knees, and aptitude for growing with their bases submerged.

The trail they followed was sort of narrow, covered in pebbles at times, and just weeds at others, and at the rate that the vegetation was growing after the heavy rains, would probably disappear soon thereafter.

Without a canopy cover, the sun was brutally hot overhead, and everyone quickly put their hats on. The puddles around them were evaporating fast, making the air more humid and unpleasant. And without the canopy cover, there was no chattering of wildlife either.

They stayed on the trail for a good while. Brett walked ahead with Josh and the young policeman—who finally Margo learned was called Mike—and Odette, Chris and herself, behind them.

Nobody said it, but Margo—who loved Agatha Christie books to pieces—did think it. And then, there were six, she told herself. She had to wonder if they were going to lose another person. And if they did, who would be next?

Brett had Sam's map in his hand, and before they entered the majestic line of pine trees ahead, he stopped to consulted with Josh. Once in agreement, Brett and Josh began to walk, and the rest of them followed.

After they entered forest lands, the tree fronds—because they grew so closely together—shut out most of the sunlight. It was kind of a pleasant change after the burning sun, despite the oppressive heat which refused to abate.

Margo took her hat off. She admired the gigantic Loblolly pine trees, whose tops seemed to reach the sky. Loblolly pines, with 22 billion base pairs—she remembered—have the largest sequenced genome size, seven times larger than that of humans. And there was plenty of twittering here, as the forest critters complained about being disturbed by them—the intruders. Groups of birds took flight, and clouds of mosquitoes fluttered over their puddles of water, their breeding grounds. Not that Margo cared anymore. That big clump of Sweetgrass she was carrying made her persona non grata in their eyes.

"Watch your feet. Don't step on a snake," she heard Brett bellow. An avalanche of forest creatures answered his voice with an angry chatter, and she could have sworn that she saw monkeys jumping from one branch to the other. The people from Wildlife and Fisheries had assured her a while back that there were no monkeys in Louisiana, but they couldn't say no for sure. "After all," they had told her, "people buy them as pets, realize they aren't meant to be domesticated, and turn them into the wild." There. For all she knew, there could be literally any number of communities of monkeys in south Louisiana where boy monkeys met girl monkeys and made baby monkeys. So yes, those furry things jumping from branch to branch, had to be monkeys. Margo grinned at the thought.

Soon, she realized that she was lagging behind the others. She could barely see them ahead. Her legs were sore, her feet were begging her to stop, and it was just so very hot. It was so humid that the leaves of the trees were dripping real drops, as if it had been raining.

She hurried on and caught up with the others. Odette and Chris were sharing stories about the strange things they had seen in the swamps and the forest lands of Louisiana, seemingly trying to outdo each other.

"My cousin Deppy was driving to Baton Rouge with a friend," Odette said. "So, they see this stray goat lying along the side of the road. It looks hurt, and Deppy has a really soft heart for animals, so he stops. And the friend starts complaining. 'You can't stop man, it's gonna kill us.' But, Deppy, well he never listens, so he stops anyway. They both jump out of the car to check on the goat. It looks like it's in really bad shape. But at that moment, Deppy sees this huge, monstrous-looking grunch that jumps out of the bushes and runs at them. Well, Deppy knows how to run, so he gets to the car in no time. But when he turns around to check on his friend, he sees it's too late. The creature has torn his friend apart and is sucking the blood out of his leg. So, my mom always says—wagging her finger—that the next time you see a stray goat wandering by the side of the road, keep going. There may be a grunch nearby, just waiting for the next foolish person to get out of the car.

"Good one, Odette, not that I believe a word of it."

"Seriously? How about the Rougarou?"

"Why should I believe in a creature that's half man, half wolf? My mom wagged her finger at me plenty as well, warning me to behave myself or else the Rougarou would come and get me and drink my blood, but I behaved badly plenty of times, and I never saw it, your Rougarou."

"In that case, never chase the Fifolet. If you ever get lost in the bayous or the swamps at night and see something at the corner of your eye, like groups of mysterious glowing lights that seem to be showing you the way to safety, don't follow them. They are not there to help you. They are evil spirits who want to misdirect and confuse. They lead their unsuspecting victims through mysterious parts of the swamp so that they will never be able to find their way back home again. So, don't ever follow the Fifolet, because you might discover that legends are sometimes true." Odette and Chris looked at each other and laughed.

Meantime, they had reached a clearing, and Brett stopped and threw his gear on the ground.

"Fifteen minutes," he bellowed with his deep, booming voice. "Good place to relieve yourselves. Girls, don't go alone. Stay together."

Chapter 51

Another One

FIFTEEN MINUTES LATER, they had all taken care of business and were sitting on fallen logs or rocks, resting.

"Time's up," said Brett, the self-appointed leader.

"Josh isn't back yet," Mike—the young policeman—told him.

"What do you mean, 'he isn't back'?"

"He went to relieve himself, and he never came back."

"That's not good. Come with me, Mike, let's go find him. Chris, stay with the girls. Be ready to defend them."

Margo huddled closer to Odette as her heart started beating treacherously in fear. Odette's eyes were big with anxiety. What if the men never came back? Margo decided that if they were not back in 15 minutes, she would start retracing her steps. Even though a cloud cover had partially obscured the sun, it was still early.

She looked up at the sky. Those were not rain clouds, anyway, just plain clouds. She was going to wait for 15 minutes. She could easily make it back to Armentor's house—and hopefully Sam—before nightfall. After all, they had been following just the one well-marked path. No way would she get lost. And if Odette and Chris wanted to come with, that would be great. If not, they could very well stay behind and make the exchange themselves.

She didn't know which, but one of those backpacks had the ransom money. And of course, neither Sam nor anyone else had bothered to share their plans with her, so whatever. She looked at her watch. 10 more minutes, and she would be out of there.

For lack of anything else to do, Margo stared at her watch getting more and more worried as the seconds ticked on. She could hear Brett and

Mike yelling for the parrain, but no voice answered them back. As the men's voices vanished into the overgrown vegetation, Margo started gathering her stuff together, getting ready to head back.

"Where are you going?" Odette asked her.

"Where do you think? If Brett and Mike aren't back within the next few minutes, I plan to get back to Armentor's house."

"They will be back."

"We'll see."

Margo watched the ticking second hand as it went around and around. "I've had enough," she said, finally. "I would prefer to get there before it gets dark. Good-bye, you two."

"Wait, Margo. Wait. They're coming, look!"

Margo turned around and watched the big, burly Brett step out into the clearing, followed by a sweating, exhausted-looking Mike.

"Josh is gone," Brett said. "We looked everywhere."

"Could something have happened to him? Could he be hurt?"

"That forest is dense. If he wandered off too far and got hurt, and he's not answering, how are we going to find him?"

"What are we going to do?" Odette asked. Her voice was shaking with stress. Chris put an arm around her shoulder, but she pushed him away. "Maybe we should all go back."

"We don't go back," Brett said with his gruff voice. We stick together. We complete the mission."

Brett never said another word. He didn't have to. He sounded so bossy that everyone just did as he said. They gathered their gear, and they followed him. No more questions asked.

Chapter 52

We Continue

ODETTE WAS PALE. She must be terrified. She was going to be the one to hand over the money. To walk into the trap. From where Margo was standing, it seemed like Odette was going to trade her life for that of the Governor's wife. Like a lamb led to slaughter. And she wouldn't make it out alive.

The bile rose in Margo's throat. Brett and Mike were going to try to shoot the kidnappers. Those others were going to shoot back. How did Brett not know that? Then, the rest of them would become collateral damage. No telling who would remain standing. But then again, better dead than being captured alive, right? God, she was watching too many scary movies. Shoot-outs? Did that really happen, like in real life?

As she talked to herself, she remembered to better pray now, while there was still time. She thought about Father Armand. He would be so disappointed to find out that his prayers for their safety had fallen on deaf ears when the authorities found them all dead. Or would they become gator fodder? Would the gators drag them underwater to feed their young? Or would they never be found until they had all turned to dust under the sweltering sun?

She prayed and prayed for a while, and she continued talking to herself, kicking pebbles or watching squirrels, already feeling the end of her life coming nigh. And then, Brett announced one more mile, and she knew that the time had come to meet her maker.

Chapter 53

Confrontation

SHE HEARD THEM BEFORE SHE SAW THEM. Voices, carried by the wind, and her heart did a somersault. This was it. Somewhere in that clearing ahead, they would all live or die.

They reached the end of the trail, and Margo turned around wistfully to look at the last of the forest lands, at the frondous tree canopy behind her, the comforting chittering of birds and monkeys, and the sense of protection she had felt under them. It was way too late to regret any of it. There was no way but forward.

It was a big clearing. An enormous open circle of muddy, sandy soil encrusted with shells, and pebbles, and a random few strands of wild grasses that reached all the way to beyond the river that bisected the clearing in half. To her left, a tributary of the Mississippi—always that muddy chocolate color—flowed along at a steady pace, foaming and splashing against the piles of a rudimentary wooden bridge that crossed the narrowest expanse of the waters. Beyond the river, beyond the clearing, more trees. Trees everywhere you looked. And overhead, that bright, relentless sun.

It was a strange feeling, walking out of the forests and into the clear open space. It had seemed like days of travel had gone by in the penumbra of the wilderness, when it had barely been a few hours. She followed the others, hurrying to catch up to them, full of angst, and yet curious, as to how this was going to turn out.

A group of men and one woman were standing way ahead, waiting for the newcomers, and Margo immediately felt that the woman looked familiar. And so did the man standing next to her. But they were still pretty far, and they were standing in the shade.

The woman looked nervous. She paced a short distance, back and forth, back and forth, fanning herself with something white, perhaps a piece of paper. The man just stood there, watching her.

Earlier—numerous times—she had complained about the heat in the forest being stifling. But stepping out into the open was so much worse, just like stepping into a burning oven, and at first impact, it took your breath away, as if you had been slapped. And the sun—reflected in the water, and the sand around it—was so bright that she had to shield her eyes.

A dozen feet or so, to the right of the man and the woman waiting for them, a woman and a child were tied to each other, sitting on a blanket under a tree at the edge of the clearing. The woman seemed to become very agitated when she saw the newcomers, but they had put tape around her mouth, so no sound came from her. The child too had been muzzled with a tape, Margo thought, although she wasn't sure. It was hard to see that far away. What was not hard to see was that they were being guarded by armed men.

Margo had no idea how these kidnapping exchanges worked. Maybe none of them really did. Brett lifted his hand and told them stay and walked over to the woman who seemed to be the one in charge.

She couldn't hear what was being said, but the voices were getting louder. They were arguing. That was obvious. The men guarding the prisoners left their charges and walked over to where the argument seemed to be getting nastier. At an order from the woman, they approached quickly, pulled their weapons off their shoulders, and adopted a menacing stand.

Meantime, Chris and Odette waited—fear written all over their faces—and Margo, right behind them, watched. Then, she looked around and realized that they were alone. Where was Mike? He had just been standing right there with them. And now, he too was gone. Oh, God, Mike missing. Mike and his gun. Did he run away? Was it just them now against these people?

Then, the woman, and the man standing next to her, stepped into a puddle of sunshine, and she recognized them. Melba Gaines, and André

Daigle. What were they doing here? Her brain scrambled to understand how that was possible. Melba Gaines, the elegant, slender, well-dressed manager of the Gallery. Almost as tall as Brett, and with that nasty rifle in her hands, almost as threatening.

"That's Melba," Odette whispered. "That's Vinnie's cousin. The one that inherits everything, or so she says."

"Yes, I recognized her from the photographs. And he's André Daigle."

"Yes. They're in it together. Quel surprise! I knew I couldn't trust her. And that sanctimonious, quiet, innocent-looking André Daigle, silent partner my foot. His dad was the original partner, you know, really good friends with Vinnie. The guy died under mysterious circumstances. Who knows, maybe his greedy kids killed him. Anyhow, Vinnie took André on as a pity project, because he was so fond of the dad."

"And now here he is with Melba, helping to ensure that the business of the forgeries continues."

"Yes, but they will not get another piece from the Two Crows site. They will have to go over my dead body."

"Shut up, girls," Chris waved at them to be quiet. "I can't hear a word."

Meantime, Brett and Melba had come to some agreement, because Brett beckoned them to come forward. Like scared rabbits, they started walking toward the others. The Governor's wife was trying to warn them as she kept shaking her head. But what was she trying to say? And what could they have done anyway but follow instructions?

They walked somberly toward Brett. They were directed to unburden themselves of their equipment, so they put all their backpacks together in a pile in front of Melba and André.

Meantime, another man walked out from behind a tree. His gloomy appearance startled Margo. She had to blink twice to realize she was not mistaken. It was the famous James Lee Reeshard, sculptor, painter, and maker of fake tribal pottery.

Instantly she understood what Odette had told her about this strange creature. Tall, gaunt, eccentric-looking, wearing all black in this impossible heat, but now, Margo also noticed the glint of cruelty in those dead eyes. Was it really Melba running the show? Or was it this strange man—whose greed must have known no bounds—who had arranged for this little afternoon event that was going to get them all killed, except of course for Odette—who would continue delivering him the goods for the sake of the safety of her people—and Chris, who by now it was obvious, would do anything to protect Odette?

They were at an impasse. Nobody moved, but the tension was there. The men working for Melba and André stood by, watching closely, holding their guns against their chest. Nobody had read the script for this charade, except that Margo knew, or at least suspected, that this type of situation rarely ended well. It was—after all—just the four of them against all these murderous hoods.

Then, James Lee Reeshard, obviously knowing what he wanted, walked over to the backpacks with the two tough-looking guys wearing camouflage and nasty guns that he had shown up with, and ordered them to find him the ransom money.

Deep down, Margo knew it already. Her instincts were screaming that this wasn't going to work out. Still, she braced herself as she watched them. The guys rummaged and rummaged and spilled all their belonging on the floor. There were bottles of water, and protein bars, and sweaters, and everything else they had packed for this trip. But none of the bags had the money.

Margo realized that she had been holding her breath. Melba, André, and Reeshard looked at each other and then at the pile of empty bags. The goons stood at attention, with their guns ready to shoot, and it was as if time had stopped for a few seconds. But then, Reeshard raised his arms to the sky with clenched fists, and suddenly, the silence exploded when he burst into screams of fury.

What was going to happen next? What were Margo, Odette, Chris, and the cousin supposed to do? They were about to get shot by these madmen. There was no backup plan. Heck, there was no plan at all. Never in a million years would Margo have thought that they were going to get stranded without the ransom money. Whatever scheme Sam had originally had, was of no importance anymore because, without Sam, nobody knew what to do. She looked at Chris and Odette. There was as much panic in their eyes as there was in her heart.

Then, James Lee Reeshard burst into a hysterical rage, screaming angrily at the world, at the guards, at his accomplices, at his prisoners. His face was red, and his whole body trembled with fury. His shaking fists threatened everyone with torture and death. The money wasn't there. But he was going to get it, one way or the other.

Reeshard's sudden explosion of rage awakened the animosity in everyone. The very thin veneer of civility that had kept the catastrophe at bay, fell away. Suddenly, everyone was pointing their weapons at each other. Even Chris. The birds and the squirrels—that had been so noisy just minutes before—had fallen silent. The expectation was so thick that you could have cut it with a knife. And Reeshard, who seemed to have gone mad, yelled, get that woman over here, pointing at Odette.

His two men—who looked more like angry gorillas than people— headed menacingly toward her, pointing their weapons at her, but Odette refused to comply. She took a step backward, and then another one. She never hesitated. It was obvious that she wasn't going to allow herself to be taken without a fight.

As Reeshard's men left his side and headed with raised guns toward where Odette was standing, Margo noticed that the girl's objective was the bridge. Surely, that was madness. She would never make it across without being gunned down. These people were out of control and out for blood. Yet, Odette kept taking cautious steps toward the narrow wooden structure, looking terrified. Her eyes, huge with terror, darted back and forth as she retreated. But she kept on going. Margo inhaled sharply, amazed at how brave but reckless the girl was. She was going to get herself killed.

The kidnappers must have not expected this move. André, Melba, and Reeshard, all turned toward Odette, and, for a few seconds, nobody reacted. It was as if the movie had been paused. And Margo watched everyone as they watched Odette, taking her careful steps backward, getting closer and closer to the bridge. But then, the tension was broken, and Melba finally reacted and ordered her men to stop.

But Odette didn't. She had obviously made up her mind. She had reached the bridge and yelled back.

"You're not going to take me alive," she screamed as she kept walking backward, never taking her eyes off Reeshard, who seemed to be in the throes of an epileptic fit.

"Stop that woman, someone," Reeshard kept yelling, pointing at Odette.

"You're going to have to shoot me. Because I'm not coming."

"Wait," André Daigle finally spoke. "We need her, Reeshard. Be realistic. You can't shoot her." He approached Reeshard and lifted a hand toward his chest, trying to reason with him. But Reeshard, in a vile mood, pushed him viciously against a tree trunk. "Leave it alone, you wuss. I give the orders around here."

"I beg to differ, Reeshard," Melba said, striding aggressively toward Reeshard, her men right behind her. She held her weapon like she knew how to use it, and it was dangerously close to the madman's face. "This is my operation. It has been from the start."

Margo watched the argument. It was intensifying. While they tried to decide with pushes and shoves who was the one in charge, Odette slowly approached the edge of the bridge. Then, she stepped on it.

At this moment, one and all finally realized that Odette was not bluffing. She was going to run for it, and they stopped arguing. All eyes turned on her.

"Where are you going, Odette?" Melba asked with a venomously cynical voice. "Surely you don't think we're going to let you escape."

"Well, you're not going to capture me alive either."

This went on back and forth for a few minutes as Odette stepped backward and they moved closer to her, trading threats and barbs. But then, Margo's eyes popped open when she saw stealthy movement to the right of the clearing. A couple of men—taking advantage of the commotion by the bridge—appeared from behind the shrubbery, crouching toward the Governor's wife.

The poor woman turned around startled when she saw the strangers, but it stunned Margo as well, because—and of course she could barely believe it—one of the rescuers was the spitting image of old Armentor, down to the stoop and everything. The other man had painted his face black, and she didn't recognize him.

Within a matter of seconds almost, the Governor's wife and kid had been cut loose, and, helped by the two men, had vanished into the forest without a sound. And amazingly, nobody had even noticed.

Margo sighed with relief and turned back toward Odette, who in the meantime had now walked further on and had reached the middle of the bridge. She was as good as trapped. On the one side, these murderous thugs with raised weapons, ready to fire, and on the other side, the unending wilderness, where she would not survive very long on her own.

It would be impossible to escape. Melba was right. There was no way they would let Odette go. They did need her alive, but nerves were so raw, so much on edge, that with the slightest provocation, any one of them could squeeze that trigger. Especially Reeshard, who looked unhinged and completely out of control. But—at least for the moment—they were at an impasse. Everyone stood still, on the alert, and time slowed down. Margo—aware that the quiet could not last forever—desperately wanted to help the young woman get away. She thought about screaming or causing some kind of distraction, to give Odette time to escape, but even if she managed to do so without getting shot, those men would pursue her relentlessly, and not rest until they had captured the poor girl, dead or alive.

She was thinking of all this—weighing her options—as the seconds ticked by when a dog appeared out of nowhere and crossed the clearing, barking its head off as if someone had lit its tail on fire.

And at that moment, the spell was shattered and all hell broke loose. The kidnappers looked at each other, baffled, and one of the muscles started shooting at the dog. Margo held her breath and closed her eyes, not wanting to see the dog's blood being shed, but when she opened them again, she saw the dog far away, safely running into the bushes.

But that just made Reeshard more furious. He was foaming at the mouth with frustration. "I've had enough of this nonsense," he yelled at the two gunmen and pointed at Odette. "Shoot her."

Both André and Melba got in front of him with their hands raised, trying to stop him, trying to reason with him. But Reeshard just shook his head angrily from side to side and pushed them away. "I want her dead. I want her dead," he just kept bellowing, shaking with anger.

Things were getting out of control. Someone had rescued the Governor's wife and kid. Why were they not helping now? Had they left? Had they abandoned Odette, Chris, and her, to their fate? Were they to be collateral damage? And where was Brett, anyway? She whipped her head from side to side looking for him in the mêlée but found not a trace of Sam's cousin. Had the coward abandoned them as well and run away? Well, somebody had to do something to save Odette from these ruffians. She was not going to let them hurt her. She thought about the man willing to die when he runs to the burning car to rescue someone and knew that she would never be able to live like a coward.

On impulse, she started running toward them, waving her arms at the kidnappers. "Stop, please don't hurt her," she begged. She reached the bridge and stepped on it, standing between the kidnappers and Odette. Melba and André seemed hesitant. Maybe they were not really killers at heart, but not Reeshard. That nasty glint in his eyes said it all. He was a psychopath. There would be no reasoning with him. He would shoot her at the drop of a hat and never regret it.

Margo looked desperately at Odette, who was just a few steps behind her. Odette was climbing over the railings.

"No, Odette, get back. What are you trying to do?"

"I can't let them capture me."

"Please don't jump, Odette. You're not going to make it. The alligators will get you, or the snakes will, or you'll drown."

"I'm sorry. I have to do this. Thank you for being my friend." She looked at Margo sadly and gave her a small wave and a smile.

"Wait, Odette. Please wait," she yelled, as her head snapped back and forth between the girl and the kidnappers, trying to think fast but unable to come up with a solution.

Meantime, Reeshard kept screaming. "Shoot her, shoot her."

And over the madman's screams, André kept yelling, "You can't kill her. We need her alive." And the world seemed to have lost all sense of reality, and then one of the guns went off. Margo stood her ground on the bridge, raising her arms, trying to protect Odette from the bullets, begging everyone to please calm down.

But it was too late. Odette was hurt. Margo watched Odette double over in pain and grab her stomach. On, no, she thought, not the stomach. Odette was gasping with pain. She turned around to run toward Odette to help her, but she didn't get to her on time. She watched—horrified—as Odette, curled up like a baby, holding her stomach, slowly left the ledge of the bridge and disappeared from her view. She heard the splash, and then nothing else.

Everyone was dismayed. They looked at each other like, what now? But it was Chris who reacted immediately. He screamed a terrible nooo and ran to the bridge. He ran to the ledge where Odette had vanished and leaned over it. "Where is she?" he kept asking. "I can't see her."

Margo bent over the bridge. "I can't see her either." She turned toward the kidnappers angrily and accused them, crying, tears running down her face. "Look what you've done. You've killed her."

"I can't see her, Margo. I have to do something. Maybe I can still find her. I'm a good swimmer." Chris put his gun down on the wooden plank and climbed over the ledge as Odette had before.

"Wait, what are you trying to do? You're not going after her, are you? It's too high, and the water is too fast. You'll never find her, and you'll drown." She grabbed Chris's arm to hold him back, but he pulled away gently. Then, he jumped over, headfirst into the water. And that was that. The spot where he had gone in stirred for a couple of seconds in ever-increasing ripples, but then, all trace of Odette and Chris was gone.

Margo began to tremble, horrified. It wasn't possible. How had everything gone so wrong? She looked accusingly at the kidnappers.

"Look what you've done," she told them, feeling the shock of losing two friends within minutes of each other. She tried to walk back toward the clearing—hanging on to the bridge's railing—but her knees were weak and barely held her up. She couldn't believe it. "How could you?" she cried at the kidnappers, shaking with anger and bitterness. "You killed my friends." And now she was all alone. "You killed my friends."

She walked sobbing, trembling with the shock, holding on to the railing, not caring any longer about anything. She couldn't do this any longer. It was too much. And it wasn't even over. The bastards were still shooting. They could all shoot each other dead, for all she cared.

With eyes full of tears and bitterness, she watched Reeshard, still screaming like a madman. Somehow, bullets kept whizzing by right and left, but she wasn't afraid anymore. She was done caring.

She felt a burning fire in her leg, and she wondered if she'd been shot. But it didn't hurt too much. Just keep going, she told herself. Get out of their way. Let them kill each other. All she had to do was curl up in a quiet spot in the forest and get some sleep. And then, everything would be fine.

From the corner of her eye, she watched with a lack of interest how people ran to the railing where Odette and Chris had gone over. But what was the point? She knew they were dead. They didn't even surface. They were simply swept away. That was a deep and angry river. Maybe days or weeks would go by before anyone found their bodies. But maybe they would never be found. The Governor got his wife and kid back, but Odette and Chris paid for this privilege with their own lives. And she had stood by and done nothing to save them. Her leg was burning. She needed a quiet spot to lie down.

She could still hear them talking loudly, nervously.

"Where are they?"

"They've been carried away. Look, the current is strong."

And then Reeshard's nasal, pretentious voice. "You two, jump into the water. Look for them."

And the muscles complaining.

"It's pointless, Mr. Reeshard. They're not there. They're dead."

"We'll never find them, Mr. Reeshard. They'll be swept into the sea."

As if in a rêverie, Margo managed to get to the end of the bridge. But without rails to hang on to, it was getting harder to stay upright any longer. The leg was really hurting now. She needed to rest. But the world was swimming around her. Something was wrong. The ground wasn't there anymore. She needed to lie down, she was falling, and she put her arms out to cushion the fall. Was she dying?

"It's over, Reeshard," she heard Sam telling him. She must be dying already. She thought it was Sam's voice. She opened her eyes a crack and saw Brooks looking down at her with his worried face.

"Am I dying?" Margo asked.

"No, you're not. You passed out for a few seconds. But not to worry. These guys are going to take you straight to the hospital. They'll take care of that bullet in your leg."

"Was that Sam I heard? I thought he was dead."

"Sam dead?" Brooks chuckled. "Never. Sam's going to outlive us all."

A heavily armed group of men with rifles appeared out of the bushes and began rounding up the group of kidnappers. Margo watched them for a few minutes.

"Odette and Chris are dead," she told Brooks, and a couple of tears ran down her face.

"I heard. I'm so sorry. And now, I must go."

"Don't leave me please," she grabbed Brooks by the sleeve and tried to hang on, but he gently detached her fingers and got up.

"Sam and I have unfinished business. But I promise that I won't be long."

Chapter 54

In Pursuit

"THEY WENT THAT WAY," Brooks said, pointing toward the shrubbery. And Sam followed, too tired to question, or almost to even care. Still nursing his barely-healed wounds, every step was becoming an agony, and it was only the sense of duty and the desire to punish the bastards that kept him going.

The vegetation was becoming denser and deeper the further they advanced. Tight clumps of bamboo, and other wild shrubberies that had to be chopped down, and the slippery, muddy, rotting leaves under their feet, made for miserable progress. Moisture ran mercilessly down Sam's face and back. The air was so humid that he could barely breathe. He kept wiping his face with his shirt sleeves, but, by now, they so wet that they provided no relief.

It was late in the day too, and the sun was about to set. Already the clouds on the horizon were turning pink and yellow, but even though the breeze was somewhat cooler, nighttime also heralded the arrival of the bugs, especially the mosquitos, the enormous, relentless, blood-thirsty mosquitos that there was no getting rid of.

They had been following the tracks for at least two hours, yet they were no closer to having any idea which way Reeshard and his goons were heading. North. That's all they knew. North, where there was nothing but wilderness. No towns, no settlements—at least as far as they knew—just trees. More trees.

"I wish they had stayed on the path."

Brooks laughed. "That would have been too easy."

Sam was exhausted. They had been going all day. First, the rescue of the Governor's wife and kid, and now, pursuing the counterfeiter and his thugs. He looked at Brooks and marveled at what difference ten years made. Brooks, in his late twenties, early thirties, was still as fresh as an oyster, even enjoying the adventure, whereas, he—Sam—could already barely put one foot in front of the other.

The moon finally came up, and it reflected its full, shining glory in the dark and quiet waters of the narrow strip of river that they were following. And with the moon, the forest land came alive with evening sounds. But with the night also came darkness, and Sam had no idea how on earth Brooks could see which way to go. Because, except for a broken twig here, or a partial footstep there, there was barely a sign that the fugitives had actually been there, and now, as the evening sky got darker and darker, those tracks would become even harder to follow.

"Why on earth are they heading further North when there's nothing there?" Sam asked.

"They must have a hideaway, or they're meeting someone. They're proceeding pretty systematically. If they were simply escaping blindly from us, they would have headed in the opposite direction, toward the populated areas. I have a feeling that they have a setup somewhere North of here."

"I guess they know that without a plan, they're heading toward certain death, just like we are. I feel like I'm going to meet my demise in these swamps. I wish we could turn back. All this seems so pointless."

"At least we captured Melba Gaines and André Daigle," Brook said cheerfully.

"Oh, yes. Cold comfort."

"You sound gloomy today, Sam. Still not back to normal?"

"No, not quite. The infection is gone, but the wounds still hurt."

"They will continue hurting until the stitches are out."

"Yeah, I'm sure."

The two men fell quiet and walked on. Sam listened to the pleasing sounds of nature, the frogs croaking, the crickets chirping, the fronds of trees and bushes rustling in the cooling breeze. Occasionally, though, he heard something that alarmed him and he shivered. That gator that nearly killed him was never far from his mind. He wondered if the feeling would remain with him for the rest of his life.

"You tired, Sam?"

"I could use a rest, yes."

The asphyxiating daytime heat had finally cooled down to a pleasant temperature, and Sam breathed in the fresh, salty, mildewy air with relief. Brooks opened his canteen and took a swig of something that made him grunt with joy. Then he passed it to Sam, who sniffed it first, and, recognizing the sweet smell of rum, he gulped from it like a man needing a lifeline. He felt better.

Brooks lighted a cigarette and leaned against a tree trunk. He inhaled happily.

"Does Margo know you smoke?"

"Heck, no. She would probably fire me." He laughed. Brooks had a pleasant laughter that made Sam smile. Fearing unseen creepy-crawlers, he had no desire to lean against a tree trunk, so he put his aching body down on a flat rock. He sighed.

"Tell me, Sam," Brooks said after a while. "Are you ever going to tell her the truth?"

"No. You know I can't. If she ever found out that I brought her along because of her sweet nature, because her compassion and kindness at the death of her friends would convince those gangsters that Odette and Chris had truly died, she would never forgive me. Never, ever."

"Poor kid. She was really heartbroken. So, she'll never know that they are safe."

"No. Nobody else needs to know, but you and I. It's best this way. But I still can't believe that we pulled it off. It was such an impossible plan."

"Yeah. And now I have to wonder if we'll pull this next one off. It sounds just as impossible. If they're meeting up with more thugs, it'll be just the two of us against God only knows how many."

"It will work out somehow. If they're escaping blind, they will eventually hit a river or a swamp, and they'll be stuck. We have rations for days and those Life Straws that turn dirty water into drinking water. But, them, what do they have?"

"Not much. I saw them take off. No backpacks, no nothing. Just their rifles."

"There you go. Don't worry, Sam. We'll get them."

Brooks dropped his cigarette butt on the ground and extinguished it with the heel of his boot.

"We're lucky to have a full moon tonight, and no clouds."

"I can barely see my own hands, though, much less which way to go."

Brooks laughed. "Not to worry. Just follow me." He extended a hand and helped Sam get up. Then he showed him a faint set of footprints.

"They went this way."

This worried Sam. "Aren't we heading toward the land of the gator's ghost?"

"Which one?"

"The one that appears from time to time to drag away people's pets and children? Many have gone to hunt it down, but none have come back."

"Do you believe in urban legends, Sam?"

"I don't know. Let's just say that I respect them. After what happened to me, I must confess that I'm scared of them. I would rather not have another encounter if you know what I mean."

Brooks nodded. "You're not alone, though. There's two of us."

Chapter 55

Haunted Lands

THE FOREST WAS ALMOST IMPENETRABLE, and the darkness didn't make it any easier to traverse it. Puddles of muddy water alternated with slippery, rotting leaves, and thick, fallen branches. Clouds of insects hounded them without mercy. And more than once, moss hanging from trees, limp like the hair of a dead woman, startled Sam to such a state of terror that he had to bite his tongue not to scream. The forest lands at night were the haunted lands of the living dead, the ghosts of the ancestors, the snakes and alligators, and poisonous spiders the size of a man's hand. He was grateful to not be doing this alone.

Sometime before midnight, they left the thickest part of the forest and they approached an area of such stench that it made them retch. Sam directed his flashlight into the tree fronds. In the play of light and darkness under the ghostly light, shapes came in and out of Sam's view. The stench seemed to get worse as they went.

"Let's get out of here. It reeks."

"No, Sam. We can't. The men came this way. Look at the footprints. One pair fancy shoes, two pairs army issue, different sizes."

"Where is the stench coming from?"

"I think there," Brooks pointed. "Look. Alligator skins." Lines of alligator hides had been hung everywhere from the trees. Some were larger, some were smaller. They looked like the sacrificial victims of some murderous madman, their cadavers hung up in the branches to terrify trespassers. The unbearable reek of death made Sam gag. Never had he contemplated such disgusting horror in his sheltered city life. He quickly averted his eyes, refusing to think about the suffering the poor creatures must have been subjected to.

"There must be people living close by."

"Not too close, I'd say. Who can live with this stench?"

"You get used to it, I suppose. Traders pay a lot of money for alligator skins. Years ago, it was like $40 per foot, back when that was real money. Even if the price fluctuates according to demand, you can make a good living with working just one or two months a year."

"How do you know this?"

"I used to have a friend in the fur business."

They reached the edge of the tree line and found themselves in a clearing of deep, mysterious darkness. But then, the massive, thick clouds that had been covering the skydome quickly dissipated and vanished, leaving a huge, enormous moon suspended above them, almost close enough to stretch your arm out and touch it. Sam gasped. Shapes on the moon, its seas, and mountains were clearly visible on the bright and translucent orb. And the sky behind it was full of milliards and milliards of stars, and Sam felt humbled by this vast, infinite universe.

They had reached the end of the road. In front of them, an immense sea of fluorescent green mossy water spread as far as the eyes could see. The air was finally clean of the foul-smelling miasma of the alligator pelts, and Sam stood for a second, breathing in the swampy fresh air carried by the cool evening breeze.

"What now?" He asked. "We don't have a boat."

"Neither do they. We'll follow the footsteps. They turn here, look, and disappear into the shrubs."

"What's that?" Sam asked and pointed to the far side of the horizon. "Looks like smoke."

Sam lifted his Sightmark Ghost-Hunter night-vision binoculars. "I see what could be the roof of a house. Not sure, though. I need to get a little closer."

Brooks was watching too, through his night-vision monocular. "Must be where they're going."

"Yeah. But, there's only one way to find out."

They followed the tracks. This close to the water, the soil around it was always moist, always willing to keep footprints, at least until the baking sun dried them again the next day. These were new. Fresh in the moist, swampy mud.

They never took their eyes off the smoke. It was obvious by now that the tracks were heading in the same direction. The column of smoke rose high up toward the sky, smudging with its quickly spreading black smoke the pristine dark blue sky.

As they got closer, Sam saw through his binoculars that he had been right. He could clearly distinguish an enormous structure with front columns that look like a big house, and a chain of people—scurrying like ants—passing to each other buckets of water that they were filling from the greenish swamp. And yes, he had been right about that as well. There was a fire. But it wasn't the big house that was burning. Numerous one-story buildings were clearly visible behind the main house. It was one of these outhouses that was being consumed by the voracious flames.

The main house was safe, at least for now. But the wind had picked up, and embers crackled and sprung from the fire and were carried away by the wind, landing—for the moment—on the wet, swampy soil. But what if the wind turned and began to blow toward the other building? It would become a conflagration.

He admired momentarily the big house. The size of an antebellum plantation home. What was such a graceful, elegant building doing out here in the middle of nowhere? This must have at one time been some ancient sugar or cotton plantation. The lands having been swallowed up by the swamps, only the big house remained. It was a beautiful thing too. Sam remembered Margo's love for old buildings and hoped the men would be able to stop the spread of the flames before they reached it.

They crept closer. Then, Brooks whispered loudly. "Careful. Watch where you step." Sam looked down and saw—to his horror—that a horde of alligators great and small was crawling in a hurry toward the swamp, ignoring him and Brooks, and disappearing into the mossy green liquid, escaping the smell of smoke, the danger of fire. The full moon shone on their oily, dark green hides as they submerged silently into the quiet waters.

Sam's heart began pounding loud and fast. So, was this the way it was going to be the rest of his life? He became dizzy with the stress. He remembered fighting the gator, running out of air, trying to escape, trying to stay alive. For a second the ground swam under him, and he broke out in a sweat. Brooks grabbed him and steadied him.

"It's okay, Sam. You just have a little PTSD. Just breathe deeply. Direct your brain to calm down and focus, and it will pass."

Sam nodded in the dark and got a grip on himself. He stepped out of the way of the fleeing beasts and followed Brooks toward the compound. He could now see them clearly, even without the binoculars. Reeshard and his goons, the man himself standing in front of the flames, directing the salvage operation.

"So, Reeshard runs an alligator farm."

"What on earth for? Isn't he already a successful artist?"

"Maybe it's just a side income. Or maybe it's a cover. Officially selling alligator hides, but delivering something extra under the table."

"True. But alligators are also a nice deterrent to trespassers. Better than vicious dogs. I can tell you from experience. Nobody would go and snoop on his business, not with alligators roaming the grounds freely like that."

"Let's go get him while he's still distracted."

"What about those men? How many are there?"

"At least seven."

"Should we shoot them all?"

"We might have no choice unless we can capture them one by one."

Hiding behind the bushes of the perimeter, they were now close enough to the men to grab one as he hurried to the water, but camouflaged enough to not be noticed. Reeshard seemed completely focused on the fire, his tall, lean frame outlined against the blaze, as he directed his men who were running back and forth from the building—braving the flames—to bring out boxes and equipment. Whatever was in those boxes had to be valuable enough to be worth their lives.

"That one. Let's grab him. He's heading for the water." As soon as one worker got close enough with his bucket, they grabbed him and pulled him into the bushes. The poor guy was about to scream, but Brooks put a hand over his mouth, and Sam showed him his badge.

"Listen to me. We don't have a quarrel with you or your friends. We just want Reeshard. This is a good time to decide whether you'll be on our side or his," he said, pointing toward Reeshard. "It will mean the difference between freedom and jail. Do we understand each other?"

The man nodded vigorously. He looked terrified. Brooks cautiously took his hand off the guy's mouth and ordered him not to scream. "Yes, yes," he said. "Don't hurt me. I just work here."

"Okay, so tell me. What's going on?"

"One of the ovens malfunctioned and caught fire. We didn't realize it until it was too late. And then the boss showed up. He said he was going to shoot us all unless we extinguished the fire."

"Do you live in the building?"

"No. There's a town like a 15-minute walk from here."

"How about the other guys? How many are there?"

"There's seven of us. We're all from the same town."

"So, they're your friends?"

"I guess."

"Loyal to Reeshard?"

"Heck, no. He's a bastard. We only work for him because, well, look around. How many jobs can you find in a place like this? And he pays well."

"Could you talk them into joining us?"

"I'll try. By the way, my name is Miguel. I'll be back."

Before they had time to discuss the plan, Miguel jumped up, grabbed his bucket, and filled it. Sam wondered if they had done the right thing by trusting this individual who could just as easily let Reeshard know that they were hiding nearby.

He watched closely as Miguel walked back toward the house, carrying his bucketful of water and encountered his soot-covered companions. He exchanged a few words with them as they approached him one by one. A couple of them nodded and stepped out of the water brigade line, but Sam watched as an argument unfolded with three of the other guys. They got louder and shook their heads, and suddenly, all seven of them were yelling and shoving each other. Miguel raised his arms and whistled. Basta, he yelled out and walked back in a hurry toward Sam and Brooks.

"That didn't go so well," Brooks said.

"No, it didn't. You better get ready to fight."

Meantime, the guys who decided to remain loyal to Miguel followed him. But the others dropped their buckets and took off running toward where Reeshard and his men were still watching helplessly the growing, expanding fire.

Sam stared at the smoke billowing in every direction. The flames had just jumped on to the next building, already licking greedily its nearest wall. He was about to ask Brooks, "What are we going to do now?" But what came out of his mouth was instead an "Oh, God." The three men who had decided to stand with Reeshard had reached the man. They were talking loudly, with big hand gestures, and they turned around once or twice and pointed to where Sam and Brooks were crouching behind the shrubbery with their new soot-covered friends.

"We can get there the back way. Follow me." Miguel and his buddies unbuckled short machetes from their toolbelts and proceeded to cut a path across the bushes.

Wild bamboo had grown so thickly by the edge of the swamp, that it kept them invisible. There was a path of sorts now, thanks to Miguel and his friends, but Sam and Brooks—being so much taller—kept getting hit in the face and chest by branches that hadn't been chopped down. Sam got a gash in his neck by one of them, and, from then on, he crouched. It hurt a lot less than being hit over and over again.

"So, Miguel," said Brooks. "We saw a bunch of gators heading for the water. What's up with that?"

"Didn't you know? This is an alligator farm. When the fire started, Garcia here opened the gates so they could escape. Garcia has a soft spot for them gators."

"What are you going to do now?"

"I have no idea, Sheriff. We just lost our jobs. And this is all we know how to do."

"Couldn't you run the farm yourselves?"

"What do you mean?"

"Well, do you essentially need Reeshard to run it?"

"I guess not. We did all the work."

"Could you recapture the gators and start over?"

"We could, I guess. The smaller ones aren't hard to grab."

"Brooks and I have rich friends. We'll send help. For your cooperation, you know?" Miguel nodded. His eyes became shiny and he smiled.

That was when the first bullet whizzed by them. Sam actually saw how it left a shiny, smoky, burning path as it headed for the trees behind him, passing right in front of his nose.

Chapter 56

Alligator Hunt

EVERYONE RETREATED INTO THE FOREST AND DUCKED. So, it was war, then. They turned their flashlights out and prepared their weapons by the green glow of the moonlight—at least what little of it managed to filter through the thick canopy above them. Without light, the forest became again that thing of mystery, with moving shadows, with slithering creatures, with giant spiders hanging from their webs, with shiny leaves and dark puddles of rotting vegetation.

Sam shivered. He was a city man. He had done his tour of duty, but never in a forest, or a jungle. He could do desert. This creeped the hell out of him.

He continued watching Reeshard as they got closer and closer by the back way. They moved in an arc, following the edge of the water, thankful that Miguel and Garcia and the other guys knew their way. Some of the ground was so soft that one foot closer to the water would have probably swallowed him in a sucking quagmire and never let him go.

Sam was surprised that all the men had pistols. Then, he realized that working with live gators required them to be equipped with all the weapons they could carry. Miguel, Garcia, and the other two stopped. They had arrived at the clearing behind the compound.

With the brilliant moonlight, and standing so close to the violently burning fire, the night was as bright as day. The two groups finally faced each other and shot to kill.

Everyone was distracted by trying to kill each other to stay alive. Meantime, Reeshard—like the true coward that he was—hurried toward the back, not quite disappearing behind the big house, but as far back and out of the path of the flying bullets as possible. Then, he hid behind a column and watched the shootout.

Sam elbowed Brooks and told him, "Let's go get him. He's alone," and they left Miguel, Garcia, and the others to keep on firing, and they slipped away.

There were no more branches, but the ground was slick with the rotting leaves, and Sam kept slipping. His whole body was in torment. If he ever survived this, he would take a month off, by God he would.

Brooks—on the other hand—alive with adrenaline, enjoying the adventure, pushed on cheerfully, a happy grin on his face. Whenever Sam slipped, Brooks quickly grabbed his arm and helped him up, and within minutes they were barely a handful of steps from Reeshard, who—still distracted by the fire, and now by the shootout—was looking in the other direction.

As if they had trained together, or had practiced the move ahead of time, Sam and Brooks pounced on Reeshard from the back. They had their prey. Screaming obscenities but handcuffed, tied safely to a tree, they let him be and looked around. All three workers that had decided to remain loyal to Reeshard, lay dead on the ground. But his two goons were still firing.

Sam and Brooks approached them, and Sam gave them the warning, raising his badge. But the two men were not impressed. They lifted their rifles and took aim. But Sam and Brooks were better than that. Before the two men could pull the trigger, they lay dead side by side. And that was that.

"Brooks, I have to rest, or else I'll drop dead like these two. Could you get the others and radio someone for help?"

"Sure thing. Just sit here."

Brooks slung his rifle on his shoulder and walked with ease on the edge of the swamp. Iridescent under the moonlight, the greenish water shone like a pool of diamonds, and Sam got lost in his thoughts as he rested. He was so tired that he would never be able to take another step.

He watched the fire, now dying off finally. The two buildings had burned to the ground. But the big house was fine. At some point, the breeze had stopped blowing the embers, and the fire fizzled out by itself and died.

He could vaguely hear Reeshard yelling. Boy, the man was angry. But that was over. Thank God it was over. Now, he just had to wait for Brooks to come back and let him drink some of that sweet rum in his canteen.

Sam relaxed more and more and almost fell asleep. Actually, he thought he was already dreaming when he saw an enormous white shadow saunter out of the forest and head toward where Brooks was leaning against a tree, smoking a cigarette.

Brooks—oblivious of the danger—looked happy, staring at the moon, and Sam told himself that he was dreaming. He willed the ghost of the approaching beast away, but it would not vanish.

Sam sat up, startled. Could it be? Could that really be the ancient alligator's ghost? The one that haunted the small towns of Northeast Louisiana? No, it couldn't be. He must be dreaming. And yet, there it was, slowly but surely meandering toward Brooks, who was unaware of the danger.

Sam stood up—completely awake now—and yelled, waved his arms at Brooks, to catch his attention, but Brooks just waved back with one hand and kept on smoking.

By then, Miguel, Garcia, and the others had also realized that something was wrong. They hurried toward Brooks, stumbling over the vegetation in their way. And Sam ran.

He was terrified. He wanted to run like the wind, to be there right away, but his body was in pain, refusing to go any faster. He was almost there, and he kept yelling, but Brooks—who had been peacefully dreaming with who knew what—was now out of sight behind the tree. All Sam could see was the smoke coming from the cigarette. And the white shadow stepped out into the moonlight and grabbed Brooks by the legs and dragged him toward the water.

He fought the bamboo and the clumps of wild cattails. If he could only get there on time. The gator wouldn't kill Brooks right away. It would drown him first. Shake him a little, sink him, and then enjoy its meal without having to fight it any longer. If he could only run a little faster.

By the time Sam got there, Miguel, and Garcia, and the others, were there as well, looking on helplessly.

"Shoot, Miguel. Shoot," he yelled.

"No, Sheriff. You know we can't do that. It wouldn't hurt the gator, but it could kill your friend."

"We have to save him. We have to do something."

"But what?"

"Jump in?"

"Oh, no. It will kill me. And I have a family. We all do. You have to let your friend go." They all shook their heads sadly and stepped back.

Brooks was in the water up to his waist, looking surprised, struggling desperately to free himself. Sam, facing the worst panic of his life felt like he was about to throw up. With shaking hands, he grabbed his head. He was going to have to jump in. He had to save Brooks. But the terror had taken hold of his body, and his muscles refused to move. He willed himself to turn around and face the men.

"I have to jump in." The men stared at him as if he had gone mad.

"You can't do that. Your friend is as good as dead. And it will kill you too."

"I have to jump in," Sam told them stubbornly, and he patted his pockets. "I don't have a knife. I need a knife."

"That's crazy. You'll die."

"Then I die."

Sam took his boots off, threw his pack, his weapons, and his Duty Belt, on the ground.

"I need a knife. Now."

Miguel looked at Sam sadly and shook his head, but he handed Sam a long, vicious-looking serrated knife. And now, there was nothing else to do. Sam took one look at the spot where Brooks had vanished, made the sign of the cross, and jumped.

Chapter 57

The Alligator

THE WATER WAS WARM AND STICKY. Holding the knife awkwardly, afraid that he would drop it, he swam in the turbid swamp toward the ever-increasing ripples left by the gator and his victim. He couldn't see them. They had gone under, and he ducked into the water, hoping to see something in the muddy liquid, but this was no ocean, no pool. And it was midnight. The visibility was zero.

He stayed under until he needed to come up for air. This was pointless. He needed to watch for turbulence. If Brooks was still alive, he would be fighting. Stirring the water. That was what he needed to look for.

He held his breath, and he watched the water, tinged by the fluorescent algae sparkling under the moonlight, holding the knife tight. The beauty of his surroundings, the pleasing warmth of the water, and the chirping of frogs and crickets contrasted surreally with the danger around him. As he stared intently, a dozen feet or so ahead toward the center of the swamp, he saw a minor stirring, and perhaps a few air bubbles surfacing. He couldn't be sure. But he had to risk it. Even as things stood, it would be a miracle. But he swam toward the wrinkles on the surface, pushing the doubts out of his mind.

Then, he saw them. The gator was enormous. How long could it be? Fourteen, sixteen feet long? Its tail was swishing slowly from side to side as it shook Brooks in its mouth. Sam couldn't tell if he was still alive. He had gone limp.

He approached the gator from behind and straddled him. He did his best to wrap his left arm around its neck but the thing was enormous. And it was beautiful. Ghostly white, looking as old as time itself, with rheumy white eyes that stared blindly at the night sky.

Sam held the jagged-edged knife in his hand and reached for the beast's eyes and was about to plunge the knife in one of them, but he couldn't. For a second he thought himself a coward. This would be such an easy kill. But the magnificent beast was blind already. Its eyes were as milky white as the rest of its body. And he couldn't do it. His arm shook as the desire to kill, and the desire to forgive fought inside his soul. And he just couldn't do it.

Instead, he slammed the hilt of the knife against the gator's snout as hard as he could, and as soon as the gator let Brooks go and turned toward him, in one swift motion, he punched the gator's snout and grabbed Brooks' head with the crook of his elbow. It was enough to warn the old gator away. He watched it swim away, and saw Miguel, and Garcia, and their friends jumping up and down, cheering wildly from the shore.

As always, Sam thought, time seemed to slow down when great things were happening to him. It had felt like a lifetime, being tossed about by the great white gator, fighting for his friend's life, but it couldn't have been more than a few minutes. He could still feel Brooks' beating heart as the vein in his neck touched the crook of his elbow. The guy—as hard as it was to believe—was still alive.

The adrenaline of the fight was enough to give him the stamina to drag Brooks to the shore. Miguel and his friends stepped into the shallow edge and pulled him and Brooks out.

For Sam, the story ended here. While the men administered CPR or something, he collapsed on the muddy bank. Everything in his body hurt. He was shivering in the hot night. His fever was probably back.

He thought about the beautiful ghostly gator, swimming away to safety. Brooks, close to him, had finally spit out the dirty water trapped in his lungs and was fighting Miguel and the others to be allowed to sit up.

He chuckled. Brooks was fine. He was just about to doze off when he heard the rotors of a helicopter coming ever closer. He sighed with relief. That was probably their ride.

Thanks for reading! Please add a short review on Amazon,
and let me know what you thought!

Don't miss the next Margo Fontaine Mystery:

The Swimming Pond

Coming Soon…